Sticks and Stones

Cat DeLuca Mysteries

Liar, Liar
Sticks and Stones

Sticks and Stones

A Cat DeLuca Mystery

K. J. Larsen

Poisoned Pen Press

First Edition 2012

10 9 8 7 6 5 4 3 2 1

Library of Congress Catalog Card Number: 2011920317

ISBN: 9781590589212   Hardcover
        9781590589236   Trade Paperback

Poisoned Pen Press
6962 E. First Ave., Ste. 103
Scottsdale, AZ 85251
www.poisonedpenpress.com
info@poisonedpenpress.com

Printed in the United States of America

For Harold and Arlene's other three daughters
Lynn Higbee, Roxanne Nelson, and Diane Westbrook

We did a good job picking our parents.

Acknowledgments

Our profound gratitude to our editor, Barbara Peters. Her extraordinary vision, guidance, and occasional flogging compel us to tell a tale greater than we'd imagined. She is no less than magical.

We wish to thank our amazing Publisher, Jessica Tribble, for her generous assistance and encouragement. The patience she affords three sisters is the stuff saints are made of.

Our affection and thanks to Cheri McManus, agent and fourth sister in crime. She is the spark behind the Pants On Fire Detective Agency. She edits, schedules signings, and penned a hilarious toothy-boy scene for *Sticks and Stones*. She also brings the pizza.

Our heartfelt appreciation to our extraordinary nephews: Marcus and Bill Higbee. They maintain an amazing website, manage marketing, and offer technical support. They work grueling hours for promises of lemon meringue and chocolate pie. We couldn't do this without them.

A special thank-you to Lynn and Amy Higbee, co-creators of all things DeLuca. And to Alan Mitchell for his generous contribution researching and proofing *Sticks and Stones*.

Our love and thanks always to Harold Larsen, our amazing Papa and number one fan. He's been with us every step of this journey. Dad brainstorms, edits, promotes, and arranges book events for us. If you're reading this book, there's a good chance he stopped you on the street and told you about it.

And our deep gratitude to Mama, whose love and encouragement surrounds us always. She adores Cat DeLuca. And she's laughing on the other side.

Chapter One

When I was seven, my second grade class made papier-mâché bunnies for Easter. Mine had big floppy ears and a white cotton tail. I gave Flopps two coats of purple pizzazz paint. When school closed for the Easter holiday, Sister Kathryn let us take our bunnies home. The thing is, I forgot.

I raced home to color Easter eggs with my brother Rocco. It wasn't until my feet hit the porch that I remembered Flopps. I threw my books on the grass and tore back to school.

I pushed the giant school doors open and ran headlong down the dark, scary hallway. The soft slap-slap of my footsteps echoed hollowly on the concrete floor. I crashed through my classroom door sucking air.

There was Flopps. Alone on my desk.

And there was Sister Kathryn. Not so alone on hers.

Our music teacher, Mr. Herbald, was making her sing.

You don't know a whole lot when you're seven. But I knew Mr. Herbald was married to Mrs. Herbald. And I knew Sister Kathryn, in good Catholic tradition, was married to—well, God.

Sister Kathryn gasped and her feet slid to the floor. I seized Flopps in my arms. Her eyes had widened since I painted them.

I raced home to Mama.

Mama was at the ironing board pressing Papa's blue police uniform. I told her what I saw, she made clicking noises with her mouth and pushed the other kids outside.

Mama shook her head sorrowfully. "Poor Harriet Herbald. "

I shook my head like Mama. "I hope God doesn't know."

Mama cut two fat wedges of honey cake and a small slice for the bunny. We carried our plates outside to the porch swing. Flopps sat between us.

"Mr. Herbald is a vampire," I said. "I saw him biting Sister Kathryn's neck."

"What other people do is none of your business, Caterina. You must never tell anyone what you saw."

"But…"

Mama cut me off with a look and a finger.

"OK." I stared down at my cake. "Mama, do nuns hide secrets under their habits?"

"What do you mean?"

"Mr. Herbald was looking for something under Sister Kathryn's skirt."

Mama made that sound with her mouth again.

"That is not something a good Catholic girl needs to think about."

I thought about that for a moment.

"Is Sister Kathryn a good Catholic?"

Mama silenced me with a look. "Just eat your cake."

Chapter Two

I'll never forget what Mama said about minding my own business. Maybe because she reminds me *every* day. When I became a private investigator and launched the Pants On Fire Detective Agency, it became her mantra.

My name is Cat DeLuca. I catch cheaters. Despite what Mama says, I'm not a snoop or a hootchie stalker. My clients come to me because they suspect their partners are cheating.

There are tell-tale signs of a cheater. Cheaters suddenly smell better. They dress better. They wear designer underwear. They groom their nose hairs.

I know these things because it was two short months into my marriage when the tweezers came out. My unholy union with run-around Johnnie Rizzo was a crash course in infidelity. But I have to tell you, it was good training for what I do best.

I scale balconies and teeter outside hotel windows to capture the perfect snapshot. One 8x10 glossy can speak a thousand words. And it could be worth thousands in a divorce settlement.

My client, Brenda Greger, was a timid, soft spoken woman who would apologize for sucking oxygen off the planet. Her husband, Steve, is the poster child for Mr. McCheater. Early fifties, six-two, all teeth, cocky as hell and so buffed and groomed I don't need to see his Calvin Klein undies to know he's wearing them.

At the moment I was tooling up the Stevenson Expressway with Inga, my beagle, riding shotgun. I'd been staked out at

Steve Greger's office since noon. My gut told me this was going to be a good day for Cat DeLuca, P.I.

At one forty-five, Greger walked out of his office, looked both ways. The perm-a-grin expression on his face screamed *booty call*. He turned north on Halsted, moving with the traffic. About a block before the on-ramp, Greger's car slowed and allowed a side-parked car to slip in front of him. He followed the car onto the Stevenson and I took caboose.

We jumped onto South Lake Shore Drive and ended up at Monroe Harbor Marina. I knew from doing background on Greger that he had a slip there. I gave the happy couple plenty of room to park and watched as a leggy, twenty-something blonde in eight-inch platforms and white hot-pants wobbled out of car number one with picnic basket in hand. Typical.

It wasn't hard following them to their dock. The marina is big enough and busy enough this time of year to keep me invisible. I just acted like a car looking for a parking spot and watched as they boarded a yacht. Not the biggest yacht in the marina but not the smallest either; just a nice, sleek vessel big enough for a galley and comfy V berth. Game on.

Once aboard, Greger and Legs scooted below deck. I guessed he was a wee bit impatient after his week of good-boy behavior and he was the greedy type. I'd have to move fast if I was going to be in position for the photo op. I doubted this would take long.

I parked illegally at the end of the pier. I tossed the binoculars on the seat, grabbed the camera, told Inga to stay, and dashed down the dock to the yacht moored next to Greger's. I took the chance that it would be empty, climbed aboard like I belonged there, and made a bee-line for the bow.

I had to trust my mark would already be preoccupied as I leaned over the side to peer into those cute little round windows through the magnified lens of my camera.

Whoa! When you're a P.I. you sometimes see things you wish you hadn't. A picture will turn in your mind and you just know it's gonna keep you up at night.

I was having such a moment.

I looked through the camera lens and a nightmare germinated deep in my brain. It was Greger's hairy, pimpled butt. And the hairiest backside I had ever seen. And in this business, I've seen a lot.

The man was a grizzly bear. Only his head was bald. He was Kojak in an ape suit. I blinked and steeled my eyes back to the camera.

There in the lens were two eight-inch platforms stuck straight up in the air. Damn. I'd have to get up higher to get a gander at Greger's hairy butt, but how?

Refusing to think, I kicked off my Converses, swung the camera strap around my neck, and climbed onto the edge of the boat. I gripped the boat's side with my toes, lifted the camera and…

Suddenly, two arms were around my waist, and a voice boomed. "Hey, hey, sweet darlin'. You here to pay me a little visit, you cute thing?"

I smelled Jim Beam and my face wasn't even turned his way. Inside the Love Boat, McCheater jerked his head and glanced behind him. It was a Kodak moment. The sweaty, flushed face filled my lens, framed by two smooth white thighs. For one glorious moment, Steve Greger was mine.

The hands around my waist tightened and pulled.

"No!"

I was dragged off the edge and my feet planted firmly on the deck.

"Didn't want you to fall in, sugar plum."

Hastily I reviewed my shot. Crap. No hairy butt, no eight-inch platforms saluting the sun. Just an unfocused pic of the stern and her name: *Steve's Obsession*.

I glared at the guy who ruined my 8x10 glossy. He was drunk off his bum, butterballish in size, and a scream for Viagra. And he was still holding me. I smacked him with my camera.

A cabin door closed and clomping footsteps hurried along on the pier. McCheater and Legs were making their escape.

Jim Beam shot a bloodshot eye on McCheater's window and back on me. It took a moment to connect the dots.

When he did, his jaw tightened. "I'm calling security."

"Already here." I waved a library card before his unfocused eyes. "Put the phone down, Jim."

He grabbed my arm. "I know the marina's security team. You're not one of them."

"I'm a little higher up on the food chain."

"The Port of Chicago?"

"Higher."

"The National Yacht Association?"

"Keep climbing."

His eyes popped and he swallowed hard. His voice lowered to a hoarse whisper. "You don't mean—"

I made one of Mama's clicking sounds with my mouth. "I'm afraid I do. Steve Gregor is the leader of a terrorist organization."

He dropped my arm and just like that, I was gone.

I raced to my car. A sparkling bottle of champagne was propped on my seat next to my binoculars. In the back, my faithful beagle slurped up McCheater's romantic lunch. I suspected the goose pate would give her farts.

Steve Gregor honked as he drove by flashing a toothy smile. *Not so fast, Kojak.*

I bumped the bottle over and scooted behind the wheel. Pumped the gas, turned the key. I got nothing.

Steve Gregor may have left his lunch, but he took a piece of my engine with him.

I beat my head on the steering wheel. And then I called Jack.

Jack is the best mechanic in Bridgeport, maybe South Chicago. He's missing a few fingers and a few more marbles. He's like a member of my family. My crazy, dysfunctional family.

"Jack. This is Cat."

"Caterina." His voice was cool as Italian Ice. I winced. He was still steamed about Dorothy.

Dorothy, a 1967 Ford Mustang, was Jack's pride and joy. He let me drive her the last time my car was in his shop. Somebody blew her to tiny bits of shrapnel and glass. It was not entirely my fault.

"I'm at the marina and I need a tow. My Honda's missing a part."

"What? You drop a tranny?"

"Nope. Definitely something smaller. Someone screwed with my car."

Jack exaggerated a sigh. "You have a gift at pissing people off."

"Hey, I was minding my own business."

"Ha! You were taking dirty pictures."

"That *is* my business, Jack. You gonna help me out here or what?"

He snorted. "I'm doing this for your mama. You know you break her heart, Caterina. She's a nice lady."

Yep. Nice and crazy.

"How long will it take to replace the part?"

"It'll be a few days before I get a chance to look at it. I'm shorthanded. Devin's still in rehab."

Devin is Jack's nephew. We went to school together. He used to steal lunch boxes. Now he's graduated to stealing cars. We all grow in our own special way.

"How's Devin doing?"

"He's changed. I think he found Jesus."

"Devin?"

"Or maybe it's the twelve steps. Anyway he's sober."

"Of course he's sober, Jack. There's no dope in treatment."

"He's sober enough. I need him at the shop."

"And I need a loaner. You gonna fix me up?"

"Fugeddaboudit. You blew up my Dorothy!"

"Hey, I sent flowers."

"I'm not givin' you a car."

"C'mon, Jack. I'll take an old klunker."

He gasped. "You're not blowin' up my Doris!"

"Doris? Seriously Jack, what kind of guy names his car Doris?"

"Hey, here's a name for you, Cat. *Hertz.*"

Click.

I stared at the cell in my hand and mumbled something worth ten Hail Mary's and a mouthful of soap. Then I jabbed in Cleo's number. I needed a ride.

Cleo's a former client. She hired me a few months ago to identify the lipstick smudge on her husband's silk boxers. I followed Walter's canary-yellow Corvette around Chi-town for six grueling days of business meetings and seminars. On the seventh day, he rested. I found him at the Marriott resting on Cleo's sister, Hotlip –Ho for short. I shot some steamy 8x10s. Cleo shot Walter's bum full of buckshot. He slunk under the radar, taking Cleo's money, dog, and sister with him.

Losing Walter was a small loss. I'm not talking about his beer belly. I have pictures. He was an unimaginative and bumbling lover. It took Cleo one week, three pitchers of margaritas, and a traveling salesman from Toledo to get over him. I gave her a job at Pants On Fire and struck a deal. I'd help her get the money and her dog back on one condition. She had to quit shooting Walter.

I gathered my bag and basic supplies of the trade out of my Accord—camera, binoculars, this month's *Marie Claire* magazine, and my cooler jammed with cold pizza and Mama's cannoli. My box of wigs, glasses and wrinkle-free clothes. Everything I needed for a stakeout. I chucked the keys under the seat for Jack and hoped he'd return my car soon. The Silver Bullet is perfect for stalking cheaters; it's small, fast, and it blends.

I set the cooler on the curb and plopped down beside Inga. We watched for Cleo's Camry to scream around the corner. Cleo drives at her one speed through life: full throttle. She doesn't blend.

A screech of tires whipped my attention to a canary-yellow Corvette boring down toward us. I grabbed Inga and bolted to my feet. I did a double take. I knew that car well. But it wasn't Walter driving. The top was down and Cleo waved from behind the wheel. Her spiked pink-tipped black hair, a recent reinvention of herself from her break-up with Walter, was unruffled. It didn't even bend in the wind. Cleo was a free bird expressing her new identity.

The sports car wrenched to a stop. I groaned.

"Omigod, Cleo. You killed Walter and stole his car."

"That's ridiculous," Cleo squawked in her grating voice. "The coward wouldn't come to the door. And don't think he didn't hear me. The neighbors were staring through their blinds."

I narrowed my eyes. "Uh huh. Well, if you didn't see Walter, how do you have his car?"

She winked. "Well, technically you were half right."

"You *stole* his car?"

"Hey, I'm just getting started. Jump in."

I loaded my stash and buckled up. Inga hopped on my lap. Cleo hit the gas and I hit the back of the seat.

She flashed a grin. "What d'ya think? Do I look smokin' hot in this car or what?"

"How does your hair stand up at this speed? I have to admit, it's impressive. But more importantly, how'd you find him?"

"This morning I was at the firing range—"

"Ah yes, your daily fantasy about shooting Walter."

"Of course," she grinned. "Anyway, I got hungry and was thinkin' pizza sounded pretty good. Then I thought about how much Walter and I loved Gino's Pizzeria. *Ding! Ding! Ding!* I knew Walter couldn't live without his emergency ballgame pizza pie."

"Wow. It's amazing how your mind works."

"I schmoozed Gino's delivery boy. It only cost me twenty bucks and a case of beer."

"That delivery kid is seventeen."

"Sixteen."

"Promise me you'll never have children."

Cleo cranked the volume up on the radio and jammed to Memphis Minnie. Here's the thing about Cleo. Her painful, nails-on-blackboard squawk transforms to a rich, sultry vibrato when she sings.

We powered down the Dan Ryan to Bridgeport, feeding every car on the road our dust. Cleo's shoulders shimmied and her hands drummed the wheel.

"I'm a bad luck woman, I can't see a reason why," her voice purred.

I watched the rearview mirror for flashing lights. "You stole a car, babe. You might want to chill a bit, or you'll be singing those blues from a cell."

"Good point." Cleo eased the gas and sighed. "I just don't get why Walter's avoiding me."

"Hmm. It might have something to do with the last time you saw him. You shot him in the bum. It could make him a little touchy."

"Pansy-ass. You should have seen him running away screaming like a little girl."

"Or maybe Walter didn't answer the door because he wasn't home."

"His car was there." Cleo's lip pouted out a little farther.

Was being the operative word.

Cleo slammed on the gas. "Okay, fine. Maybe he caught a ride with my sister, the Ho."

A low hiss issued from between clenched teeth.

"You do realize everyone in Walter's neighborhood now thinks you're dangerously unbalanced."

"I hate to shock you Cat, but people thinking I am 'unbalanced' is no newsflash. Besides, what else could I do? I had to call out his lying, cheating, sneaking around, dog-stealing ass."

I flicked open a mirror from my purse and began slathering my lips with Dr. Pepper Lip Smacker. "Not when you work for me, you don't. The Pants On Fire Detective Agency is a first-class organization. We have an image to uphold."

"What image? You say 'Pants On Fire' and I see tighty-whities and a whole lot of flames."

"Discretion, Cleo. Our clients need to know we keep their secrets. We don't scream in the street and we don't draw attention to ourselves. We discreetly let ourselves through the door."

"What if I don't know how to pick a lock?"

"Then shut up and learn."

Cleo drove in sulky silence almost a block.

"You of all people should know how I feel. Your husband cheated with half of Bridgeport right under your nose. He played you like a violin. Can you honestly say you never wanted to choke the life out of him?"

My head whipped right, then left. "Not even *once*...in front of witnesses."

Chapter Three

It was after three by the time we arrived back in Bridgeport. Cleo was mastering the parade queen wave for Walter's neighbors. That's a sure way to get a one way trip to the slammer for grand theft auto. I, on the other hand, was mastering my "invisible" look.

Our mission for returning to the scene of the crime was an easy one. Get Cleo's dog back. Walter's house was in Bridgeport Village, a tree-lined street with newer, high-dollar homes. It seemed Cleo's liar liar husband was doing well for himself.

Cleo muttered under her breath, coasted to a stop behind her Toyota Camry, and pocketed the key.

"Well, I'm dividing our assets. From now on Walter can drive the Camry."

"You look hot in a Corvette."

"Better than Walter."

"Damn straight. Now focus. In and out with your dog."

I palmed my lock and pic set and followed Inga onto the curb. Cleo scooted around to join us, her eyes scanning the street.

I flashed a smile and reached down to pluck a weed from the lawn. "When you B&E, act like you own the place." I said.

Cleo tried to smile. She mostly showed a lot of teeth. I thought her smile looked like a chimpanzee's grin of fear and I told her so.

She snorted. "Easy for you to say. The men in your family are Chicago cops. Your cousin's a prosecuting attorney. If you get caught, odds are your case disappears, your troubles go away, and you get awarded some sort of medal."

It was true. The DeLuca men are cops and the women breed more cops. Somewhere there's a glitch in my genes. I never fit into the family mold.

Papa is something of a local hero. He was wounded in the line of duty by friendly fire. That rookie cop's future is now cemented in traffic duty. I have three cop brothers and one crazy sister. Mama rules us all with staggering amounts of pasta and guilt.

My shoes clacked on the stone walkway as I led my entourage to the door.

"Observe, Grasshopper," I said. With a flick of the wrist the door swung open. I pushed Inga and Cleo inside kicking the door closed behind me.

"Walter, are you home? It's Cat DeLuca. Nobody's going to shoot you. Isn't that right, Cleo?"

Cleo waggled her hand and lifted her shoulders. "Maybe… Maybe not… I guess he has to ask himself one question…"

I gave her an eye roll. "Your Dirty Harry impression needs work. Besides, the house feels empty."

A shrill howl, sounding oddly like Cleo, wailed from upstairs. She screeched back and a frenzied bundle of black fur hurled down the winding oak staircase, taking flight and landing in her arms. Cleo clung to the dog, sobbing.

"I gotchu now, Beau," she cooed. "You're coming home with Mama as soon as I divide more of Papa's assets."

Beau was a Tibetan terrier with soft black hair and bright, happy eyes. I stroked his head and pulled my hand back. He felt sticky.

"Eeuw! You need a bath. You are disgusting."

"Hey! He has ears you know. Don't worry, baby. Mama's taking you home and giving you a good, long soak. You can't help it that your kidnappers have you a flippin' mess, now can you?"

Cleo set Beau on the floor and wiped her hands on her leopard print spandex.

"This is Inga," she said. "Make nice."

The ritual butt sniffing began.

"Oh." She made a face. "Maybe not that nice."

I turned to my assistant. "OK, Cleo, you have what you came for. Let's hit it before Walter gets back."

"Not so fast." Cleo strolled through the modish living room. She scooped up a Tiffany lamp and placed it by the door.

"Uh, Cleo? Whatcha doin'?"

"I'm dividing our assets. Last month Walter cleaned out our bank account and ran off with my dog and my sister. I'm taking my stuff back. He can keep my sister."

"That was your lamp?"

"It is now."

She added an antique Waterford Crystal candy jar and an ebony and ivory chess set to her haul. Then she ducked into a coat closet.

"You don't want to piss off the judge before he divides your property."

"Like that coward is going to say anything," she called from the closet. "Aha! My wine- colored leather jacket. The Ho borrowed it last winter."

Cleo flung the jacket out and I tossed it by the door. Next came Beau's leashes, his winter coat, and rain jacket. I added them to the pile.

"Ooooh," Cleo gushed. "Here's Beau's Chicago White Sox tee shirt and his itsy bitsy baseball cap."

The beagle and I exchanged glances.

"Find your rubber ducky, " Cleo said.

The fast friends raced up the winding staircase.

Cleo smiled. "Beau loves his rubber ducky. He refuses to take a bath without it."

"Uh huh."

Cleo's voice muffled as she moved deeper in the closet. "Mmm, what's hiding back here? I'm likin' this." Cleo hauled a RB designer leather travel bag and heaved it onto the cream colored chaise lounge chair. "It's heavy. And it's locked. Open it."

"Ok. But then we are leaving."

I stomped my foot for good measure, bent over the case, worked the pick until the lock popped opening the top. I choked on a gasp. The bag was stuffed full with cash. I blinked, temporarily blinded by a veritable fortune of dazzling green bills.

Cleo squealed and looked up to the heavens. "Thank you, Jee-sus."

"Oh my god, Cleo."

She clapped her hands and snapped the bag shut. "We're finished here. Walter can keep his Corvette. There's not enough room in his trunk for my assets."

She loaded her arms and darted out the door to the Camry.

"Right behind you," I said and called the dogs. "Inga! Beau! We're leaving!"

The beagle bounced down the steps, tail wagging, with Beau hot on her heels. Inga carried something in her mouth and dropped it at my feet. A man's white athletic sock, stained a hideous red.

I smelled blood, wet and fresh. My stomach lurched. I looked closely at Beau's hair that had felt sticky when I'd touched him. It was too dark to tell but when I took a whiff, he smelled like the sock. I had a really bad feeling this was not going to end well.

Cleo called from the door. "Let's go! We have a wild night ahead of us, and Chicago's never gonna be the same."

"You're half right. I'm thinkin' we've got trouble. Put the dogs in the car and come back in."

She called the dogs to follow her. "Listen, girlfriend, the only trouble we got is blowin' this joint before Walter comes home."

I reached down and pinched a white edge of the bloody fabric with two squeamish fingers. Then I extended an arm in front of me and followed the sock up the winding staircase. Hardly breathing, I forced one foot in front of the other and hooked a left at the top of the steps. I barely glanced into the master bedroom and exercise room as I passed. I was following the dark red paw prints to the office at the end of the hall. The door was ajar.

I took a deep, steadying breath and entered the office. An early summer breeze gusted through an open window, billowing the lace curtains. A gnarled old maple would have many tales to tell. But the only story I cared about told of the stains on the soft white carpet. I followed the grisly tracks around the side of the desk to where Walter lay in a gooey mass of blood. His shock of black hair was slicked back as if he'd just combed it. His dark eyes were wide open with shock. My stomach lurched and I tasted vomit.

What I knew about Walter wasn't pretty. He stole from his boss, pocketed donations from an MS fundraiser, and abandoned his wife, leaving her penniless. Walter was a man void of scruples and he certainly had his share of enemies. It appeared he finally pushed one too far.

A fat wad of bills rested beside a jewelry box on the dresser. On his wrist a gold Rolex shimmered in the sun. This wasn't a burglary it was personal.

I stood there hardly breathing with the bloodied sock limp in my hand. I scanned the room for the smallest clue the murderer might have left behind. There were blood and beagle prints everywhere. Great. The Pants On Fire Detective Agency was first to discover a grisly homicide and we contaminated the crap out of the crime scene.

I knelt beside Walter and felt for a pulse. I knew I wouldn't find one and didn't. His body was still warm. I felt a deep sadness in my chest.

"You were a schmuck, Walter. But Cleo saw something good in you once. If you had more time, maybe you would've turned yourself around." I thought about that. "Yeah, right, here's for hoping."

"Cat!" Cleo yelled her cat-on-hot-coals screech and her footsteps pounded the stairs. "Quit screwing around. We gotta get—"

Cleo skated through the door and froze. Her eyes took in the bloody carpet and me standing behind the desk, sock in hand. Every drop of color drained from her face. Her body swayed and I rushed over to catch her arm.

"Walter's dead, Cleo. You don't want to see him like this. Go wait downstairs."

"Knock it off, Cat," she squawked, pushing me away. She began moving quickly around the desk. "He is not...." When she saw him her face contorted.

And then she kicked his leg with her boot. "Get up, you big piece of crap. Get up! Do you hear me, Walter?"

Walter wasn't going anywhere. He'd taken a chest hit from a large caliber bullet.

Cleo's lip trembled. "Why'd you always have to go and piss people off? I warned you you'd get yourself killed. You made me so mad I could've killed you myself."

I grabbed Cleo by the shoulders and shook her. "Now would be a really good time to quit saying that."

"Ah, you know I don't mean it, Cat. Sometimes I say things I don't mean. Walter understood that. He was good to me that way. Probably the only way he was good to me, now that I think about it."

I pulled my phone from my pocket. "I need to call this in. Listen to me, Cleo. Be careful what you say when the cops come. Answer their questions honestly but carefully. Do you understand what I'm saying?"

"Not at all."

"Nine one one. What is your emergency."

"This is Caterina DeLuca. I want to report a murd..."

The hair bristled on the back of my neck and suddenly I knew we were not alone. Maybe my subconscious detected the slightest brush of fabric on the stairway or maybe this house that felt empty earlier, didn't feel so lonely anymore.

Had the murderer returned to the scene of the crime? There could be only one good reason to do so. It was in the trunk of Cleo's Camry.

"911," the voice repeated with more urgency. "What are you reporting?"

My hand dropped the phone in my pocket and emerged with a pistol. The murderer's gun, judging by the size of the hole in Walter, was bigger and meaner than mine. I'd be a fool to pretend size doesn't matter. In fact, I never do.

Cleo sensed a hostile presence in the house too. Or maybe she just took her clue from the hot shot detective with the trembling nine millimeter in her hand.

Her lip curled and she seized a golf club from the bag by the door, swinging it over her head. "He's not taking *my* money," she mouthed.

I gotta give it to Cleo. She looked freakishly calm in a totally crazed kind of way.

I motioned for her to move behind the door. She refused until I pointed the gun at her.

It was his arm I saw first, wearing a pressed and starched long sleeve blue shirt. Two steady, beefy hands gripped the hard cold steel of a Glock, a standard police issue. It's the gun of choice for the old timer Chicago cops. The tattoo on his right hand was a lion. Leo. That was his sign and his name.

I lowered my gun.

"Come in, Leo, and don't shoot. It's Cat DeLuca."

"Cat?"

Leo rounded the corner, gun drawn. His face crumbled with relief when he saw me.

"Jeezus almighty, Cat, I could've shot you."

Leo was a tad shorter than me. Compact but strongly built with short brown hair and shrewd blue eyes.

Cleo came out from behind the door with her golf club. His eye flickered to the blood on the floor and his face tightened.

Leo raised the gun again and leveled the barrel at Cleo. Moving guardedly, he circled the desk to the body. He crouched and pressed two fingers on Walter's neck.

"He's dead," I said.

"And still warm," Leo noted.

He pulled the radio from his belt and called in a one eighty-seven.

Leo jerked his head. "Get out of here, Cat. Go out the window. Back-up's on the way."

"She didn't kill him, Leo. Walter was dead when we got here. What are you doing here anyway?"

"A neighbor called about a disturbance. A woman fitting your friend's description was overheard threatening to kill a man named Walter."

"Well technically many women fit Cleo's description."

"This woman was wearing leopard print spandex and a sparkling gold shirt."

"Not many women can pull that look off," I admitted.

Leo cocked his head toward the body. "Is it safe to assume the victim was one of the many Walters in the world?"

"Chicago Police," a voice bellowed from downstairs.

"Up here, Tommy." Leo's eyes gleamed, gun trained on Cleo. "You know Tommy," he said to me. "I'm breakin' him in."

I knew Tommy alright. He's a rookie from rural Wisconsin, hardly more than a kid. He was there the day somebody blew up Dorothy, the Mustang Jack gave me for a loaner. It was Tommy's first day on the force and he was way too close to the fireworks. You could say I did my share of *breaking Tommy in* too.

Tommy's boots pounded the steps, taking two at a time. "What the heck, Leo. I was around back. You were supposed to call me before—"

Tommy stomped into the room. He glimpsed Leo's weapon trained on Cleo and fumbled for his gun. Waving the forty caliber Glock between Cleo and me, he tracked the bloody paw marks to Walter's lifeless body. The red headed rookie's lips paled when he saw all the blood. He wrenched his eyes from the body and saw me for the first time.

"*Cat?*" Tommy stammered. "What's going on here?"

"Don't you point that gun at her," Leo said. "That's Tony DeLuca's daughter. Show some respect."

"Oh. Sorry. I wasn't thinking."

"Put the gun away, Tommy," I said. "Cleo and I are trained detectives."

Leo snickered.

"Pants On Fire Detective Agency," Cleo said crisply. "It's a highly regarded operation."

Leo let out a bark of laughter.

I ignored him. "My assistant—"

"*Partner*," Cleo said.

"Cleo Jones was worried about her husband, Walter," I said. "We stopped by to check on him. The door was unlatched so we came in."

"Your husband?" Tommy said. "I'm sorry for your loss."

"Walter was a putz."

I kicked her. "She's overwrought with grief and she doesn't know what she is saying."

A tear tumbled down Cleo's cheek. She dashed it away and sidled up next to me. Then she dropped something in my hand. I felt the keys to her Camry.

Cleo leaned over and whispered in my ear. "This isn't looking good for me, Cat. You know they always blame the wife. Promise me you will bail me out. You know where I keep my assets."

A siren wailed with increasing ear-shattering intensity, stopping cold on the street outside.

"Listen guys," I said. "I found the body before Cleo even came upstairs. I was calling it in when you arrived."

"Uh huh."

Leo snapped the handcuffs on her wrists.

"What are you doing?" I demanded. "A murderer is getting away."

"For the last time, Cat, *go home.*"

"You have the right to remain silent," Tommy began.

"Yeh, yeh," Cleo said. "You think I don't watch television?"

I followed the three of them downstairs. "You're making a big mistake. I was with Cleo the whole time."

Leo glared at me. "She didn't say that, Tommy. Cat DeLuca doesn't know this woman. In fact she isn't even here."

"Wait," Cleo said. "I want to make a call."

"You can call your lawyer from the station," Leo said.

"Who said anything about a lawyer? I'm calling my sister, the Ho. I want her out of my house. Walter's dead. It's all mine now."

The rookie's jaw dropped and Leo stopped on the stair to write something in his notebook.

I groaned. "Don't write that down, Leo. Does anybody have any duct tape I can borrow?"

The cops looked at each other.

"When did you first decide to kill your husband?" Leo asked.

"Don't answer that." I turned to the cops. "My assistant has nothing to say without a lawyer."

"Partner," Cleo piped in.

Tommy shrugged. "If she's innocent she won't mind answering the question."

"I'm not that innocent," Cleo said. "When Walter left me, I wanted to kill him. Somebody just beat me to it. That's all."

I threw up my hands. "Super glue, anything? I am begging here." I looked at the grinning cops and turned to Cleo. "I'll call a lawyer and meet you at the precinct. Do you think you can manage to keep it zipped that long?"

Cleo pressed her lips together in a thin line and nodded as we stepped onto the porch. The house was surrounded by cops, gawkers, and a neighbor waving a video camera. Leo angled his chin in a way that said, "Get outta here." I began walking to the Camry.

"Yoo hoo, Cat," Cleo called. "Don't forget I'm singing this weekend at All Things Blue. Bail me out in time to shop for a dress."

A ripple of snickers erupted from the crowd.

"Flames," I muttered. "She's going down in flames."

I slid behind the wheel and eased the Camry into the street. My breath came shallow and fast. A knot lurched in my gut. I needed a miracle.

I called my Uncle Joey.

Chapter Four

Joey called in a favor from Tony Beano, one of Chicago's fiercest criminal defense attorneys, to represent Cleo. The way Uncle Joey tells it, Tony's son was once looking at a nasty stretch in Joliet for drug trafficking when the evidence against him vanished. Uncle Joey vowed it would reappear if he messed up again. He didn't. Tony's son graduates from the University of Chicago Law School this month.

"Maybe the kid got his shit together," Joey said. "But with lawyers, eh, who knows."

I dropped by my house to stash away Cleo's assets behind a false wall I discovered last fall while painting my pantry. A few dusty bottles of gin and whiskey were all that were left in my new hiding place when I found it. A hold-over from the days of Prohibition. In my line of work, secret compartments are quite handy. Those dusty bottles have much more interesting company now.

My stomach snarled, reminding me I'd missed lunch. I didn't know how long I would be at the station. In fact, I wasn't entirely sure Captain Bob wouldn't arrest me. I made two sandwiches with meats and cheeses from Tino's Deli. I cut one in half for Inga and Beau to share. I finished mine with one of Mama's cannoli and washed it down with a swig of chocolate milk from the carton.

The matted mess of dried blood in Beau's dark hair wasn't visible to the eye but thinking about it nearly made me toss my cannoli. The dogs would stay outside until I could give them a bath. I left alone to face Captain Bob.

Tony Beano beat me to the station. Cleo was meeting with the lawyer when I breezed in.

I gave my statement to Detective Ethel Opsahl, a recent transfer from the Fifth District in Calumet. She was a slim, scrawny woman with waves of curly dark hair, cut short. I had hoped to be interviewed by someone I knew. Somebody I drank beer with at Mickey's. But no such luck.

Detective Opsahl made no bones about it. She didn't believe my story and I thought it was a good one. She sipped weak tea and assessed me with shrewd, skeptical eyes. I couldn't see meeting her at Mickey's anytime soon.

Captain Bob's face was pinched with a barely contained rage when I entered his office. My signed statement was clenched in his hands and there were more papers on the desk. Notes, I guessed, from my interview with Detective Opsahl. I tried to read upside down and thought I made out the word *anti-Christ* but I couldn't be sure.

The captain's words were carefully measured, his face red and poofy. For Captain Bob, keeping his temper in check was a challenge.

Bob is like a member of the family. Back when they were beat cops, he and Papa were partners. Their careers took different paths but they've remained close. Bob has been eating burnt chicken since Papa got his first grill.

I sat in the chair across from his desk and watched a tick jerk Bob's right eye. I suspected it might have something to do with me.

"Captain," I said.

"Caterina." His eye twitched again. "I've read Detective Opsahl's report."

"What? It doesn't look good?"

"It would look a hell of a lot better if your name wasn't in it."

"I want you to know I'm here to offer my assistance, Bob. Speaking as one professional to another, I'll do anything I can to clear my assistant's name. I will aid you in finding the real perpetrator of this heinous crime."

"Assist? Excuse me, did you say you were going to 'aid us'?" The Captain burst out laughing.

"What are you saying, Bob?"

"I'm saying you are a walking, talking crime spree, Caterina DeLuca. In the past thirty days Bridgeport has had two bombings and three murders. Oddly enough, you've been present or involved in each one of them."

"I'm a victim of crime, Bob."

"*Victim*? Hah! You *inspire* crime. You're the cheerleader on the sidelines rooting it on. I don't know how you do it."

"You were present at my baptism, Bob. Don't spit on the baby."

Captain Bob's face went into a full spasm as he raked his fingers through his hair. "Last month, oddly enough, you were having lunch across the street when one of Bridgeport's most influential citizens—a man you had a personal vendetta against, I might add—was killed. That very fact alone would leave one open to questions."

I frowned. "I wasn't brought in for questioning."

"It's not the Ninth District's problem. In fact, I'm not sure I *want* the answers." He glanced at my statement on his desk and pushed it aside. "Suppose you tell me what really happened today. But if you keep covering for your friend, I can't help. Ya got me?"

"I'm not covering, Bob. I swear on my Grandpa DeLuca's grave, Cleo didn't do it."

"Nice try Cat. Your Grandpa's alive and kicking. Got a call on him just last Tuesday for starting a naked conga line at the senior center. Ya know, if they would just stay in their building, I wouldn't have to arrest all those nice old people."

There's a visual. "You know what I mean, damn it. Cleo's innocent."

"Fine. I'll bite." He leaned back in his chair, lacing his hands behind his head. Except for the nervous twitch, the Captain appeared relaxed. "Let's have it."

"OK." I took a breath. "If Cleo had killed Walter, she wouldn't have picked me up at the marina and brought me back there to rescue her dog. If it were me, I'd head straight for Cuba."

"She went back because you were her alibi. She let you find the body so she could act shocked."

"Oh she was shocked, Bob. And I know this was the first time she and her dog were reunited. Animals don't fake it."

"Did you know this dog?"

"No."

"Maybe the dog's like her owner, a major drama queen. That's all you got?"

"Oh no, I've got more. If Cleo killed Walter, she wouldn't leave his money on the dresser. She'd take his watch, his jewelry, his—"

Twitching eyes lit up. "You're saying she's also a thief?"

"I'm saying he owes her. Besides, he's her husband. They hadn't filed for divorce."

"So maybe Cleo was scared. She panicked and forgot to clean him out. I'm sure she regrets that now."

"You don't know Cleo."

"That greedy, huh? Well, I've seen the coldest, most calculated killers make bigger mistakes. As far as we know, this is her first time killing. It's understandable how she could forget to grab the money. She was too busy snuffing her husband."

"Bob, whatever you got, it's gotta be crap. I was there."

"I'll tell you what I've got. I've got a freakin' headache from her screeching voice. I got seven witnesses who heard her threaten to murder him. I got a restraining order issued six years ago by an ex-boyfriend who says she assaulted him with a frying pan."

Oh, that Cleo was full of surprises.

"I got gunshot residue all over her hands and her gold shirt."

"That's nothing," I waved a dismissive arm. "Cleo's at the shooting range every day."

"Practicing her aim to kill Walter." He gave me a knowing glance.

Okay. So he had me there.

"The best part I saved for last. Cleo's husband was recently shot in the ass. His girlfriend—that would be Cleo's sister and motive enough to kill him—will testify Cleo pulled the trigger. What do you know about *that* shooting?"

"Zip. Nada. Nothing. I am thrilled to say I missed that episode. What does the police report say?"

"Walter claimed he accidentally shot himself…. *in his own ass.*"

"Alrighty then. There you have it."

Bob's voice raised an octave. "That's not even possible."

"Cleo isn't a murderer, Bob. She's passionate. I think we are losing focus here on finding the real killer."

"She's not passionate. She's psychotic. And we have the killer, in lock up."

"What about all of Walter's enemies? Don't you want to investigate them as well?"

The phone on the desk rang. Bob picked it up. He grunted a few terse syllables and dropped it back on the cradle with a cat that ate the canary grin.

"That was Detective Opsahl. She found traces of blood on your friend's clothing. We're waiting for the lab results to confirm that the blood belonged to her husband. And when they do, we'll have our ace."

Stunned, I shook my head. "It's not possible."

"Your friend is being charged with murder. You're damn lucky I'm not charging you with breaking and entering, accessory after the fact, and obstruction of justice."

He kicked back his chair, walked around, and sat on the desk in front of me. When he spoke again his voice had lowered to a soft roar.

"If you're smart you'll use this experience to reexamine your life. Cleo Jones played you, Cat. When are you gonna figure it out." He rapped his knuckles against my head. "I'm telling you this as a friend. Your life is a mess. Your family is worried about you. You're involved with killings and bombings, and now what? Your *partner* is a murderer? You're a good girl, Caterina

DeLuca, and you're attracting bad things to your life. You need to ask yourself why."

Captain Bob pulled me up from my chair and guided me to the door.

"She's my assistant." I muttered stumbling over my feet. Just as I reached for the knob I jumped. "Wait! The dog!" I squawked, sounding a lot like Cleo. "Cleo was holding the bloody dog!"

The right side of Bob's face flinched in an unsightly, spastic seizure.

"Don't you get it?" I said. "There was *blood* on the dog!"

"Don't push it. Now get out of here before I change my mind!" Bob slammed the door behind me.

The dogs had a bath that night, after a paralegal from Tony Beano's office took Beau to an independent lab where his hair was tested for Walter's blood. I took them to my groomer for two emergency full package treatments. They came out icky free. I added an outrageous tip to the bill to show my gratitude.

I tried not to worry about Cleo in jail. I tried not to think about Walter's killer who was, at this moment, getting away with murder. Mostly I tried not to panic about how, with all the evidence against her, I was going to prove Cleo innocent. I took a long, hot shower to scrub away the day. Then I tugged on flannel pajamas, climbed into bed and held Inga close. Beau curled into the crook of my legs and together we chased the boogie man away.

Chapter Five

Cleo Jones was arraigned first thing the next morning. Her lawyer, arranged for her to wear a powder pink polyester skirt that hit right below the knee, along with a cream colored button up blouse and oval framed glasses. With her hair slicked back, you wouldn't recognize her as that crazy psycho woman screaming, "*I am going to kill you, you son-of-a-bitch, you can't hide forever,*" on videotape. He instructed Cleo to look modest and demure and above all, keep her squawking mouth shut.

The prosecutor argued against bail. But Tony Beano addressed the court with eloquence and passion, stating she had lived in Bridgeport all of her life and had a lifetime of ties to the community. The guy's a real schmoozer. It probably didn't hurt that he and the judge have a standing golf game every Saturday. The judge set a high bail, and Cleo had to surrender her passport, but with the money from Walter's stash I was able to pay the bondsman.

I rescued Cleo from the Bridgeport slammer, drove to her house, saw the press camped outside, and kept on cruising. In the past 24 hours, Walter's murder had become a media frenzy. Every Chicago news channel was promising exclusive video coverage of Cleo screaming on the street. I anticipated a lot of bleeping. For the time being, Cleo's dog and her squawking voice would have to stay with me. But, on the plus side, she's amazing in the kitchen, and when I wear my hair down, it covers my ear plugs.

I watched my new live-in chef dancing at my stove, making a late lunch of chicken with artichokes and angel hair pasta.

I pulled romaine, cucumber, tomato, purple onion, and jicama from the fridge and made a salad. "So how was the big house?"

She gave a crooked smile. "To tell the truth, I made some friends and slept like a baby."

"You may have to get used to it. I saw Captain Bob yesterday. They've got a mountain of evidence. And that's just what they collected in the first two hours. Ya know, funny it never came up in conversation in all the hours we've worked together. You beat the crap out of an ex-boyfriend with a frying pan."

Cleo scrunched her nose to drudge up the memory. "Oh, *him*. Yeah, he was a loser too."

"Yep. You know how to pick 'em."

I knew she was torn up over Walter's death. Her eyes were red and puffy in court this morning and I saw her expression when she found Walter on the floor yesterday. Cleo spends more energy than anyone I know disguising her true feelings. I just don't get why.

The meal she prepared was amazing. I finished every bite and wanted to lick the plate.

"You should open your own restaurant," I said.

"In Bridgeport?"

"I was thinking more like Cuba. Balmy weather, tropical fruit, the rumba, and the best part is no extradition."

"No speako Españolo. Besides, I'm a hotshot detective now. I'm your partner. You need me."

"Assistant. And believe it or not, Pants on Fire Detective Agency will survive without you in its employment."

I brought Cleo fresh coffee, paper, and pen. "Make a list of everyone who would have a reason to want Walter dead."

Cleo tapped the pen on her teeth. "There's his boss, of course. Walter has been skimming the books since starting there. That must be a boat load of cash. If the boss caught on, he'd have one hell of a motive."

"I'll check him out first. Who else?"

"There was a neighbor Walter sued a few years ago when he fell off his porch. Walter claimed his back was broken. The neighbor lost his house. Walter bought a cabin in Colorado for skiing and snowmobiling."

"With a broken back?"

"Are you kidding? It was a con. Walter's life was one con after another. He liked slipping on wet floors at supermarkets. Mostly insurance scams. At first he hid his cons from me. Then after a while I caught on. It was the court papers and process servers and the endless appointments with lawyers and doctors. It's like he was addicted, ya know? I told Walter he needed help. But he wouldn't listen to me, that stubborn fool."

"Focus on the ones the insurance companies didn't pay. Give me everything you can remember. How about personal grudges, long held grievances?"

"Walter was a card hustler. He won big at poker. He made a few enemies there. He cheated."

Big shocker. "Keep writing it down, even if it seems irrelevant."

I left Cleo bent over her paper, documenting Walter's miserable life. She wrote feverishly. It appeared she needed a notebook. I ducked into my bedroom and changed into a green hoodie that matched my eyes, white shorts, and tennies. My brother Rocco was coaching his girls' soccer game at five. If I hurried, I could check one name off Cleo's list today.

Wrapping my hair up into a ponytail, I walked into the kitchen and found Cleo staring bleakly at the list in her hand.

"Walter was witty and charming. People adored him. That's what made him a great con-man. I'd like to think he would've done things differently, if he had more time."

"Wouldn't we all." I pried the list from her hand finger by finger. "I'm taking your car. Why don't you come with me to the soccer game?"

"Nah, I'd rather stay home and hide out. Walter's dead, I'm on trial for a murder, and thanks to a video, I'm the most notorious woman in Chicago."

Yep, she hit that one on the head.

"Ok, why not pour a glass of wine, take a hot bubble bath, and read some V.I. Warshawski? She always gets her man."

Cleo almost smiled.

"And it wouldn't hurt to make your peace with Walter. He might help us find his killer. We're gonna need all the help we can get."

Walter had managed the books for Millani Construction almost three years. Owner Ken Millani was one man on Cleo's growing list of suspects. According to Cleo, her husband's embezzling had escaped Ken's detection. But an anticipated independent audit had Walter in a dither. Last winter he asked Cleo to help him cover his tracks. When she refused, he was furious. Walter actually used that as his excuse for porking Cleo's sister.

Cleo had always disapproved of the way her husband played people. She had tried to change him and couldn't. In time, she excused his character flaw as a result of early childhood abandonment issues and the years he spent in foster homes.

I drove to Millani Construction, located on Archer. The Millani's are friends of my parents and members of Father Timothy's parish. Ken remodeled my house when I bought it, updating the kitchen and converting the front bedroom to an office with a side entrance for clients. He's a member of the Bridgeport neighborhood council and a generous contributor to community fundraisers.

I caught Ken in the parking lot. He was headed to a construction site in Chinatown.

"Cat. How is your office working for you? When you marry and have children I'll put another story on your house with lots of bedrooms."

I made a face. "Thanks Ken, I'll get right on that. Actually, I'm on my way to a soccer game."

"At the school?"

"Yeah. My nieces are playing. Rocco's coaching."

Ken chuckled. "Your brother won't give those girls any slack. He's too much of a competitor."

"Rocco's like you. He hates to lose. And so far, they don't very often."

I walked with Ken to his truck.

"I came by to ask you about Walter."

"We're saddened by Walter's death. It's a big loss for the company."

Loss was the word, alright.

"The last several months took a toll on him," Ken said. "Walter was having problems at home. His wife was a real whack-job. She tried to kill him twice."

"Twice?" *Oh that Cleo, she's a bundle of surprises.*

"When they split, I sold Walter a house I built in Bridgeport Village. He began working from home. When his wife called the office, she was told Walter was no longer with us. You have to understand it was for Walter's safety. Walter said his missus could star in Bridgeport's version of *Psycho*. I thought it was typical divorce talk. You get me? Then I saw the video, and yeeoza."

"Oh, I get you. I understand Walter managed the company's books."

"Yeah, he did."

"Were there any discrepancies with the books?"

"Why you wanna know?"

"I'm a detective, Ken. I'm detecting."

He squelched a smile. "Yeah. I remember my nephew hired you to find out why his missus was tramping out every Thursday night."

"I remember. I caught her red-handed. She was 'tramping out' as you so elegantly put it, taking dance lessons to surprise him for their anniversary."

Ken laughed.

I smacked the truck's hood with my hand. "I'm a damn good investigator."

"You hooked the dancing diva, I'll give you that."

"I do serious cases too, Ken."

"Sure you do." His voice dripped with disapproval.

I knew where Ken was going with this. Ken Millani is an active member of the Parish. He is a hard core, traditional Catholic. His job is building homes. He suspects mine is destroying marriages.

Ken unlocked the door of his white work pick-up and climbed in.

"Anyways, you asked about the books." He looked down at me from the cab. "It was Walter who discovered the screw up with the financials. A dirty employee was stealing from the company. I fired his sorry ass. He won't find work in this town anytime soon."

"You didn't press charges?"

"Pressing charges is not gonna get my money back. Why drag Millani Construction through the newspaper and get nothing for it?"

He fired up the truck and put it in gear.

"Listen, Ken. I know for a fact that Cleo didn't kill Walter."

He talked slowly like maybe it would be easier for my brain to catch up. "Not according to Captain Bob. We talked last night at the bowling alley."

"And?"

Ken smiled broadly. "Our league is going to the state championship."

"Oh. Yay."

Ken waited.

I mustered up some enthusiasm. "Congrats. Really, that is fabulous." I plastered a grin on my face. "So, do you know of anyone who might have a reason to kill Walter?"

"Walter got along with everybody, except for that nut job ex. He was a good guy. If you saw how that no good embezzling business broke him up…"

"Oh, I'm sure it did." I felt my teeth grind.

"Everybody liked Walter."

My eyebrows shot up.

"Well," he amended, "I guess *somebody* didn't."

Chapter Six

I arrived at the girls' soccer game shortly after it started. Maria, Rocco's wife, had organized a potluck for the families. Papa burned burgers on the barbeque and Mama orchestrated the event and kept the potato salad coming. My brothers, Vinnie and Michael, roasted the weenies. It was a good job for the twins. They hang out wherever the food is anyway.

My cousin Stella waved from the stands. She had a big, top-of-the-world smile on her face. I used to babysit Stella. Next Saturday I'll be her Maid of Honor. She's marrying her childhood sweetheart.

Stella and Jake have been valentines since the second grade. They exchanged promise rings in the seventh. Jake's an only child. His dad's out of the picture. His mom, a registered nurse, works long hours to support the two of them. Jake was a lonely kid until Stella brought him home one day for supper. He's had a seat at the table ever since. Jake grew up with the DeLucas. He's been at every family event anyone can remember. It's not as if he doesn't know what he's getting into.

Jake's mother is a staunch Southern Baptist. When her son converted to Catholicism, she was mildly horrified. Uncle Joey assured her Jake will retain all the guilt Baptists provide along with the new perks of dancing, drinking, and the kind of unleashed sex that produces large families.

When Stella was in high school, I talked to her once about dating other guys. I said, "life is like Mama's buffet. How can you know chicken alfredo is your favorite dish if you never tried the cacciatore?" Stella told me what I could do with my chicken cacciatore.

But then, who am I to give advice on relationships anyway?

Maybe some people just know where they belong. Jake is a great guy. He has two more years of college to complete a degree in Law Enforcement. Stella works for minimum wage in a little flower shop that she dreams of buying someday. They have a hard road and a lot of cheap pasta dinners ahead of them. They're just too damn happy to care.

I heaped my plate shamelessly and joined Mama and my crazy sister, Sophie, to watch the game. Walter's murder was all over the news. Mama would have plenty to say about my assistant's arrest, as would all of Bridgeport. But at least my friends were loyal enough to talk behind my back.

Mama pinched her lips. "So, your Uncle Joey said you bailed *that woman* out of jail."

"Yes Mama, and you know that woman's name. We have dinner with you and Papa every Wednesday night. You like her."

"That was before I knew she killed people," Mama said, all snooty.

"Cleo doesn't have to kill people. She makes them crazy."

Sophie hugged the infant she was nursing. "*Some* of us have children to protect. Thanks to you, a murderer is loose in the city."

My sister is quick to point out I don't have kids of my own. Her fertile uterus is a triumph to our parents and the Pope. The fact that I'm thirty and divorced makes her positively giddy.

"I spoke to Father Timothy," Mama said.

"Of course you did."

Mama has Father Timothy's number on speed dial.

"With *that woman* all over the news, I thought Father Timothy should know the DeLucas do not consort with criminals."

"The DeLucas consort, Mama. We're cops and P.I.'s. Consorting pays the mortgage."

My sister sniffed. "By enabling a murderer?"

"I know for a fact Cleo didn't do it. I was there. *I* found the body."

Mama's voice rose as she threw her arms up in the air. "What has happened to my sweet Caterina?"

Sophie took a big bite of potato salad and made nummy noises in her throat. "No one makes potato salad like Mama."

"You're such a suck-up," I said.

The soccer game was a decisive victory for our team. Rocco and Maria's oldest daughter made a goal. There would be ice cream sundaes tonight at Gio's Deli and Restaurant and all the DeLucas would be there.

I hung around after the game and helped Rocco pack up the equipment. My brother is a year older than I am and he's my best friend. I lived my entire life with the certain knowledge that we had each other's back. That is until that very moment.

"Great game," I said.

"Happy you made it. It means a lot to the girls."

"I wouldn't miss it. I wanted to ask if you—"

"No."

"What?"

"Sorry Cat. I can't help you with your friend's case. You're on your own with this one."

"Cleo is innocent. I can prove it."

He shoved a bag of soccer balls into my arms. "Ya can't. 'Cause she's not. I've seen the evidence. If there was a chance in hell she didn't do it, I'd be with you. The last time you interfered with a murder investigation, you could've cost Captain Bob his retirement."

"Interfered? Really? Let me tell you something, Mr. Police-man. I'm a licensed detective. I was investigating, just like you."

"You're not just like me. I investigate. You stalk. You're a—"

"Don't say it, Rocco."

"Hootchie stalker."

I made a face. "Sticks and stones, bro."

"Captain Bob is up for retirement next year. He can't afford another screw up. I won't help you tarnish his reputation."

"I'm only asking you to run some fingerprints."

"It's a little more complicated than that. You don't get it, sis. It's not just Cleo they're looking at. You were at the wrong place at the wrong time. And you're not home free yet."

"Hello? What are you talking about exactly?"

A vein in Rocco's neck throbbed. "For once in your life, trust somebody, Cat. Bob is trying to keep you out of this. Stay out of his way and let him do his job."

I was bummed after my conversations with Rocco and Mama and my switched-at-birth sister. I skipped the ice cream sundaes and stopped by Tino's Deli on my way home. My ears burned as I stepped from the car. Somewhere in Bridgeport, my big fat Italian family was talking smack about me.

I breezed into the deli and Tino's round face broke into a smile. "Caterina! You came for my cannoli."

"You heard."

Tino laughed. "Your mama cut you off. She says you consort with criminals."

"I've consorted with worse." I winked.

I took a table by the window. Tino splashed wine in two glasses and sat beside me. Outside the steady hum of traffic lit up the street with red and white lights. I inhaled deeply and let the ruby red liquid warm my throat.

"Cleo didn't kill her husband," I said. "He was dead when I found him."

"Take the advice of an old sausage maker."

"Who was once a spy."

"And you know this how?"

"I'm a hotshot detective. I know how to keep a secret. You can tell me and you won't even have to kill me."

It was true. Before Tino opened the best deli on Chicago's south side, he was a covert operative for the U.S. government. He denies it, of course, but I have my sources. I just wish I had his. Tino always knows what goes on in Bridgeport, and often before the cops do. Hushed backroom meetings and a bulletproof car add to his intrigue.

"Cat, you have a vivid imagination."

I smiled. "What's the advice?"

"Stop telling people you found Walter's body."

"But I did."

"Stop saying that."

"What should I say?"

He shrugged, palms up. "You were in Vegas. Like they say, 'everything stays in Vegas'."

"The cops saw me with Walter's body."

"Leo? Psssh." Tino made a dismissive sound.

"And I went to the cop shop. I saw Captain Bob and the evil—"

"Detective Opsahl?" He waved a hand. "Cops can be persuaded to forget things. Airline records will prove you were in Las Vegas at the time of the murder."

"See! Right there, you're not talking like a sausage maker."

"Let's say I know a little about spies and a lot about cover-ups."

"And you know this because…?"

"James Bond. I'm a huge fan."

I laughed. "Thanks, Tino, but my butt isn't on the line here. I'm worried about Cleo. Can you get her to Cuba?"

"Right now it's your sweet little bum I'm worried about. There's a big fat line attached to it."

I felt my stomach sink. Tino knows things.

He stuffed sausages and a small box of cannoli in a bag. I added a crunchy loaf of bread, camembert cheese, and a bottle of Chianti. He tossed in a fistful of chocolates.

"I need your help, Tino." My voice sounded small.

"I know," he said softly. "I've already asked around. I'll let you know what I hear."

I nodded. "What are Cleo's chances?"

"The prosecution doesn't have the murder weapon. That can be problematic. But they have motive and opportunity. And a video every potential juror in Chicago has seen. They say their case is a slam dunk."

I sighed dismally. "I need to find Walter's killer."

"What you need is a signed confession. And then you can only hope it's half as convincing as that video."

Chapter Seven

I drove home on autopilot with a sense of impending doom. There was a sick feeling in my gut. Like you get when the dentist says *root canal.* Or you just slipped off the Sears Tower. For some reason the investigation into Walter Jones' murder had turned an eye on me. My butt was on the line with Cleo's. And that line had *Cuba* written all over it.

A shiny metallic gray Toyota Highlander Hybrid was parked in front of my house when I pulled into the driveway. Brand new with a temporary license posted in the back window. I got a whiff of new car smell when I opened my door.

I climbed out with my goodies and shut the door with my booty. A beagle's unmistakable bay broke through the night. A moment later Inga emerged from the darkness, her white-tipped tail wagging joyfully. A man jogged behind her and his feet pounded a steady rhythm on the concrete. I couldn't make out his face until the floodlight from Mrs. Pickens' yard picked it up. My breath caught.

He was tall, broad shouldered, and he exuded testosterone.

He stopped beside the new Highlander. The street light lit the cobalt blue eyes. A wolfish smile touched his lips. I dropped Tino's groceries and walked into Savino's arms.

Chance Savino is my very own gorgeous FBI agent. He has one of those amazingly chiseled bodies that should be put on display as a piece of art. I recently began seeing him after a long dry spell in the dating department.

We're still in that early, honeymoon stage of a relationship when your lover makes you giddy. Everything he does has a certain charm. So far Chance hadn't done anything that could, given time, make me crazy. He didn't snore, chew tobacco, or leave the toilet seat up. Based on my experience with three brothers and more cousins than any Protestant I know, I expected the quirks to come.

Chance wrapped his arms around me. The last two days had been like a rollercoaster ride on steroids. I held tight.

"You OK, DeLucky?"

I pulled back and tilted my head to look at him. His face was adorably appealing. Chance Savino was, in a word, magnificent.

The curtains parted at the Pickens' house.

"Please tell me this is your new car."

"Do you like it?"

"You're so much hotter without your boat."

Chance chucked a fist to his chest. "The Eldorado is a classic. It's not a boat."

When I met Chance Savino he drove a Porsche Boxster. Turns out the car wasn't his. Chance drives a 1959 Cadillac Eldorado Biarritz. A boat with wheels.

He grinned. "You want to break in the new seats?"

"Another time. I can feel Mrs. Pickens binoculars already. So where's the Titanic?"

"I dropped the car off with Jack. He agreed to restore it under *one* condition. He says you can never drive it."

I gasped with mock dismay. "How will I be able to stop myself?"

"Smartass."

He traced the outline of my lips with one finger. A shudder swept through me. I leaned into him, savoring the hot, sweet scent of eye candy.

"Zero to sixty in two seconds," he breathed.

My arms went around his neck and I kissed him. "I wasn't expecting you until next week. Did Rocco call you?"

"He didn't have to. Cleo's video is all over the net. The media has tried and convicted her. It's more than you can handle."

"What?" I pushed at his chest with both hands. "Wait a second. So you came back because you thought *I couldn't handle* this?"

"Is that a trick question?"

I stomped my foot. "I'm a detective, Savino. A damn good one."

He smiled easily. "Your detective cases involve people who may *want* to kill each other. But they hook up with a neighbor or co-worker instead. This is cold blooded murder."

"Thanks for the support!"

I turned on my heel as he grabbed my arm.

"I am supporting you. That's why I'm here. I thought you might need a hand. Or at least a shoulder."

Okay. So he had a point.

He took my arms and wrapped them behind his neck and leaned down and kissed me.

"What about the baseball game tomorrow night? You had tickets."

He winced. "The White Sox at Yankee Stadium. I had box seats."

"Ouch."

"You can make it up to me." He picked up Tino's bag from the driveway. "I have ideas."

"So do I. I'll share my ice cream with you."

His cobalt blues sent a shiver through me. "Later, babe. First, I have something else in mind."

"Oh really…" I hooked a finger in his belt and steered him inside.

Chance was gone when I awoke the next morning. He'd left a note on the pillow.

Hey, Beautiful, we'll be back soon.

"We?" I patted the bed around me. No beagle.

The sound of pans banging in the kitchen meant something wonderful was happening. With Cleo in the house, my refrigerator brimmed with gourmet foods and fresh ingredients. By her own admission, Cleo cooks when under stress. Considering her present circumstances, I could count on a boundless source of shameless gluttony; something I'd missed since moving away from Mama's kitchen.

I squinted at the clock on my nightstand and groaned. Eight fifteen. I'd overslept. I scooted out of bed and into the shower. I dressed quickly in a pair of DK Jeans, tucked in a silky lavender tank, and slipped on a pair of ballet style flats. I did my emergency two minute makeup routine and ambled down the hall to join Cleo in the kitchen.

I made a bee-line for the coffee pot. "Where did Chance and Inga go?"

"They're meeting Captain Bob at the station. I guess it's some kind of 'professional courtesy' thing." You could almost see the light-bulb over Cleo's head. "Hey, do you think Chance will put in a good word for me?"

I sipped my coffee. "It's *so* cute you think that would help. There aren't enough *good* words in the dictionary to smooth over that video circling the Internet. Did you see Jay Leno last night? You made the dialogue."

She glowered. "I hate that video. It makes my ass look fat."

I gripped my cup with two hands to keep from throttling her.

"Really, Cleo. Your ass? That's what you are worried about? You might consider being a little more concerned about screaming *I'm going to kill you, you cheating bastard and hang you by your—*"

"Stop!" Cleo's eyes welled with tears. "You think it's not hard for me to know those are the last words I said to him? It's something I'll have to live with the rest of my life. No matter what anyone thinks, I loved Walter. I couldn't have killed him."

"Yeah? Well the only way to save you from slinging tamales in Havana is to find the real killer."

Cleo chewed her lip. "Do you think we can pull it off?"

I lied shamelessly. "Absolutely. We're top rate detectives. Nobody gets past the Pants On Fire Detective Agency." She smiled, relieved.

"But," I added, "I wouldn't be afraid to bone up on my Spanish."

Cleo made brunch. Potato pancakes with smoked salmon, capers, and dill cream. She was pulling an almond plum pastry from the oven when Savino walked through the door, Inga trotting at his heels. If it wasn't for a messy murder and my crazy family, I'd think I'd died and gone to heaven.

Chance pulled me to him and kissed me. "That was from me," he said.

I kissed him back. "That's from me."

"Get a room," Cleo said.

"And this is from Captain Bob." Chance slapped my behind.

I pushed him away. "Captain Bob smacked me?"

"Police brutality," Cleo said.

"The captain says you lied to him. He's fuming."

"What? I was straight with Bob. I told him exactly what happened."

"Exactly?"

"I may have left out a few of the details—like saying Walter's door was open—but I didn't *lie* to him, exactly. What did you tell him?"

"I wanted to hear it from you."

"But I told you everything last night."

"Everything?"

I looked hard into the cobalt blue. This time I didn't melt. I didn't even thaw a little.

"You should've told Captain Bob I didn't lie to him. The fact is you didn't believe me. That's a lot worse than snoring."

"Snoring?"

"Time out!" Cleo squawked and lifted her frying pan into the air.

I resisted the urge to duck for cover.

"If there's one thing that's worse than lying and snoring, it's cold potato pancakes," she said. "Sit down, shut up, and eat something before you both say something you'll regret."

My appetite was gone. I played with the food on my plate, shuffling the smoked salmon around with a fork. Chance, on the other hand, ate like a big fat pig at the trough.

He laughed and his eyes crinkled around the edges. He leaned back in his chair, his long easy posture and hard muscular build stirred up those tingly feelings. I looked away, reminding myself how angry I was. Once, I had to think about dead kittens.

Cleo told funny stories about Walter and her eyes softened. I believed her when she said she couldn't kill him. I glared at Chance. It appeared I was the only one.

After brunch, I loaded the dishwasher and Chance washed the pans in the sink. Dishwater hands are something you rarely see with DeLuca men. *Dead kittens, dead kittens*, I reminded myself.

When Chance had tucked the last pan away in the cupboard, we joined Beau and Inga in the back yard.

"We'll finish our conversation out here," he said. "The air is a little thick in the kitchen."

Cleo chortled. I threw her a look.

Chance suppressed a smile. "Ethel Opsahl is the lead detective in the investigation."

"She hates me," I said.

"She wants to fry me," Cleo said indignantly. "Whatever happened to the presumption of innocence?"

I waved a wrist. "That was before the age of videos. Before you announced to the world how you intended to kill Walter using several very creative instruments."

"Does that video give me a fat butt?"

Chance opened his mouth, closed it, and turned his attention to me. "According to the autopsy results, there's a serious problem with the time of death."

"What are you saying?"

"Captain Bob originally believed Cleo killed Walter before she fetched Cat from the marina."

Cleo snorted. "How dim-witted do they think I am? Like I would return to the scene of the crime? I mean, give me some credit!"

"The department bought into this scenario because Cat claimed Walter was dead when she found him."

"I didn't *claim* anything," I snapped. "Walter was dead!"

"Well, according to the autopsy results, the timeline doesn't fit. Walter was alive and well when Cleo left the house for the marina."

"Woo hoo!" Cleo squawked. "I couldn't have killed him!"

Elated, I hugged Chance. "Why didn't you say so? Do they have another lead? Any suspects."

"Uh huh. That would be Cleo. Or more accurately, both of you."

"What?"

"Cleo didn't kill Walter *before* she picked you up at the marina. But according to the medical examiner, she could have killed him when you were both in the house."

"That isn't possible. I found the body first. Cleo was never out of my sight."

"Captain Bob doesn't know what to think. The facts suggest you were in the house when Walter was murdered. Not involved, necessarily. He suspects you are covering for your friend. At the very least, that makes you an accomplice after the fact. Their case against Cleo is pretty solid. Nothing has changed there. As things stand, Captain Bob will be forced to bring charges against you too. You'll go to jail. At the very least, you'll lose your investigator's license."

I was stunned. "I'll lose Pants On Fire Detective Agency?"

"Unless you strike a deal and testify against Cleo."

"And it didn't occur to you to tell the captain this is bullshit? That I was telling the truth and Cleo is innocent?"

We both looked at her. "In a manner of speaking." I amended.

"If it makes you feel better, I told Bob I'm behind you one hundred percent. He's trying to keep you out of it, but the forensics creates a big problem for him. Anyone else would be facing charges already."

"Why can't Bob accept the obvious fact that someone else murdered Walter before we arrived?"

"With that video? It's better than a signed confession. Besides, after the commotion Cleo made, no one could have entered the house without a neighbor noticing."

"The killer must have skulked through the back," I said.

"Yeah. Killers skulk," Cleo said.

Chance smiled. "Don't see you as a skulker, Cleo. You'd kill Walter on Main Street with a hundred witnesses and half a dozen video cameras."

"Damn straight," Cleo said.

"If I'm going to help you girls, I need to know everything. Did you see anything at Walter's house that might suggest another person had been there recently?"

"Nope," I said.

"Yes. There was a designer bag." Cleo whirled her head back to me. "I'm not going to let you lose your business, girlfriend. And I sure as hell can't speak Spanish."

"Oh, you'll learn fast with that big mouth of yours," I said.

Savino's breath, irritated, hissed out of his lungs. "Tell me about the bag."

"It was in the coat closet by the front door. Someone had to have dropped it off that day. Walter would've taken it to the bank almost immediately."

"The cops didn't find the bag. I assume you have it."

Cleo winked.

"What, exactly, was inside?"

"Do you really want to know?" I said.

Savino sighed. "No. That way I'm not withholding crucial evidence from the Captain."

Inga dropped a Frisbee at his feet. He picked it up and flung it in the air. Inga and Beau charged after it.

"Did you get fingerprints off the bag?"

"Rocco won't help me. Can you believe it?"

"Did he say why?"

"He has this wild idea I'm going to screw up Captain Bob's retirement."

Savino grinned. "I wonder where he would get an insane idea like that."

"Exactly!"

"Bring me the bag. I'll send the prints to the FBI lab, to see *if* there are any left after you two were done with it. We should also interview the neighbors behind Walter's house. Maybe somebody saw something."

I headed inside and stacked the rest of the money on a shelf behind the pantry wall and delivered the bag to Chance.

"So I guess I acted stupid earlier, huh. I thought you didn't believe me."

"I believed you, DeLucky. But it's a two way street. I need you to be straight with me. What is it with you and these stupid little secrets? I get that it's hard for you to trust people. But don't stick me in a league with your ex. I'm not the same guy that hurt you."

"Shut up."

His hands settled around my waist and he pulled me against him. "You shut up and kiss me."

Chapter Eight

Chance took off with the bag and Cleo's list of people Walter pissed off. He also intended to snoop around the Millani Construction Co. I explained I had it handled, but Chance said he wanted to talk to some of the employees.

I dressed Cleo in a pastel pink sundress that hugged her generous waist and bust like a second skin and flared out at the bottom. Did a little make-up magic with thick black eyeliner and topped it off with a sexy blonde wig. After this little romp through my trusty box of disguises, I hardly recognized the crazed video woman myself. We drove back to Bridgeport Village and stood in the alley behind Walter's house. We decided three houses had a possible view of traffic moving in and out of Walter's house.

We struck out on the first two. If the neighbors saw anything, they weren't talking. The last was a large white, three story home. The curtain in the upstairs window moved. I could make out an old man, eyes fixed on the alley. I waved to him and rang the bell but he didn't come to the door.

We tromped back in the Camry. I scooted behind the wheel and turned the key. The engine groaned twice before firing up.

I dropped my head on the steering wheel. "I think the starter's going out," I groaned. "I'll call Jack but he's not giving up Doris."

Cleo grinned, dangling a key. "Forget Doris! We have Walter"s Corvette. It belongs to me now."

I threw her a look and shoved the Camry in drive. "Captain Bob may disagree. Unless you're running for the border, the Corvette stays here."

We were tooling our way north on Ashland when the back pocket of my DK's started vibrating. Hank Williams belted *Your Cheatin' Heart.* I dragged out my cell phone.

"Pants on Fire Detective Agency. We catch liars and cheats."

"We're not having this conversation," Jackson said.

Jackson is my brother's partner. He's Samoan and he's massive in body and in heart. He was going to tell me something that he didn't want coming back.

"Works for me. Is Rocco there with you now?"

"He is."

"Why doesn't he talk to me himself?"

"He promised Captain Bob he wouldn't assist you with your obstruction of justice."

"I'm a private investigator, dammit."

"No, you investigate people's privates. Big difference."

My brother cracked up in the background.

I rolled my eyes. "Tell me what you've got, Jackson."

"I pulled Walter's phone records."

"You didn't make Captain Bob any promises?"

"He didn't offer me a paid vacation at his cabin on Bass Lake."

"Sweet."

"Rocco says you're babysitting."

"Fine. But the girls get ice cream every night."

"Rocco says there's no need to tell Maria."

"Deal. Whatcha got?"

"Walter Jones had enemies."

"Tell me something I don't know."

"After his marriage fell apart, he began gambling heavily. He owed money to people you don't even want to know your name."

"Do we know *their* names?"

"We know one. The last call Walter made was to a bookie named Jake Manovich. The guy's on parole so his address should be current."

Jackson read off an address on South Fifty-third and I jotted it down. "Thanks. I'll check it out."

"Rocco says take Cleo with you. The guy's a scumbag. If he makes trouble, Cleo can use him for target practice."

"My brother's hilarious. Why was Jake Manovich in the tank?"

"He rearranged a customer's face with a crowbar. One of his high rollers didn't pay up."

"Short fuse. I won't let Cleo piss him off."

"That would mean not letting Cleo open her mouth."

"Gotcha."

◇◇◇

The bookie, Jake Manovich, lived in Cicero not far from the Hawthorne horse track. I knocked on the head smasher's door and elbowed my assistant. "Let me do the talking on this one."

"OK."

"No argument?"

She zipped her lips.

I glared into her eyes but she seemed to mean it.

A man with long blond hair answered the door holding a can of Schmidt beer in his hand. He was shirtless and a beer belly hung over his belt. If he turned around, we were sure to see a crack.

"Are you Jake Manovich?"

"Who wants to know?"

"I'm Cat DeLuca, private investigator."

Cleo whipped out her agency identification card. My head did a double take. A tin badge was pinned to the ID. It looked like she picked it out of a cereal box.

"Pants On Fire Detective Agency," Cleo quipped.

"Let me see that," he said.

I shoved her aside. "We'd like to ask a few questions about your relationship with Walter Jones."

"What do you want to know? The guy owed me twelve large. I want my money."

"Your number was the last call Walter made before he was brutally murdered. What did you two talk about?"

"The dude said he had my money. He was supposed to meet me in an hour. He never showed."

"And that's why you killed him," Cleo said.

"What?"

"Cat, arrest this man."

"You arrest him. You're the one with the badge."

"Screw you lady. I ain't goin' nowhere with ya. I ain't killed that low-life. How stupid do I look?"

Cleo looked at Jake and then at me. "Okay, tell Rocco to arrest him."

"We don't need Rocco."

"Why not?"

"Cuz he didn't do it."

"Thank you," Jake Manovich said sarcastically.

"How do you know?" Cleo said.

"He's a money-grubbing bookie. Walter died with his Rolex on. And a fat wad of cash on his dresser."

"Hey," Jake said. "That's my money!"

Mickey's in Bridgeport is a serious cop hang-out. The locals call it "The Pig Trough." You don't have to be a cop to drink there but you should at least enjoy their company.

The Sox game was just starting when Cleo and I cruised through the door. We got a few cat calls and whistles and the hot new blonde got plenty of looks. I told Cleo to cover her bum and scoot along behind me. We made it through the crowd with three slaps and a pinch.

Chance had chosen a table close to the big screen TV. He stood and kissed me when we arrived. His eyes never left the screen.

"I had box seat tickets for this game," Chance reminded me.

"Let it go, Savino."

I ordered drinks at the bar and two big stuffed-sausage pizzas. I stopped by Papa's table and gave hugs all around to my brothers, cousin Frankie, and my Uncle Joey.

"Who's the blonde?" Papa said.

"Uh, Chance's cousin, Amy. I don't think you know her."

Uncle Joey grinned. Cleo's disguise wasn't fooling him. "She looks like Marilyn Monroe in *Some Like It Hot*."

"I like it hot," Frankie said and waggled his eyebrows at Cleo.

"Don't let her talk," Uncle Joey said.

Papa squinted. "She looks familiar."

"Think of Wednesday night supper," Rocco said.

I kicked him.

My brother Rocco is smarter than the twins and cousin Frankie put together.

"Chance's cousin is visiting from LA," I said.

Frankie broke into song. "Wish they all could be California girls."

The beer he swung in his hand wasn't his first. Frankie has a long history of mental health issues. That's why he was turned down by the FBI. The family took the snub as an insult to all DeLucas. Luckily, for my unbalanced cousin, the Chicago PD welcomed him with open arms and gave him a really big gun.

This long-standing family grudge against the FBI prompted an emergency family meeting to determine what to do with my FBI boyfriend. The vote was inconclusive. Frankie's mother, my Aunt Fran, is frosty, if not downright rude to Chance. However, most DeLucas consider my case desperate. They know I'm thirty, single, and I suck at dating. They stand behind Mama who will embrace any man reasonably sober and capable of breeding grandchildren.

"Enjoy the game," I said. "I ordered a pizza for your table."

"Woo hoo!" the twins said waving hot wings.

I made my way back to our table and watched the game with Chance and Amy from LA.

We cheered the Sox, chomped gooey slices of pizza, and drank beer. Chance recounted his day in bits and pieces during the ads. It had taken him longer to knock off the names on Cleo's list than he'd expected. In the end, some lived out of state or were at work when Walter was killed. Two guys were over Walter and had put the experience behind them. Another man was savagely bitter and would've cheerfully killed him if given half a chance. He just didn't have that chance Friday. The final man on Cleo's list had the most convincing alibi of all. He was as cold and dead as Walter.

In the seventh inning, Chance got a call from the FBI lab with the results of the fingerprints on the bag. He grunted a few times and hung up. We had to wait for an ad to hear what he learned.

"After eliminating our prints and Walter's, one more person was identified."

"Who is it already?" Amy from LA squawked.

"Keep your voice down," he growled. "It's Roxanne Barbara."

"The famous designer?" the star-struck blonde gasped. "The First Lady wears her gowns."

"It's an RB bag," I reminded her.

Roxanne Barbara grew up here. She's one of Bridgeport's biggest success stories. She hosts *Fashion Runway, Chicago*. Her cutting-edge designs have changed up-and-coming trends everywhere. RB boutiques are peppered around the United States and Europe.

Cleo sighed. "I've always dreamed of working with Roxanne."

Cleo amazes me with her wide scope of interests.

I, on the other hand, am far less diversified. I tried several careers and only discovered what I love doing when I started the Pants On Fire Detective Agency. I didn't know what I'd do if I lost my license.

"Here's something else," Chance said. "The fact that RB's prints are on the bag doesn't mean she had anything to do with it ending up in Walter's closet. This particular bag was a sample. Only a few were made. Apparently Roxanne wasn't pleased with it and cut the bag from production. You'd expect her prints to be all over it."

"It still narrows the playing field," I said. "Roxanne may not have delivered the bag but someone with access to her did. Tomorrow I'll check it out. She's expanding her factory in Bridgeport."

Chance nodded. "You may want to pay another visit to Millani Construction. Your friend lied to you. The guy he fired last week was Walter Jones. Ken wasn't going to press charges for embezzlement. I'd like to know why."

"Blackmail," Cleo said grimly. "Walter needed leverage if his boss found out he was skimming. He wanted me to look into Ken's personal life. I refused."

"He found what he needed without your help," Chance said.

I topped our beer mugs. "I need to get back inside Walter's house. Who knows how many people he was blackmailing. Chances are one of them killed him. He must have left a trail somewhere."

"Forget it, DeLucky. The house is wrapped in police tape and the door is sealed. I'll stop by and talk to the Captain. He'll listen to me."

"You have a meeting at the FBI office tomorrow and Cleo is seeing her lawyer. I'll drop by the cop shop and talk to Bob myself. I want to bring him up to speed on how our investigation is coming along. I think he's starting to see me in a different light. You know, not the little girl growing up, but a capable professional."

"Bob doesn't *appreciate* your professional opinion, DeLucky. He says you're a—"

"Don't say it."

He grinned. "It's your call. But when he arrests you, try not to piss off the judge. I have a government salary to bail you out on."

Amy from LA leaned forward, spilling boob out of the sundress. Even her whisper is shrill. "Screw the government salary. We got a crook's big ol' bag of cash."

"*Ick-snay on the ash-cay,*" I low-growled at Cleo. I could have pretended it was the wig cutting off circulation to the brain, but that would've given her too much credit.

I squeezed Savino's thigh to get his attention. "While you're out tomorrow, stop by Walter's alley. There's an old man in the big white house. Maybe he'll talk to you. I'd like to know if he saw anything the other day."

"Old man, white house, got it." Savino's cobalt blues electrified the air between us. His finger reached up slowly and touched my lips. "Shhh. We're missing the game."

Chapter Nine

I was all tangled in my sheets when a hammer woke me the next morning. I pried an eye open, listened, and closed it again. I blamed Amy and the last round of tequila. The memory of her squawking 'Ole!' grated in my skull like nails on a chalkboard.

The aroma of coffee and bacon lured me from bed. I tugged my robe on and glanced in the mirror. The smeared mascara had glued one lid shut and gave me raccoon eyes. My hair was smushed to my head in clumps. I stuffed my feet in bunny slippers and shuffled down the hall after the paper.

Shielding my open eye from the sun I stepped onto the porch. The paparazzi charged the door with flashbulbs going off in my face.

"Isn't that Cleo Jones' car outside your house?"

"Is she staying with you?"

"What did she tell you about her part in the vicious slaying of her husband?"

"Does the Pants On Fire Detective Agency assist in the murder of cheaters?"

I forced the other eye open and regretted it instantly. Suddenly there was twice as many.

I answered their questions. "Yes. No. She didn't do it. Are you freakin' insane?"

I snatched the paper off the porch and scooted inside, slamming the door behind me.

I dropped the paper on the table.

"Good morning!" Cleo's shrill voice gushed. "You have—"

I held up a hand. "Hold that thought."

"But you—"

"Hey. Give me a minute, will ya. I need to wash my face and find my eyes." I sauntered down the hall.

"Have Tony Beano release a statement to the press," I called over my shoulder. "Tell them you're staying somewhere—anywhere. Just get those vultures off my porch."

I took one step into my room and screamed. A man was in my bed.

Hard chest, six pack abs, this guy was a half rack. The kind of body you read about in steamy gothic novels. An inferno stirred in me, somewhere south of the border. Inga sighed on her back and his hand massaged her pink tummy. Lucky bitch.

"I came in the back," Max said. "There's a war party circling your wagon."

I tore my eyes from his chest to the chair with his Levi's and black tee draped over the back.

Max smiled.

"What are you doing here?" I said in a voice two octaves too high.

"Tino called me. I flew in this morning from Rio."

"Spy work?"

"Vacation."

"Gotcha." I winked.

"Check out the tan," Max said.

I was checking it out alright.

"Captain Bob called you a walking crime spree. He's talking about an arrest warrant. You're going to need some help with this one."

Max, a friend and former colleague of Tino, a.k.a. the spy-turned-sausage-maker, was my bodyguard recently after someone tried to kill me.

"Thanks Max, but no one's trying to kill me now."

"Honey—" he laced his fingers behind his head—"if no one's trying to kill you, you just haven't found Walter's murderer yet."

"Thanks for the pep talk." I made a face. "So whatcha doin' here—in my bed?"

"Shaking off some jet lag. I need to sleep for a few hours, then you can tell me about your latest crime spree and I'll do what you need." He glanced over at the empty side of the bed and our eyes locked. "In fact, you can tell me what you need now."

"You and I…" my pointy finger darted from him to me. "we never—" I attempted to check the regret from my voice.

He grinned. "And that, love, is the biggest crime of all."

I grabbed my toothbrush and clothes and dressed in the main bathroom. Cleo was all smiles when I joined her and Beau in the kitchen.

I poured a cup of coffee and split a piece of bacon with Beau.

"I tried to warn you. Where's Max?"

"In my bed."

She whistled low. "You go, girl. The man has a body of a Greek god."

"He's Danish. And he's sleeping."

"Make that a Viking god. If only I wasn't a widow in mourning, I'd—"

"Not a chance, chica. Max doesn't do crazy. He saw the video."

I dragged Cleo to my office for revamping. I made her a redhead this morning with a pulled back ponytail and bright red lips. When I was finished, I eyed my creation with satisfaction. *Damn, I'm good.* From my magic bag of tricks I'd pulled out a full skirt, a light summer sweater set, and flats. She looked like *I Love Lucy.* I didn't let her in on the fact that my inspiration came from Lucy's husband, Desi, and her likely relocation to his homeland, Cuba.

We tromped back to the kitchen. Cleo whipped up brownies and popped the pan in the oven. I drank coffee and counted her name in the morning paper.

"Seventeen times," I said. "You're more popular than the President."

"Holy shit. I'm like a celebrity."

I made a face. "That's what John Gacy said."

She plopped down beside me. "Did they put my picture in the paper?"

"Don't even ask me about your butt."

The front door opened. The paparazzi's shouts drifted inside and the door closed again.

"Who's here?" Cleo mouthed.

A wave of Catholic guilt hit me. Only two people wield that power. And it wasn't Father Timothy. He always knocks.

Mama's voice wailed from the living room. "You see what your life has become, Caterina? And now the whole world knows."

"Cleo and I are in the kitchen," I called.

"She's with the knives?" Mama gasped.

"That hurts, Mrs. DeLuca," Cleo said.

Mama appeared at the kitchen door. "I brought cannoli," she sniffed. "When *that woman* slits your throat, you should die happy."

I squealed with joy and made a dive for the Tupperware.

Mama's grip was fierce. My gaze traveled from Mama's Tupperware to my dear, troubled friend and back to the cannoli again.

"If *that woman* touches your cannoli, I'll kill her with my bare hands," I said.

Mama smiled happily and surrendered the Tupperware.

I lifted the lid and peeked inside. Chocolate.

"I have never loved you more," I said.

Mama beamed.

Cleo scowled. "I'm not feelin' the love."

A door opened down the hall and Inga raced to the kitchen. A nearly naked man charged behind her, wildly brandishing a gun.

"I heard you scream."

Max's darting eyes were blurred with sleep.

"Yowza," Cleo said. "A boxer man."

Max's smoky gray skivvies flew open like a cape as he slid to a stop in front of Mama. "Good morning, Mrs. DeLuca."

"Indeed," Cleo breathed.

Max lowered his weapon and stumbled back to bed.

Mama reached over to me and held out her hands.

"Caterina," she said. Her disapproving voice was surprisingly calm as she commandeered my cannoli.

Mama didn't say goodbye. She marched through the living room and out the front door. I watched helplessly through the window as she served up my cannoli to the vultures on my porch. When she drove away, I stomped to the kitchen.

"Mama hates me," I said.

"That's ridiculous. Your mother loves you. That's why she makes you crazy."

"Yeah? Well your mama must love you a helluva lot."

Cleo pulled chewy double-fudge brownies from the oven. She tossed the pan and two forks on the table. I poured coffees and we had breakfast.

It was almost ten and the paparazzi were still on my porch. I called my cousin Frankie. He's always looking for the opportunity to shoot someone.

"I can't get to my car," I said. "There's a mob outside of my house."

"Gang members? Terrorists?"

I heard a click. Frankie cocking his gun.

"I dunno. I overheard someone saying something about *'a vicious slaying'*."

"Stay in your house until I get there. And for chrisake, keep away from the windows." He panted between footsteps.

"Thanks, Frankie. I owe you."

"Remember that when you talk to your FBI boyfriend. I want my job back."

This wasn't the time to tell Frankie there's no Santa Claus and he never worked for the FBI.

"Uh, sure, cuz," I said. "I'll see what I can do."

I joined Cleo in the living room. She glared at the paparazzi through a slit in the curtain.

"Can't we just take them out?" Her trigger finger twitched. "We're wasting a perfectly good day."

A siren screamed and a white and blue cop car skidded to a halt, blocking the street outside my door.

My cousin Frankie tumbled out his door and squatted low beside the car, using the car's steel frame as a shield.

"Smokin'," Cleo breathed.

"You know the drill," Cousin Frankie yelled. "On the ground, hands behind your heads." His voice raised a little higher. "Where I can see them, dirtbags."

"He's sooo hot. Is he married?"

"No. He's one fry short of a happy meal whack-job."

"Really?" She drew a breath and wet her lips. "He's so fearless."

"Huh?" I lowered my eyes and glimpsed beneath the squad car. If squatting knees are courageous, I wasn't seeing it. "My cousin Frankie was turned down by the FBI for general insanity."

"Bastards," she said hotly.

My gaze flickered through the glass to Frankie's knees and back again to Cleo's wet lips. She purred.

I shuddered.

Cleo downed the last swill of coffee. "It's show time," she sang and shimmied out the back.

I slung my bag over a shoulder, grabbed my keys, and strolled out the front door.

Across the street, Mrs. Pickens gawked through binoculars. I wondered vaguely if the people on the ground were the only ones with video cameras.

I couldn't see Frankie crouched behind his car. But his gun was propped over the front fender and his trigger finger twitched. Sort of like Cleo's.

I zig-zagged around a maze of sputtering, horizontal bodies, waved to Mrs. Pickens, and hopped into the Camry. Then I swung around the back, and picked Cleo up in the alley.

Chapter Ten

I pulled in front of Tony Beano's office and turned off the engine.

"Where would Walter hide something?" I said.

"Whoa," Cleo said. "You mean you're not seeing Captain Bob?"

"Am I insane? He and Detective Opsahl are itching to lock me up and throw away the key."

"But you told Chance—"

"It was for his own good. With no prior knowledge, he's not an accomplice."

"You better hope he doesn't find out. It'll be ugly."

"That's an understatement."

Cleo thought a moment. "Walter has an old wooden tackle box that belonged to his grandfather. He took it with him when he went into foster care. It's the only thing he has that connects him to his family. He's very secretive about that box. You might want to look there."

"Where does he keep this box?"

"He used to keep it in our office. It could be anywhere now but I'd check the office first. Walter was a creature of habit."

"Thanks. When you're done with Beano, wait for me at Connie's. Order me a Rueben. If I'm not back when you finish eating, bring bail money."

Cleo climbed out and I called my mechanic.

"Jack. This is Cat. Cleo's Camry has problems starting. When can you look at it?"

"Not before Monday. *She* can't have Doris either."

"You're a real pal. How's the Silver Bullet?"

Jack grunted. "I ordered the missing part this morning. If Devin was here I would've done it yesterday."

"Devin is a good mechanic." *And a psycho,* I added to myself. He and I had an unpleasant encounter when he crashed my thirtieth birthday party and tried to choke me to death. Little things like that tend to bother me.

Jack sniffed. "My nephew has his faults, I grant you that. But at least he's not implicated in a homicide."

I took a steadying breath and forced my voice to sound cheerful. I knew from experience if you piss off Jack, he'll hold your car hostage.

"It sounds like you read about Walter's murder in the paper," I said.

"Who has time to read? My customers talk about nothing else. They think you and the wife were in on it together."

"That's crazy talk, Jack. What do you tell them?"

"I say you break your mother's heart."

"Tell me something I don't know." I blew a sigh. "When can I pick up my car?"

"Call me tomorrow. If Devin was here—"

"Yeah, yeah. I could have had it yesterday."

Click.

◇◇◇

I parked the Camry on the street adjacent to Walter's, adjusted my mousy brown wig in the mirror, and cut through the neighbor's yard. I cut the police seal on the back door and waved to the old man in the white house as I closed the door behind me.

Walter's computer was in his office and the hard drive was still in it. The prosecution thought the case was sewn up. They didn't need the hard drive to nail the killer. But I did. I inserted a flash-drive, hit the power, and downloaded the good stuff.

Cleo was right about the tackle box. It was in the office closet behind some reams of paper.

I took a moment to look through his desk. Nothing unexpected. Lots of paperclips and post-it notes.

The download onto the flash-drive said *two minutes, fifty-four seconds remaining* when a key rattled in the lock. Someone was at the front door. I stopped breathing. I was trapped. I turned an ear and listened.

There was a muffled sob.

"Come in, Ms. Harrison. We'll go through each room and I'll make a list of everything that belongs to you."

I groaned inwardly. The voice belonged to the evil Detective Ethel Opsahl. That would be the woman itching to put me away. The sobber was Cleo's sister, the Ho. As I recalled, she didn't have Cleo's shrill, nails-on-a-blackboard voice. She was a whiner. And a nasally one at that.

"It's not fair," the Ho whined. "I don't understand why I can't live here. This is my house. Wally wanted to marry me. *She* stood in our way."

Puh-leeze.

"Your sister was legally married to the deceased and neither party filed for divorce. As far as living here, the house doesn't belong to you. Your name isn't on the mortgage papers. The furnishings and virtually everything in the house was purchased by the victim. What I need from you is a list of any gifts and items the deceased bought for you. You won't be able to take those things with you today. You will only take personal items like clothes and jewelry."

"If I don't get the house, who does?"

"I'm not a lawyer, Ms. Harrison, but I'd expect the victim's wife will receive the bulk of his assets. Unless, of course, a jury convicts her."

"Cleo killed him all right. She shot him before."

"And you'll have an opportunity to testify to that effect in court."

"Can I keep the house then?"

Detective Opsahl was quiet just long enough to count to ten. I know because I counted with her.

"Look around and tell me what belongs to you in the living room."

The Ho let out a blood curdling scream. "She stole my Tiffany lamp and"—there was a pause while she opened the closet—"my leather jacket."

Drama queen.

I pulled the flash-drive and wiped my prints away with my shirt. I moved across the room to the window and opened it. The big giant maple was only a few feet from the window. If I jumped and held on for dear life, I should be able to shimmy my way down the trunk. I jammed Walter's tackle box down my jeans and tightened my belt around it. I tried to recall the saint of no broken bones—there was certainly one out there—and was poised to leap when my cell phone blared "Your Cheatin' Heart." *Oh Hank.*

The nasal gasp downstairs was audible. That would be the Ho.

"Chicago Police. Come out with your hands up!" Detective Opsahl blared.

I soared out the window, scooted down the gnarled old maple like my pants were on fire, and hit the ground running. The race was on. With one hand on the tackle box, I sped toward the white house. My eyes found the old man in the window. I swear I could see him laugh. It gave me a burst of speed and I crossed the alley and had one leg slung over his fence when the screech of brakes suspended my flight. I turned my head and gawked at Chance Savino. His astonished mouth was wide open.

"Oh shit."

"Stop! You're under arrest!" Detective Opsahl screamed from Walter's window.

I flung a second leg over the fence and hot-footed it through the old man's yard, past smells of mint and lavender to the parallel street where I'd parked Cleo's Camry.

Cleo's car had been having starting problems. *Not now,* I murmured and inserted the key. With a poof of burning rubber,

I put Walter's neighborhood behind me. I didn't stop until I could breathe again.

At the first red light I changed my ringtone. "Say good-bye to Hank," I told Inga and Beau in the back seat.

I stuffed the wig in the glove box and zipped to Uncle Joey's to drop off the flash-drive. My cousin, Joey Jr., is a computer genius. He's suspiciously smart for a DeLuca. It's just as well he's a spitting image of his dad. Otherwise, my uncle would demand a DNA test.

I told Junior what I needed. "If it's there, you'll find it. How's the college search going?"

"I'm leaning toward Harvard. Dad wants me to go to the Police Academy—or at least a school that can play football," he said unhappily. "Dad gave me a Notre Dame jacket for my birthday."

The subtlety trait is inherently missing in the DeLuca gene pool.

I hugged him. "Don't worry about your papa. He'll come around."

Junior shook his head. "He didn't even know where Harvard was."

"He's pulling your leg," I laughed. "Hey, would you keep something for me until tomorrow? A certain detective might hunt me down and I don't want her to find it on me."

"Sounds intense, dude."

"Yeah, maybe a little."

I gave up the tackle box and scooted out to the Camry to snag something to wear for the afternoon's activities. When you stalk people for a living, you have an outfit for almost any occasion.

I changed and bagged the wig and clothes I was wearing when Detective Opsahl wanted to shoot me from Walter's window. I called Inga and Beau to the car. They had been running through the sprinklers. When I opened the door, they jumped in the back seat and shook themselves dry.

"Don't ever try that in my car," I said.

Cleo would be waiting for me at Connie's Restaurant. I pointed the car that way and a wave of exhaustion washed over me. I was running on fumes.

I hadn't slept much since the whole Walter mess started. I'd been too worried about Cleo. I told her we were hot shot detectives. I promised we'd find Walter's killer. And she believed in me.

After two solid days I had *nothing*. Captain Bob, on the other hand, had a conviction sewn up in two hours.

The day wasn't half over and I was on a roll. I ticked off my boyfriend. My mother wasn't speaking to me—again. And a cop threatened to shoot me. A day starts like this, a voice screams in my head. *Abandon ship!*

I wanted to go home, take a long hot bubble bath, and drown my sorrows with a bottle of wine and a pint of Ben and Jerry's. But I had a little thing—like my assistant being charged with murder—that couldn't wait for my own personal meltdown day.

So, I put on my big girl panties and drove down an alley where I found a big dumpster to deposit my clothes and the brown wig.

And then I drove to Connie's where my Rueben was still hot.

Chapter Eleven

Ken Millani's assistant, a gorgeous redhead, sat behind a large oak desk. She had been with Millani Construction for the last five years and knows the ins and outs of the business. Page Pullman schedules jobs, bills customers, and pays the workers. She's a capable, no nonsense woman and she isn't easily fooled. I didn't try.

I was dressed in a black suit and my hair was clamped in a bun. I marched through the door and slapped my card on her desk.

"Pants On Fire Detective Agency. I'm investigating the death of Walter Jones."

"I saw the movie," Page said. "The wife did it."

"That was a video."

"Whatever. I'd volunteer for jury duty if I could. Walter was a nice guy."

"He was a schmuck. You know it, I know it. Ken fired him for stealing from the company."

Page opened a drawer and pulled out a slip of paper. "Walter was a valued employee. We'll miss him." She slipped the paper back and closed the drawer.

"What was *that*?" I said leaning over the desk. "Did Ken write that?"

"No. Ken said it. I wrote it. It's my answer for all Walter questions."

"You've used it before?"

"Cops were here, the press was here, and now it's you."

"And you have to write it down to remember? Geez, he was worse than I imagined. Keep practicing, maybe you'll convince someone to actually believe it."

Her face pinched. "What do you want?"

"Did Walter's work here involve contact with the designer, Roxanne Barbara."

Page's eyes shifted to the drawer and I waved a hand to stop her.

"Please. Just tell me so I can leave."

"We're presently contracting with Ms. Barbara's company. It's possible they may have run into one another."

"Thanks. Is Ken in?"

"You said you were leaving."

"I did. I just didn't say when."

Page mumbled under her breath as she dialed Ken's office.

"Detective Hot Pants here to see you." She dropped the phone in the cradle.

Ken met me at the door and motioned to a chair.

"What, you stalking me now?"

"I'm a private investigator, Ken. That's what I do."

He sat behind his desk and laced his fingers behind his head. "Whatchu got this time?"

"You lied to me about Walter, Ken."

"So what? I had a beef with Walter."

"You had a beef and a key to his house. That's what we call motive and opportunity."

"You forget yourself, Caterina. You're not a cop. You're a hootchie stalker."

I blew a sigh. "Does my mother talk to everyone?"

Ken stood and leaned over his desk. "You know I'm no murderer. I've known you all your life. You used to play house with my daughter for god's sake."

"We played Nancy Drew, not house."

"The difference is, she's all grown up. She's not playing anymore."

"Oh yeah? I bet she reads a mystery a week."

I winced. That was so lame.

His eyes did that thing people do when you talk crazy. I looked down at his hands. There was bruising on his right knuckles. "In a scrap, lately?"

Ken crossed himself. "You could test the patience of a saint, Caterina DeLuca."

I picked up my bag and corralled a notepad and a pen. "Just one last question and I'll be on my way. What were you doing the Friday afternoon Walter was killed?"

His jaw tightened. He marched around his desk and detached me from my chair. His hands clamped on my shoulders as he pushed me out the door.

"That's none of your business." I heard a whack on the door that closed behind me.

I smoothed my suit, held my head high, and strolled past Page Pullman's satisfied smirk.

◇◇◇

"You may've noticed Chance hasn't called," Cleo said.

I looked up from my office printer where I was laminating a plastic ID. The special printer was a gift from my Uncle Joey. He confiscated it from a guy he arrested for identity theft and making false documents. Uncle Joey thought I could use it. And he saved himself some paperwork by not hauling it in as evidence.

I sighed. "Savino's really ticked about seeing me at Walter's."

"I warned you. What do you expect? You BS'd him."

"Shut up."

"On the plus side, Detective Opsahl isn't here with handcuffs. At least Chance didn't rat you out."

"That's a good thing."

Cleo drummed her fingers. "Well?"

"*Well… What?*" I said.

"Are you calling Chance?"

"Alright, fine. I'll give him a ring. Geez get off my back."

I reached a hand out and my cell phone blasted "Run to The Hills" by Iron Maiden.

"You're hilarious."

I took the call. "Pants On Fire Detective Agency. We catch liars and cheats."

"Cat?" a meek voice said. "This is Brenda Greger. I'm wondering if you learned anything about my husband, Steve."

Steve is the funny guy with the Love Boat. He disabled my car at the marina. I still had my reputation to uphold as hootchie stalker extraordinaire. I'd been trolling by his place of business when I could. "I'm still on the case, Brenda. I'm working on a murder investigation but I expect to have your 8x10 glossies within the next few days."

Brenda sniffed. "Steve's a good provider for the kids and me. I'm almost ashamed to suspect he would ever behave…"

I recalled my view through the boat window. "Like a dirty dog?" I said. That covered it well. I'd give her the glossies, all right.

"It's just Steve often works late and when I phone his office, he's not there. They say that's a red flag."

More like a three alarm fire.

"He just called to say he's working late again tonight. If you could maybe…" Her voice trailed off.

"I'll be there. If he goes anywhere, I'm right behind him."

Brenda sighed and hung up.

The Iron Maiden jammed again. "Run to the Hills." This time it was Chance. The last time I saw him, was in Walter's alley. I was scaling a fence.

"Hey," I said. "I was just going to call you."

"Uh huh."

"We need to talk," I said.

"You lied to me, Cat."

"That's what I want to talk about."

"Liar."

"You're angry. Got it. We can talk about it later, and we can clear that whole mess up. I promise. Uh, did you speak to the old man in the window?"

"I did."

I gave Cleo the thumbs up. She delved into a bowl of chocolates from the antique candy dish she snagged from Walter's.

"And…?"

"He claims he saw nothing. I'm not sure I believe him."

"Why? Does he have beady eyes?"

I heard him smile. "We'll discuss it over dinner. I'd like to try that new Indian restaurant in Bridgeport. Ettie recommended it."

"Ettie? If you mean Detective Ethel Opsahl, I thought she only ate small children."

"She's an interesting person when you get to know her."

"I don't see that happening, unless it's through bars in a cell block."

His voice smiled. "I'm starving. And I've finished the assignments you gave me. Now if you're home, I'll swing by and pick you up."

"Uh, nix on the dinner. I have to work tonight."

"Sure you do."

"No, really. But I won't be late though and—"

He exhaled slowly. "Forget it, DeLucky. We'll talk tomorrow."

"Chance, I—"

Click.

I winced. "I hate fighting."

Max walked in, hair damp from the shower. "Who's fighting?"

Cleo's eyes raked over his muscled chest.

"Come to Mama," she purred.

I rolled my eyes.

Cleo sucked the gooey center from one of Tino's chocolates, her eyes hooked on Max.

"But, there's no sex like make-up sex."

Roxanne Barbara's designer bags and signature clothing were made in her Bridgeport factory, not far from White Sox's Cellular Field. Her offices and boutique were on Chicago's Gold Coast, one of the wealthiest strips of real estate in the country. The Gold Coast crowd may lunch on chilled salmon with herb mayonnaise, but in Bridgeport we do redhots and italian beef sandwiches.

Roxanne Barbara's commitment to one hundred percent American-made fashion had made her something of a local hero and American icon. In the last five years, she'd seen her line explode. An expansion to her Bridgeport facility was currently under construction by contractor Ken Millani.

Despite my prior call to RB's downtown office, two freshly laminated press ID's, and my hunky sidekick, Max, we didn't make it through the door of her Bridgeport factory. The fashion police slammed it in our faces.

"Where's Cleo when you need her to shoot somebody?" I said.

Max smiled. "Put your weapon away, babe. We have company."

A steamy man in an Italian suit and Ray Bans emerged from the unfinished building under construction. I jammed my camera in Max's hands and walked purposefully toward him. *Gorgeous.*

I stepped right up to the Italian suit and whipped out my press card. "I'm Maddie Goldstein and this is my photographer, Max. I'm writing a piece for *NY Mag* on Roxanne and the opening of her Fifth Avenue Boutique."

He lifted his Ray Bans and I stared into his eyes. They were an almost liquid shade of amber. His energy was electric. Standing still, he seemed to be in motion. My initial impression of AJ Nelson can be summed up in three words. *Oh My God.*

He had an easy smile. "Yes. The office said you called. I'm AJ, RB's assistant. I admire your work."

"I admire your shoes."

"I particularly liked your piece on art-deco-inspired design in February's *NY Mag.*"

"Actually *Encore Magazine* picked up that piece. In April, I think. Something tells me you knew that." I batted my eyes. "Are you testing me?"

AJ had done his homework, as had I. I'd chosen the name of a relatively unknown, up-and-coming freelancer. There was a picture of Maddie Goldstein in a recent *First Design Magazine,* interviewing Michael Kors. It wasn't a direct face shot. I figured if I wore my hair the same way, I'd pass.

"Guilty," he flashed a smile. "Espionage is a big problem in the fashion industry. With the unveiling of our fall line next week, we're particularly cautious. No offense."

"None taken."

Something about him made me think of dark jungles and forbidden passions. There was a "bad boy" appeal about him. Sort of like James Dean in designer clothing. I tried to analyze his attraction and couldn't put a finger on it. Hell, maybe it was the shoes.

"Have you been with *NY Mag* long?" AJ asked.

"I freelance for several publications. Just another starving writer without insurance," I said, as if he didn't know.

He gave me a luscious smile. "So, are you single?"

"And how does that affect my getting an interview with RB?"

"It doesn't. It will, however, affect whether I ask you to dinner sometime."

"I'm assuming we will both be invited?" Max growled.

Dry amusement gleamed in the simmering golden eyes. "Does your photographer accompany you everywhere?"

"Definitely," Max chimed.

"Not," I laughed.

"Ah. Hope springs eternal. I'll show you around." AJ held out his arm and I took it.

Max snarled and followed two steps behind us.

AJ was a curious mixture of sophistication and boyish charm. Even without the Gucci shoes, the suit he wore cost more than my entire wardrobe.

"Roxanne Barbara *is* American fashion," he said. "Her vibe is about an easy urban cool, both powerful and feminine. Her little black dress is something you can wear forever."

I wanted RB's timeless little black dress for Cleo's Blues debut. I mentally calculated the damage it would inflict on my credit card.

AJ grinned looking even more appealing. "Like I said, you'll wear it forever."

I made a face. "I just don't want to pay for it forever."

I wondered if Uncle Joey could figure a way to write it off on my taxes.

"It's your turn," I said. "Tell me about yourself."

"I'm single."

I laughed. "How long have you been with Roxanne?"

"Ten years. I started at the bottom and clawed my way up the ladder. I take care of everything for her. No one talks to RB without charming me."

Blink, blink. "How am I doing."

"I'm suitably charmed. I think I can arrange twenty minutes with her the day after tomorrow. Shall we say eleven-thirty?"

"Perfect." I waved a hand at Max. "Take a picture of AJ and me together."

AJ grinned and threw up his hands. "No photos, please. I work hard to protect my anonymity. It allows me to move around without the hassle of fans trying to get to RB. Roxie's had people throw their designs at her over the bathroom stalls."

"That's disgusting," Max said dryly. "Some people are like… stalkers."

"Imagine that." I flashed AJ a smile.

We got a few photos of the warehouse and new construction before thanking AJ, climbing in the Hummer, and driving away. When I checked my rearview mirror, he was jotting down the license number.

"It's OK," Max said. "The Hummer is registered to a dummy corporation. It's legit enough and it won't take him any further."

I exhaled and lay my head back.

"That arrogant bastard is the luckiest man alive. To be able to work with Roxanne, one of the hottest woman on the planet." Max gave me a sidelong glance. "She's right up there with you, babe. She could have anybody as her assistant. Why she keeps that SOB around is beyond me."

"How cute are you, Max? You have a crush on RB!" I laughed. "And AJ's not arrogant. He's intense, I grant you. But he has charisma."

"It's not charisma. There's something off there. I don't trust him. I want you to stay away from him."

"Excuse me?"

"I could tell the moment he walked up—with those beady eyes of his."

"He was wearing sunglasses."

"I see through everything except kryptonite."

"Right. And I'm Lois Lane."

His gaze fixed lazily on the nape of my neck and traveled south.

I caught my breath.

"Blue leopard print bra with a racer back, unhooks in the front, delicious cleavage, high rise bikini…"

My face felt hot. I bolted up straight, shielding my breasts with crossed arms. "How…" I sputtered.

Max smiled. "No kryptonite, babe."

Chapter Twelve

Once the mark makes you, your job gets a lot harder. Steve Greger had been on to me before I chased him off his yacht at Monroe Harbor. But rather than skulking back into the shadows, like any other self-respecting cheater, this guy was upping the ante.

He was making it a point to meet up with Legs—as I knew her—during his lunch hour. But it was only for a quick grope.

It was always at a different location, usually a park. It was always far enough away from the street so that I had to follow on foot. He kept the rendezvous to five minutes of grope-time so I couldn't set up my camera.

This guy was obviously enjoying the cat and mouse chase. He was a cocky little mouse. He always laughed climbing back in his car. I began to wonder who the mouse was here and who was the cat? This guy was having way too much fun at my expense.

Why Legs was putting up with a five minute feel, I had no idea. But finally I realized I was getting felt up too. Time to change my tactics. So I let Greger think I was leaving him alone. The Silver Bullet was in Jack's shop, but I switched Cleo's Camry with Rocco and then with Papa. Papa's car is a jet-black Cadillac, 2009 model. I have no idea how he landed a Caddy on a cop's pension after he retired. I suspect my Uncle Joey had something to do with it, but I don't ask questions. I even switched cars with my switched-at-birth sister, Sophie. That hurt big time but at least I stayed under the radar. And once I saw it was another park destination, I just drove on by and left it alone. Greger has a lot of teeth and I was sick of looking at his laughing pearls.

I had promised Brenda I would stake out her husband tonight. Steve told her he was putting in a long night at work. I suspected he was putting in something else.

We left AJ at the construction site and Max drove to Greger's office. He opted to go along and keep me company. The gold Hummer doesn't exactly blend but Max could pull it off. He was, after all, a spy. I was hoping he'd pass a few tricks on to me.

I cruised by the office earlier that day but Greger didn't bother to leave during his lunch hour. It was five-thirty when Max and I trolled back there. Greger's car was still in the parking lot. At seven-thirty, he came out of the office building, looked both ways, and trotted to his car. *Pay dirt.* So I thought.

The Hummer is big and flashy. It's rather obvious on a city street. Max stayed on him. He was in spy mode. Toothy boy never saw him coming.

And then Greger reached his destination. The Bridgeport Café. *Crap!*

Johnnie Rizzo is my ex and the owner and top chef of The Bridgeport Café. It's an excellent restaurant. It's arguably the best there is in Bridgeport. Hell, it's probably the best there is on the south side. Johnnie is a god in the kitchen. His gorgeous body, his gorgeous face, and his gorgeous hotness, all figured into why I married the man. And I love food.

When I first brought Johnnie home to meet the family, Johnnie ended up in the kitchen with Mama. He walked away with Mama's cannoli recipe. This is the power of Johnnie Rizzo. Nobody in the whole world has stormed the gates of Mama's cannoli recipe and lived to tell the tale. I've tried. Beloved family members have tried. It took Johnnie Rizzo less than three hours. That's when I knew I would marry him. I considered it the family blessing. What a mistake that was.

I don't have a lot of absolutes in life. Maybe three. One. I don't kill people. Two. I don't get drunk and sing karaoke naked. And three. I avoid my ex at all costs.

The last time I saw Johnnie Rizzo was a complete disaster. I can feel my face flush every time my mind dredges up that embarrassing moment. How Johnnie thought I was stalking him. How I couldn't get over him. How I needed therapy. It was *so* humiliating.

I hoped Johnnie would be cooking in the kitchen. Or better yet, home with an excruciating case of herpes.

I took a serious, deep breath and sent out a prayer to Our Lady of Perpetually Embarrassing Moments. I really hoped she'd get back to me on that one.

I pulled my hair into a ponytail, put on some fake eyeglasses from the glove box, and grabbed my camera. Max dropped me off in the alley and circled around to park on the street. I walked through the employee entrance and turned left. There's a small walk-in closet the employees use to dump their stuff and change into uniform. I snagged an apron off a hook and donned a beanie cap. Then I walked down the hallway, past the restrooms, and onto the floor.

The place hadn't changed. Johnnie was trying to do some refinancing with his brother-in-law. He wanted to add a sports bar on to the restaurant but the deal obviously hadn't gone through yet. I didn't know why nor did I care.

What I did care about was finding Greger, getting my photo and getting the hell out of there before anyone saw me. I grabbed a bus tub and towel from the side station and started prowling the room. I figured I knew where they'd be. They were in the far back corner table with their backs to the wall. No surprise there. The lighting was dim and they had a clear view of anyone entering the restaurant.

The two of them were snuggled up real tight and Greger, at least, was pretending to look at the menu. Legs had her hands under the table and her tongue in Greger's ear. I'd have to be fast. I stepped to an empty booth with a good line of sight, dropped the bus tub onto the table and snatched my camera out of it. Then I dropped to my knees like I was picking up a fallen napkin and eased my head around the booth's side.

Perfect. Legs was still planted on Greger. She was working down his neck now and I had a full frontal shot of Greger's slack jawed, bleary eyed mug. I lifted my camera, sighted it and….

Uh oh. What were a tight pair of jeans doing in my lens? Wait a moment. I knew that fly.

I slowly lowered the camera and there, standing in front of Greger's table, was my ex, Johnnie Rizzo. His face was furious. In three long strides he was on me. He wrenched the camera from my hands, lifted me off the floor, and strong-armed me through the restaurant. Just as we rounded the corner for the restroom hallway, I craned my neck back to see Greger's full rack of glowing teeth tipped to the ceiling as a loud bark of baritone laughter split the air.

Johnnie hustled me through the restaurant, grabbing the skull cap off my head and throwing it behind the bar before shoving me out the door, onto the sidewalk. He was breathing hard and I could tell he was trying to get a hold on his temper.

I looked up at him and batted my eyes. *Blink. Blink.*

Johnnie said nothing. He just held out his hand and waited. I untied the apron and shrugged out of it. Then I ceremoniously handed it to him. Still silent, Johnnie dropped the apron on the ground, reached over and took the faux-glasses off my face. He held them up so I could see and broke them in half at the nose. Then he dropped them onto the apron.

I felt like one of those soldiers being stripped of his uniform.

"I see you, Kitten." Johnnie growled in a low voice. "I will always see you. That will never change."

"It's not what you think, Johnnie. I'm working a case. I had no idea I'd be here tonight!"

"My god, look at yourself. I hate seeing you grovel this way. I gotta say, Kitten, it's a turn-off."

My face burned. "You- you…" I sputtered.

I was livid and humiliated beyond words. At least I couldn't find any. I opened my mouth and darted my index finger in front of it. Not real mature, I know.

Max, enjoying the encounter way too much, appeared at my side. His grin was ear to ear.

"Max," I blurted gratefully. "Explain to Johnnie I'm on a case."

Max smiled. "What?"

"This isn't the time to joke around. Tell Johnnie I'm a detective, for godsake. I'm not stalking him, I'm stalking—"

The restaurant door flew open.

"*THEM!*" I cried. I threw my arm and wagged an accusing finger at Steve Greger and his hootchie.

Johnnie sucked a breath. "For godsake, Kitten, get a grip on yourself."

Steve Greger bellowed a laugh and quickly ushered his date to the car.

"They're getting away!" I flew at Johnnie, trying to wrestle the camera from his hands.

He twisted around, tightening his hold. "Whatever lame excuse you have come up with, you may not photograph my customers as part of your ridiculous charade."

Steve Greger and his hootchie woman honked as they drove by. Johnnie released my camera and waved.

I punched his arm.

Johnnie shrugged. "They've probably been married twenty years."

"*He* has. *To another woman.*"

Johnnie's eyes searched my face and stopped on my mouth. I felt his breath, hot on my lips.

"I understand it's hard for you to get over me. I gave you what no other man could."

I turned my head and wiped my mouth with my sleeve. *Blach! Blach!*

"You gave to half the women in Bridgeport," I shot back.

"Good comeback, babe." Max said. "Too bad he didn't hear it."

I looked. Johnnie was gone.

"But *they* did." Max nodded behind me.

I cringed and slowly pivoted to see a small crowd gathered to watch the crazy lady.

"Oh god," I groaned. "I'm becoming Cleo."

"Why, yes you are." Max hung an arm around my waist. "Come, Kitten. I'll take you home."

Max dropped me at my door. I undressed, slipped into a White Sox tee, and climbed into bed, eyes wide open. I was humiliated after my encounter with Johnnie Rizzo. I pulled the covers over my head and squeezed my eyes shut. When that didn't work I padded to the kitchen and melted a chocolate bar in a cup of warm milk. I waited. Not even a yawn. I followed the warm milk with chamomile tea, two glasses of wine, and three trips to the bathroom. I lay down again and tried counting sheep. My sheep wouldn't stay in the pasture. They romped in the alley behind Walter's house and climbed all over a spanking new Highlander. The old man in the white house laughed. Detective Ethel Opsahl dangled from Walter's window and tried to shoot the sheep.

I gave up and reached for the phone beside my bed. I punched some numbers and Chance's sleep-slurred voice answered. I looked at the time and winced.

"Hey. I didn't realize how late it was. Were you sleeping?"

"I was reading," he mumbled groggily.

"Liar. Go back to sleep. We'll talk tomorrow."

"Don't hang up. Is everything OK?"

"Yes…er, no," I amended. "I'm sorry you missed your Indian dinner."

"It's OK. The food was overrated."

I was stunned. "You went without me?"

I heard his smile. "No. I had a greasy hamburger. I thought we'd try again tomorrow."

I was shallow enough to be pleased. "Sometimes I work late. But it's what I do. Did you know most sex occurs late at night?"

"Come over. I'd like to test that research."

"Ha! You'll be asleep before I find my keys."

"I'll be reading. Tell me about your day."

I briefly reviewed my trip to Roxanne's factory and my brief encounter with the designer's assistant.

"And I might have found Walter's blackmail cache. Cleo tipped me off. I snagged his fishing tackle box from his bedroom closet."

"No comment."

"You're upset because I lied to you. I couldn't help it, Savino. I didn't want to involve you. Knowing I was going in would make you an accomplice. Don't get me wrong. I'm not apologizing for what I do. I'm a private investigator."

He wasn't making this easy.

"Savino, are you listening?"

I heard a grunt on the line.

"Come again," I said softly.

Heavy breathing and a snort.

"My god, Savino, are you asleep?"

He answered with another snort.

I dropped the phone and plopped on my back beside Inga. Her head lay on my shoulder and her big brown eyes watched me questioningly.

"He snores," I sighed.

We rolled over and this time I slept.

Chapter Thirteen

The phone woke me before seven. Eyes closed, I grappled for the receiver.

"Pants On Fire Detective Agency. We catch—"

"You're catching zzz's," Uncle Joey said. "I'm in your kitchen. Where's your coffee?"

I threw off my covers and pulled on a robe.

"Some watchdog," I said to Inga. Her eyelids fluttered and she closed them again.

I jammed my hair in a clip on top of my head and padded to the kitchen. Uncle Joey sat at the table hunched over a deli box of Tino's cream puffs. Tell-tale sugar outlined his mouth.

"These ain't your Mama's boconnotto," he said with regret.

I kissed his cheek. "I'm cut off. I embarrassed her with Father Timothy."

The dark eyes smiled. "At confession?"

"I should have something so juicy to confess." I pushed the brew button on the coffee maker. "No, I guess my assistant being charged with murder somehow reflects poorly on her."

When the coffee was ready, I poured two steaming cups and slid in the chair next to Uncle Joey.

"Thanks for taking care of Cleo's lawyer," I said.

"Tony Beano's the best. He thinks Cleo didn't do it."

"She didn't."

"An hour ago I wouldn't have believed you. Now, I'm not so sure."

Uncle Joey reached under the table and brought up Walter's tackle box and a cassette player. "Where did you find this thing?"

"In Walter's closet. It's his grandfather's fishing box."

"Captain Bob said a woman broke the police seal on the back door. She was seen running away."

"Just a woman?"

"A woman in a mousy brown wig and navy stripe capri pants. Her cell phone plays 'Your Cheatin' Heart'."

"Mousy, nothin'. That was an expensive hair piece," I said in a huff. "Detective Opsahl's frizzy helmet hair should look so good."

Uncle Joey laughed. "Ettie didn't suspect a wig. It was Bob. You didn't fool him. You're the only woman he knows who can swing down a tree like a snot-nosed kid."

"I'll take that as a compliment."

"Don't. He said you're a menace and you should be locked away."

I chucked a fist to my chest. "Show me the box."

Walter's box contained a handful of marbles, a GI Joe, Transformer, remnants from a childhood before his birth family unraveled. A few letters from his dad promised to pull him out of foster care as soon as he got out of prison. There were also three small manila envelopes. Each envelope contained an assortment of photos, tapes, newspaper clippings or videos. The envelopes were unmarked, with no identifying names.

"I'm thinkin' Walter Jones blackmailed these people," Uncle Joey said. "That's motive for murder."

"Do we know who they are?"

"We know this one." He emptied the contents of one envelope on the table. A single cassette tape tumbled out. He slipped it in a recorder and pushed play.

"Forgive me Father for I have sinned. It's been six weeks since my last confession."

Uncle Joey stopped the recording.

My jaw dropped. "*Oh my god!* Walter Jones bugged the confessional?"

"Oh yeah. He's burning in hell. Do you recognize the voice?"

"It's familiar but I can't—Ken Millani," I gasped. "Walter's boss."

Uncle Joey grinned. "Now that's someone with something juicy to confess."

"Cleo said Walter stole from Ken for years. He was looking for leverage to keep Ken from pressing charges in case he caught on. It seems he got it."

"I called a guy I know who works for Ken. He said Millani is predictable like a timex. Leaves early every Friday night for Mass, never misses."

"Walter would know some Fridays he'd be in the confessional. Given enough time and confessions, he got something with teeth in it."

"The teeth are gnashing on this one." Uncle Joey pushed the play button. I pushed stop.

"Because it was said in the confessional, I'd like to respect Ken's privacy. It's enough to know he was being blackmailed. And that's motive for murder."

"You're a better person than I," Uncle Joey chuckled. "Don't worry. Ken's secret is safe with me."

"Ken lied to me about his relationship with Walter. I want to know why."

"I'd talk to him for you but it'll be a while before I can look at him without laughing."

"What about the other envelopes?"

Uncle Joey put Millani's envelope away and shook out the contents of the second one. A few old newspaper articles and two yellowed obits from the *Chicago Tribune*.

"I'll save you some time," Uncle Joey said. "Twenty years ago, a young student named Courtney Kelly was studying for finals. It was just before Christmas in her junior year. She left the library for her dorm a little before midnight. She never made it.

A grounds keeper was shoveling snow the next morning when he found her body.

"The young woman had not been sexually molested. Courtney's body was laid out on a soft bed of ground cover. Her hands were crossed on her chest. Her coat was carefully straightened and the killer smoothed her long wool scarf around her neck. After he strangled her with it."

A chill went through me. "To position the hands like that can suggest regret. Did the killer know the victim?"

"I made some calls this morning. The case went cold. It was never solved."

"That's gotta be tough on the family."

"Courtney was an only child. She grew up here. Her parents, John and Donna Kelly, lived in Bridgeport at the time of her death."

"Are they here now?"

Joey shrugged. "Shouldn't be hard to find out."

He slapped a photograph of six college-aged kids by a river. They were laughing about something. An object in the background could've been a raft.

Joey made a face. "Looks like a camping trip."

My uncle's idea of roughing it is a weekend at the Hilton without 500 cable channels.

I studied the river picture against the young woman's obit. "This looks like the dead girl here. And the woman next to her could be Roxanne."

"Everyone knows Roxanne Barbara grew up in Bridgeport. She and Courtney may have gone to school together."

He tapped a cluster of articles concerning a missing man from Wisconsin.

"The guy's name was Hal Bjornsen. Twenty-one years old, paranoid schizophrenic. Off his medication. He left home twenty years ago and never came back."

I picked a clip from the table. "It says here that hunters found Hal's body three years later. Was he murdered?"

"The coroner determined the death was accidental."

I studied the playful image of six friends by the river. Something awful happened twenty years ago. Something that Walter used to scare the cash out of Roxanne Barbara. It was right here, hidden in the papers spread on the table. Did the secret belong only to Roxanne? Or had Walter blackmailed the others as well.

"I don't get it," I said. "How are a camping trip, a dead college student, and a mentally ill man connected?"

"You'll figure it out," Uncle Joey said with a confidence I didn't feel. "You're a damn good detective. Find the thread and follow it."

I topped our coffees and took two oranges from a bowl on the counter. "May I peel one for you?"

"You're kidding. Right?" Uncle Joey scooped up another cream puff.

When he had brushed the last traces of sugar from his hands, he opened the last envelope.

"A video of a guy in a hotel room, probably cheating. The man is wearing a wedding ring and the woman is far too attentive to be his wife."

I laughed. "Don't let Linda hear you say that."

"I'll do whatever I can to help you—but Captain Bob has all DeLucas on a short leash. Ask Savino to run a facial recognition on the guy in the video. I'd like to know where he was when Cleo picked you up at the marina."

"I'll talk to Chance. Did Joey Jr. find anything more on what I gave him?"

Uncle Joey shook his head. "Nothing related to these envelopes or other blackmail victims. Walter's bank and financial info is there. Cleo should live well if she can beat this."

"She's singing Sunday night at All City Blues. Chance and I will be there. You and Linda should join us."

"Count us in. No one beats Melvin's ribs."

Cleo appeared in the doorway, her eyes swollen, nose red, wrapped in a terrycloth robe. She searched for the largest cup and filled it with coffee, turned on her heel, and headed back to her room. I had a sneaking suspicion she finally realized the seriousness of her situation.

Seven seconds later her head was back in the doorway. "Hey. That's Walter's box."

Cleo went through the contents without speaking. A postcard from the prison stopped her in her tracks.

"What's that about?" Joey said.

"I dunno. Walter got some collect calls from Joliet. I could tell it upset him. When I asked him about it, he said it had to do with his dad going to prison."

"What did the caller say?"

"He said, 'You lied'. And something about getting even. That's about it."

"That's creepy," I said. "When was that?"

"Last year sometime. Walter never talked about the incident that sent his dad to prison. All I know is Walter was there when it happened. He was ten and it damaged him big-time."

"What's Walter's dad's name?"

"James Walter Jones. I think he was born in Toledo."

Joey gruned. "I'll ask a guy from the Twenty-third to check it out. Captain Bob will be none the wiser."

Uncle Joey dropped me off at the garage. Jack gave me the keys to the Silver Bullet and a bill. Four hundred bucks. I winced and gave up a card.

"What part did you have to replace?"

"A coil wire."

"Three days and four hundred dollars to replace a flippin' *coil wire*?"

Jack gave me a patronizing look. "Devin could've replaced the coil wire right there, while it was sitting at the marina. But do I have that option? No. I gotta tow your car into the shop, park it here with all the other cars, and it's gotta wait for me to get around to it."

"Well I'm sure everybody appreciates Devin's talents in treatment. And in prison."

"You're quick to criticize my nephew." Jack tapped his foot on the cement. "Once again you're all over the papers, Caterina. Murder—Murder—Murder."

"My name wasn't in the paper." I said righteously. Captain Bob promised to keep me out of it.

"I read between the lines. You take dirty pictures. You hired a killer. You found a dead body. It adds up to trouble. Your mama told me everything. And then she gave me your cannoli."

I gave the small refrigerator in his office a sidelong glance.

"Not gonna happen," Jack said. "She warned me about leaving it here overnight. The cannoli comes home with me."

I was getting into the car when Melanie called. Melanie and I were best friends when we still thought babies came from Kmart. In fifth grade, we gathered Mama's gardening shears and a wad of toilet paper and became blood sisters. It's a recipe for gangrene. In a solemn ceremony we promised to die for each other. That very summer at camp we almost had our chance. Our canoe tipped over and Melanie and I spilled into the lake. We nearly drowned trying to drag each other to safety. The camp counselor jumped in and smacked us both in the head. We swam to shore.

The camp director wasn't impressed. He sent us to bed without supper. We thought we deserved a badge for courage and told him so. He said it was a damn shame we were so stupid.

"Ooo-yay are-hay uh-they upid-stay un-way," I said.

Melanie and I were fluent in pig-latin. We told all the kids we spoke French.

The director's eyes narrowed to slits. *"I-hay ate-hay ids-kay."*

Apparently he spoke French too.

Smiling at the memory, I answered the phone.

"Hey, girlfriend. What's up?"

"I've finished my errands and I'm leaving the liquor store now. What time do you want to set up?"

Set up? I racked my brain. I got nothing. I played it safe.

"Uh, what do you think?"

"Well, the girls are coming at seven, I've got tons of decorations and those cute little party favors. I bought enough tequila and limes to stagger a horse. If you need help setting up your appetizers…"

Panic sliced me like a knife. I whipped the car out of Jack's parking lot and jetted home. How could I forget my cousin Stella's bachelorette party?

It was low of me, I know, but I blamed the dead man. Walter made a bucket load of trouble when he was alive, and now that he was fettuccine al dead-o, he just kept piling it on.

"Who did you get for entertainment?"

Holy crap, I forgot to order the stripper.

"Uh, it's a surprise." *For all of us.*

"You can tell me."

"No. I really can't."

Melanie laughed. "I'll see you at five with a fistful of ones. We can sample the margaritas before the party."

I grabbed my phone and punched numbers. My weekly Merry Maids agreed to an emergency house call. I bribed them to bring flowers and candles. I found that Twelve Loaves Catering puts out an amazing spread, and an employee would deliver my order on her way home.

The stripper was harder to find. It was eleven when I finished. The last minute party arrangements were spendy but Stella would have her big night. I breathed my thanks to every unfaithful schmuck in Chicago. Infidelity is a thriving business.

One of the first things an investigator learns in this business is how to find someone. I have a seven stage plan that will pinpoint almost anybody. If I bomb at stage eight, I call in reinforcements. It helps to have friends and family in law enforcement. Their guns aren't always bigger. But their computers are.

Locating John and Donna Kelly was a stage one deal. The parents of the murdered college student were listed in the phone book. They lived in Bridgeport. According to Courtney's obituary, they hadn't moved in twenty years.

I punched the number on my cell.

"Hello. Is this Donna Kelly?" I said.

"Yes." She had a soft, melodic voice.

"My name is Lara. I was a friend of Courtney's. I'm in Bridgeport visiting friends. If it's convenient I'd like to stop by and say hi."

"Oh, do come," she said eagerly. "We enjoy meeting Courtney's friends."

Donna gave me directions to their home. I didn't need them. I've lived in this neighborhood all my life. It's a good thing I like it here. Because there's a troll that keeps me in Bridgeport. She lives in Mama's house.

I dashed into my bedroom for a quick redo. I needed to look older if I was going to convince Donna Kelly I went to college with her daughter. I brushed my hair back in a French twist and applied the faintest smudge of smoky eye-shadow under my eyes. I snagged a pair of faux-glasses from my bag of tricks, circa nineteen-ninety, and stepped into the dated peach pant suit I'd found at last year's church rummage sale. With a pair of sensible taupe flats, I was ready to go.

Donna Kelly had soft porcelain skin and kind blue eyes. She poured tea in delicate china cups and set out a plate of biscuits.

"I don't remember meeting you at Courtney's funeral," she said.

"Uhm…"

"You must forgive me. Those horrible first months are a blur." Donna stirred honey in her tea. She took a sip. "You said you went to school with Courtney?"

I squeezed a slice of lemon in my cup. "We were in Hawkins Dorm together." I got that much from the newspaper articles in Walter's envelope. "We had some things in common. We both wanted to be famous designers." I laughed. "I was never as good as Courtney. She was brilliant."

Donna smiled.

"We both played piano." I took my cue from the baby grand in the living room. "And we talked about going white water rafting in the spring."

Donna rose and caught my hand. "Come with me. I have something to show you."

I followed her down the hall to her daughter's room. It was, for all practical purposes, a shrine. The story of Courtney's life was told in the collection of Smurfs, Barbie dolls, and photos on the wall. A picture of Courtney selling Girl Scout cookies in the rain. Courtney playing soccer. Courtney on the high school swim team. On the cheerleading squad with a young Roxanne Barbara. And heading off to college in a red Subaru.

"I want you to see this." Donna pulled a photo from an album. It was like the one in Walter's blackmail envelope.

"This was taken a few months before Courtney died. You may know these kids."

Three girls, three guys and a river.

"I know Roxanne."

I flipped the picture over. The names were written on the back.

"Yes, Aron Sikes was in my Biology class. I can't recall how he hurt his arm."

"He fell off a cliff on this very trip. Courtney said he joked about it later. The scar on his arm looked like a Mercedes logo."

"That's quite a feat. I wonder who's missing from the photo. Did Courtney say who took the picture?"

"Not that I recall. Courtney had many friends. A few drop by from time to time. I couldn't bear to think they'd forgotten her."

I gave her a quick hug. She felt small and fragile. "No one who knew Courtney will ever forget her."

Donna's finger touched the glass over her daughter's face. "They never found the monster that took her life. There's no justice for my little girl. How can she rest in peace?"

Donna put the picture back in the album and we returned to our tea.

"At first, John and I didn't know if we would make it. I don't know how we could have without Roxanne. She's become a second daughter to us. She always calls. She stops by to check on us. Every year she sends us on a cruise."

I saw the first genuine smile on Donna's face. "In fact I'm expecting her any minute. We're going out for lunch."

Awkward.

"You must come with us. You two will have a lot to catch up on."

"Wow." I forced my lips to curl.

I heard a car door close in the alley. I jerked the phone from my pocket and glanced at the dark screen.

"I have a text. There's been an accident and I'm needed at the hospital."

I high-tailed it to the front door.

Donna scampered after me. "But Roxie will be so disappointed."

"I'm devastated myself, Donna. There's a lot of blood. I'm needed in surgery."

"Oh my." Her eyes went wide. "I thought you said you're a designer."

"I'm a doctor," I said soberly, "and I design scrubs."

A voice rang from the kitchen. "Mom, I'm here!"

I escaped through the front as Roxanne Barbara came in the back.

I had Max on the phone before my wheels rounded the corner.

"AL-LO, Kitten," Max purred into the phone.

"Ah, Max, you're *so* funny." I said, trying not to snap. "I need your help." He was still enjoying my humiliation at Johnnie's way too much.

"Name it."

"I have a twenty-year-old photograph that Walter used to blackmail our favorite designer. I need to know why."

"Alright, fine. Who's in the pic?"

"Six college kids and maybe one more behind the camera. I have names. I need everything they can remember about that weekend."

"Got it."

"Walter's blackmail package included newspaper articles about a missing man named Hal Bjornsen. Find out if they knew him. There's gotta be a connection somewhere."

"Is that all?"

"One more thing. We need to know if Walter was blackmailing Roxanne's friends as well."

"Done." He said it easily, as if I'd asked for a carton of milk.

"I'll email everything to you. Thanks Max. Is there nothing a spy can't do?"

"If you want to be impressed, Kitty, at least give me a bit of a challenge." He laughed and lowered his voice. "And if you *really* want to see my skill set, babe, I will rock your world."

Oh boy! Time for a conversation change, pronto.

"Cleo made crumpets this morning for Uncle Joey. When you come by, she'll give you some."

Max let out a deep throated chuckle. "Well, if that is all I would be getting, I'd rather grab a burger. Your partner scares me."

"She's my *assistant*. Where's that big tough guy who was here a minute ago?"

"*He* saw *Fatal Attraction*. And compared to Cleo's video, it's a Disney flick."

"Um, if you're free later, why don't you drop by?"

"Sure. Can I bring anything?"

"A pizza."

"OK."

"And, uh, dress like a pizza delivery guy."

"You're not serious."

"Think of it as role play."

Max let out a deep throated chuckle. "Hot damn, Kitty. You surprise me."

"Oh I have a much bigger surprise in store for you."

"I can't wait. But a pizza delivery guy? It's not exactly a sexy look."

"Surprise me."

"OK." I heard him smile. "May I take your order, ma'am?"

"Yes. I'd like one large pepperoni pizza delivered about eight-thirty this evening."

"I'm sorry ma'am. Our pepperoni is only available in extra large."

"Uh huh, that's what all the pizza guys say."

Chapter Fourteen

I drove by the church and rectory twice, slow enough to merit three honks and a hand gesture from the driver behind me. I skipped the horn and returned the gesture.

I wanted to be sure Father Timothy's car wasn't anywhere around. It was the day Mama and a few church ladies accompany Father Timothy to hospitals and nursing homes to visit sick parishioners. For the first time in my life, I hoped there were a lot of them. When the coast was clear, I parked on the street and skipped up the church steps. Walter put a bug in the confessional and I intended to take it out.

Three people were praying in the sanctuary when I entered. I took a seat and waited for them to leave. Two were fast talkers. They left shortly after I arrived. The third man lingered nearly a half hour. I shuffled my feet. I counted the panes in the stain glass windows. No one has that many people to pray for.

He rose to feet slowly and gave me a sad smile on his way out. I groaned inwardly. His daughter plays soccer with Rocco's kids. His wife has cancer and the prognosis is bleak. I felt like a putz. I gave myself seventy Hail Marys and three days without chocolate to save Father Timothy some time.

When the coast was clear, I raced up the red carpeted aisle and swung a left to the confessional. Slipping inside the door on the right, I shut myself in. It was dark and small inside with limited space to hide something. It would have to be somewhere

where it wouldn't be brushed or kicked or seen. I felt along the ceiling with my hands, and scanned the walls without success. I poked my head out the door. Still clear. I dropped to my hands and knees, my derriere hanging out the confessional door. I ran my fingers underneath the back of the bench and—*wha-laa*. I peeled off the two-by-two inch audio recorder and palmed it in my hot hands. Just then, I heard a low "Ahem" behind me.

I winced. Kneeling on all fours, I slowly peered over my shoulder and saw black. A lot of black, with a little white on the collar.

"Caterina," Father Timothy said severely. "What on earth are you doing down there?"

"Uh, praying." That was dumb. "And um…looking for my earring. I thought I dropped it here."

"It's been a long time since your last confession."

"It's been a long time since I wore those earrings."

I squiggled backwards out of the confessional, bolted to my feet, and brushed myself off.

"Do you wish to make confession now?"

For lying to my priest? Not good.

"I already took care of it. I'm off chocolate for three whole days." That didn't include lying to a priest. "Make that four."

"I am concerned about you, Caterina, and your struggle with addiction. Your mother says you have a problem with pornography."

I heard my teeth grind. "Oh, that's not me. That's my sister, Sophie. You know how crazy she is. She practically lives in this booth."

"But…"

"With a little prodding I am sure Sophie will tell you all about her horrible obsession."

A woman rushed into the church and caught Father Timothy's eye. I knew her. She's the wife of a client of mine. I followed her to the Chicago South Loop Hotel last week for a one-on-one evaluation with her boss.

"Now there's a woman who *really* needs your help." I patted Father Timothy's arm.

With that I made my exit.

◇◇◇

I pulled in front of my house and jabbed Savino's number on my phone. For a moment I imagined I was on a tropical island with Fabio, sucking Mai Tai's from coconut shells. It was more fun than weaseling out of a dinner date, the second night in a row.

"Hey Delucky," Chance said. "How's it goin'?"

"I just met Donna Kelly. It seems Roxanne Barbara took on the daughter role after Courtney's death. She takes care of them. She sends them on trips."

"Is that love or guilt?"

"There's a difference? The mother/daughter relationship is complicated."

"So I've noticed. What do you need?"

"I need to know everything you've got on two people who died twenty years ago. Courtney Kelly and Hal Bjornsen. If the detectives are still around, I'd like to talk to them."

"All right. Send what you have and I'll see what I can do."

"Thanks, Savino. I owe you."

His voice smiled. "I will collect. By the way, did you call me in the middle of the night?"

"Nope. You must have been dreaming."

"Huh. I swear you apologized about missing our dinner date."

"Yeah, like that would happen."

"And when I woke up this morning, the phone was on my pillow."

"Maybe it was one of your other girlfriends."

"You're funny, DeLucky." His paused. "Uh, about dinner tonight…"

I braced myself.

"I'll have to take a rain check. My parents are in town."

Phew! Er, wait a minute!

"You have parents?"

"Of course I have parents."

"You never talk about them."

"Maybe that's because we're always talking about yours."

"What's wrong with your parents, Savino?" My forehead crinkled in concern. "Do they hold satanic rituals?"

"Don't be ridiculous." Savino chuckled like he adored me. "They're just—different than your family. That's all."

"Oh, you mean they're not dysfunctional and somewhat insane?"

"Insanity has many faces, DeLucky."

"Parents don't scare me, Savino. You've seen mine."

"That kind of reckless courage will bite you in your cute little butt someday."

I ended the call just as my friend, Melvin, of the All Things Blue bar, beeped in.

"Cat, love. How's my rising blues star doing?"

Melvin Michaels was Johnnie's best man at our wedding. He truly was the best man. He was the best thing I got out of that disaster called *my marriage.*

"Cleo's hanging in there, Mel. She's had a rough couple days."

"I can cheer her up. Tell her we're packin' a mega crowd here for her big night. She's a show stopper."

Nothing like being a suspect in a murder investigation to bring out a crowd in Bridgeport.

"Cleo will be thrilled."

"I'm counting on you to keep her ass out of the pen until after the show."

"I'm doing my best to keep all asses concerned slammer free, Mel."

It was no small feat. Detective Opsahl had it in for me. I wouldn't be able to avoid her forever.

"I'm billing Cleo as 'The Black Widow Sings All Things Blue'. Get it? The media will be here in droves. I can't buy this kind of publicity."

I cringed.

"I even bought props for the show. Cleo's mic looks like a pistol and I got handcuffs for her to wear as a bracelet on stage."

"I'm willing to bet those handcuffs are yours." I paused. "Visions are dancing in my head, Melvin. They're not pretty."

"All right, fine. She can have a new pair."

"No. Cleo isn't using props, she's got talent."

"Black and white stripes at least. It's a classic look."

"Nope."

"You're a tough agent, Cat."

Oh great, I've found my fall-back profession. "Hey, save us a table for eight o'clock. My Uncle Joey and Linda will be joining us."

"Your uncle's coming? I'll save the best seat in the house, of course."

"Uncle Joey will be pleased. He's a freak on the dance floor."

Chapter Fifteen

My house was magical when the guests arrived at seven. It was a warm summer evening. Melanie and Cleo and I had transformed the back yard with streams of heart-shaped lights and wedding-bell paper lanterns. Two bride and groom mannequins with Stella's raven black hair and Jake's auburn flat-top kissed on the porch swing.

Half of the outside bar was covered with trays of meats and cheeses, tapenade, stuffed mushrooms, and puffed pastries. The right side was lined up with jello shots, a full selection of alcohol and mixers, and a blender for the margaritas.

Our bachelorette opened her mountain of presents. The gifts were mostly fabulous lingerie. It didn't take long for one of the cousins to dress Inga in a soft pink corset. Beau ran and hid, afraid he would be next. But Inga didn't mind as long as food was involved. She is such a food whore.

Melanie waved me over to the blender. "I haven't seen the stripper yet," she whispered. "Tell me what he isn't wearing and I'll keep an eye out for him."

"Nice try. Don't worry. You won't be disappointed."

"How could I be disappointed? I've been married a decade. I've only seen one man in a g-string. I can tell you right now, the stripper looks better than Rapher."

"You married our high school football hero. You were the envy of every girl in school."

"You know something funny? You wake up next to someone every morning and you never see him change. Then one Sunday afternoon he's manning the TV remote, cheering the Chicago Bears and calling for a beer. And there it is."

"What?"

"The dreaded Buddha belly where his six pack abs used to be. How does that happen, Cat?"

"Oh please. You wouldn't trade Rapher for anything."

"That's true. I'm a sick woman."

The back gate swung open and Max walked through carrying a pizza box high over his head. He looked fine in low rider jeans and snug shirt unbuttoned to his navel. He wore a pizza delivery cap angled jauntily on his brow. He must have snagged it at the restaurant picking up the pizza. His eyes widened as he took in the lights, the liquor, the lingerie strewn across the backs of chairs and the gorgeous Italian women. He froze, in awed reverence.

A wide grin slowly spread across his face. One of the many things I admire about Max is his ability to adapt. For one glorious moment he thought he'd died and gone to heaven.

"Pepperoni, anyone?"

"Stripper!" Melanie screamed.

The screams erupted as twenty-five women descended on Max. The pizza was the first casualty, landing ten feet across the yard. Long manicured nails were yanking on his buttons, others had his cap off and fingers raked through his hair.

"Cat! Get them off me!"

"What? Sorry, I can't hear you."

Melanie paused with her hands spread across Max's six packs. She looked over her shoulder at me.

"So, Max isn't the stripper?"

The heartbreak in Melanie's voice was tragic.

"Um....nope."

I didn't even try to keep the smile off my face.

"Damn," she sighed and let go of Max.

"I thought we needed a designated driver," I said.

"That man can drive me anywhere."

"He will. Straight back to Budda."

She winked. "The kids are at my mother's tonight. I might go home early."

Right then the gate kicked open. A fireman charged into the yard carrying a hose, jacket open exposing tight black leather pants and a smooth bare chest. He strolled straight to the bride. Stella was a dead ringer in the veil she'd taken off the mannequin.

He set down his boom box. "Hot In Here" from Nelly started playing as Mr. Fireman started working his hose.

Max fled in relief. He grabbed my hand and dragged me to the drinks counter.

I handed him a coke. "I need a designated driver, Max. I figured you wouldn't mind. Unless you want me to call a couple cabs."

Max was thoroughly enjoying himself. "I'm your man. But you owe me, Kitty," he mock growled.

"And I always pay my debts." I pulled a short list from my pocket with the names of three partiers. "You've been in a dating slump lately."

"I blame you for that."

I kissed his cheek. "I'm going to make it up to you."

I pointed to three women in the crowd.

"These women are the hottest women here. Next to Mel and me, of course."

"All single?"

"And looking."

Max plopped an icy margarita on a silver tray. "Excuse me. I'm buying a lady a drink."

Melanie watched bug eyed as he made his way into the crowd. "He's going for Tiffany," Melanie giggled. "How do you spell *easy*?"

"Shut up," I said.

Chapter Sixteen

Ken Millani was on the phone in his office the next morning when I stopped by the construction company. He waved me in.

"I'll work out the numbers and get back to you," he said ending the call.

"Come in, Caterina," he said warily. "What do you want now?"

"You lied to me, Mr. Millani."

He shrugged. "If I lied, you asked me something that was none of your business."

"I know Walter was blackmailing you." I sat in the chair facing his desk. "Where were you the morning Walter died?"

His face hardened. "Get out."

"I'm sorry, Ken. I have to ask."

"I've known you since you were born. You don't come into my business and disrespect me this way."

I opened my bag and placed the manila envelope and bug on his desk.

"I found this in Walter's closet. And this was in the confessional."

His face flushed scarlet.

"I didn't listen to the tape, Ken. What you say in the confessional is between you and the big guy. I'll find out who killed Walter, but I won't do it this way."

He stared at the envelope.

"Walter was a snake," I said. "I wouldn't blame you for killing him. But I won't let Cleo do your time either. I'm laying it out there, Ken. I'm letting you know where I stand."

I was three steps down the hall when Ken spoke behind me. "I was with Father Timothy. The ladies want a new church kitchen. Ask him."

I nodded.

"Walter's embezzling hit me hard. I'm broke. With the recession, I don't know if the company can fully recover."

Deflated, Ken turned on his heel and closed the office door behind him.

My step was a little lighter as I walked to the parking lot. I felt enormous relief to scratch Ken's name off the list

The Millani's light up their house every Christmas as bright as the Milky Way. Their annual holiday party is the one highlight of Mama's social calendar that doesn't involve bingo. Every year she wears her red coat with the sable fur collar. And she brings Mrs. Millani panettone, an Italian Christmas bread. Mama would never forgive me if I sent Ken to prison. She doesn't know that many millionaires.

AJ was waiting for me when I walked into RB's downtown office, a camera swinging around my neck. I was solo on this one. Max was off chasing down the friends who accompanied Roxanne and Courtney on the rafting trip. Something extraordinary happened that weekend and I fully intended to find out what that was. The images in Walter's blackmail envelope scared the bejesus out of Roxanne Barbara. At the very least, it inspired her to cough up a bundle of cash.

AJ leaned back, completely at ease, against the receptionist's desk. His cocky, boyish grin was out of place with the all-business blue pin-striped suit he wore.

"Maddie! Where's your monkey?"

Call it my obsession with spy flicks or my enormous crush on Jason Bourne. I was confident Max could turn AJ to meatloaf with his bare hands.

I smiled. "Max had another photo shoot."

"I hope it's in Paris. He's uh, oddly... possessive. Are you two...?" AJ let the sentence hang.

"We're good friends."

"Better yet." He pushed off from the desk. "Come with me. You can wait for Roxanne in the lounge."

The lounge was a warm, open space with large windows, hand-crafted beech wood furniture, and bright accent pillows. I flipped through fashion magazines but my thoughts circled the little black dress I saw downstairs in Roxanne's boutique window. I was crazy about it.

The dress was perfect to wear for Cleo's debut at All Things Blue. But it was expensive. I hadn't made any money all week. Not since Walter bought the farm. And I didn't know when that would change. Who knew how long it would take to clear, convict or smuggle Cleo to Cuba? And to divert Detective Opsahl's evil eye away from me.

Roxie met me at 12:48. Not bad for a diva. She spilled apologies.

"I'm sorry to have kept you waiting. A pipe broke at our new construction site and we have water *everywhere*."

She was smaller than she appeared on television, with bursts of energy that can leave you breathless.

I liked her at once.

I stood and she took my hands in hers, looking me over with frank appraisal.

"Have you modeled? You certainly have the body for it."

OK. I loved her. Roxanne Barbara was my new BFF.

We went to her office. I snapped pictures of Roxanne standing in front of a wall covered with awards and photos of her favorite runway shows in Paris. Someone appeared with sparkling waters and a platter of fruit and cheeses, crackers and macaroons.

The designer gave me a crooked smile. "My blood sugar gets low this time of day. My staff feeds and waters me. They're really saving themselves. It took me a while to catch onto what they were doing."

"I love it when people feed me," I said through a mouthful of coconut.

Roxanne kicked her heels off and sighed deeply. She wasn't at all what I expected. If she would stop calling me Maddie, I'd take her to Mickey's for a beer.

She talked about growing up in Bridgeport. Staying true to her Chicago roots was important to her, despite international fame.

She smiled. "I love this town—the people, the history, the culture. It's truly one of the sweet spots on earth."

"You've been good to Chicago. RB Design has created training, jobs, and boosts the tourist industry."

"The people of Chicago have been good to me. It's only right I give back."

"I understand Bridgeport High School is planning a tribute to you at their next reunion."

I like to make it up as I go.

Roxie cocked her head. "I didn't know that."

"There'll be a memorial as well, honoring your friend, Courtney Kelly."

Now she smiled, enormously pleased. "Courtney was my best friend. And a brilliant designer." Her arm swept the room. "All this, everything I've created, we planned together."

Her face was open. I knew one thing for sure. Roxanne had nothing to do with Courtney Kelly's death.

AJ tapped at the door and poked his head in. "Roberto Cavalli is on line four."

Her expression was one of genuine regret. "I'm sorry to cut this short. I have to take this."

I thanked her and snagged a macaroon for the road. AJ walked with me to the elevator.

"You hungry?"

"Not really," I wiped my mouth with the back of my hand. I hoped I didn't have coconut in my teeth.

He checked his watch. "I have an hour before my next appointment. We can grab a bite at Hugo's."

I'd never been to Hugo's Frog Bar and Fish House. I stopped by a few months ago and couldn't get in without a reservation.

"We'll never get a table."

The elevator door opened and AJ followed me inside.

"I called this morning. Our table is waiting."

The elevator door closed on my astonished face.

Hugo's is a spectacular restaurant on Chicago's Gold Coast. The maître de led us to a choice table by the window with a view of the lake. A waiter appeared and cracked a bottle of wine. AJ leaned over the table and murmured in my ear.

"I'm sure you saw Nanette Lepore when we came in."

I looked around at the tables and sucked in a breath. I hadn't seen this many stars in one place since that field trip to the planetarium.

He smiled. "Ground rules. No working, scouting, or hustling interviews. No questions about Roxanne."

"OK, fine. But if Oprah walks through the door, all deals are off."

"I've got one hour to impress you. This is about two people who just might, if they give themselves the chance, be crazy about each other someday."

"Really?"

"No. It's all about the wine. I don't want to waste a two hundred dollar bottle."

"You paid two hundred bucks for a bottle of wine?"

"Are you impressed?"

"Not even a little bit," I laughed.

"Good."

The waiter opened the bottle. He dropped the cork on the table and I eyeballed it for gold.

I have to admit I was loving all the attention from this sexy guy. But when you're a doubling as someone else, you have to cover your story. I knew more about the real Maddie Goldstein today than I did when I first met AJ in Bridgeport. I'd been stalking her on Twitter. I was her new Facebook fan. If AJ was a Facebook fan, he'd know that she was, at this very moment, in

LA interviewing Sarah Jessica Parker for her new movie. This was not good.

I gave AJ the Facebook version of my family. A brother at NYU, a sister in Germany with her Army husband. Then I diverted the conversation to his life. I haven't met a man yet who wasn't enormously interested in himself.

AJ's parents divorced when he was a baby. His mother worked two jobs and raised AJ alone until she remarried when he was eight. The step-father adopted him. He eventually connected with his birth father and took his name back.

"How did the name-switch work for your mom and stepdad?"

"Let's just say Santa doesn't bring much at Christmas."

I thought of Christmas at my parent's house with the dizzying smells of honey ginger cakes and Mama's pork crown roast with apple stuffing. Papa dresses up as Santa Claus. My switched-at-birth sister pounds *Silent Night* on the piano and her devil children screech along on their band instruments. Everyone sings in a pastiche of English and Italian. To me, it's the perfect Christmas.

"How about your dad?" I asked. "Do you spend much time with him?"

He laughed bitterly. "My mother was right about him. He comes and he goes, but mostly he's just gone."

Something dark flashed in his eyes. I felt a wave of energy that jolted me. I suppose everyone has issues with family. But what I felt from AJ in that unguarded moment was a raw, explosive anger. There was more family drama than he was telling.

"That's tough," I said.

He shrugged. "That's life."

And just as quickly the shadow was gone. His mood was light and I wondered if I'd imagined it all.

He grinned. "Let's eat. I hope you're famished."

"Always."

AJ loved food. His eyes glazed over studying the menu. He ordered expansively off the appetizer menu: baked goat cheese with tomato, kalamata olives, and basil, an order of oysters

Rockefeller, and two sides of their famous jumbo lump crab cakes. He could pack a meal away like the twins. Unless his Canali jacket covered a multitude of sins, I had no idea where it all went.

We had almost finished with our late lunch and were contemplating dessert when AJ dragged his cell from his pocket. He eyed the caller ID and glanced up at me apologetically.

"Excuse me. I should take this." He swiveled in his chair, facing the other way for privacy, and answered the phone. "Yes?"

He was deep in conversation when my cell vibrated in my pocket. I thought AJ looked important talking to somebody on his cell. I figured I should answer mine. I was Maddie Goldstein, after all, an up-and-coming investigative reporter from New York City.

"I should take this," I mouthed breezily when AJ glanced over at the ringtone. AJ turned back, engrossed in his phone call.

"This is Maddie."

"Maddie?" The man had a voice like a truck horn. "I'm looking for Cat DeLuca."

"Speaking. How may I help you?"

"I heard you're lookin' for the guy who done Wally."

My breath caught and I gave a sidelong glance over at AJ. He was talking away, totally absorbed. "Yes. I am looking for that guy. What do you know?"

"I know the crazy dame didn't do it."

I lowered my voice to a hoarse whisper. "Who then?"

"That kind of information ain't free."

"Nothing of value is. Tell me what you know. I'll pay."

"Do you know The Bridgeport Café on Morgan? Meet me there in twenty minutes."

Johnnie's restaurant? I shuddered at the thought. "Um, not there. Let's meet across the street at Ozzie's. One hour."

"Johnnie's has better burgers."

"Fine. I'll buy you a steak."

"Johnnie's has better steaks."

"Then buy one yourself with the money I give you. What are you drinking?"

He laughed softly. "A double Crown Royal on the rocks. I'm wearing a red plaid shirt and a baseball cap."

"Red plaid shirt and baseball cap. Got it."

"Bring lots of cash, Miss DeLuca. And come alone. This is a private conversation."

"If you're worried about protection, I'll see that you're safe, Mr—?"

"Oh I ain't worried, Missy. I ain't testifying."

Click.

I stared at the phone in my hand, heart racing.

I waited for AJ to finish his conversation.

"Shoot me an email. I'll let Roxie know the dates." AJ clipped his words. "No, I'm heading back now."

He grunted twice and tucked the phone back in his pocket.

"Duty calls," AJ smiled apologetically. "Please stay and finish the wine. I intended to order the torte, myself. Perhaps you'll have a piece for me. It's Hugo's specialty."

"I spotted the dessert tray when we came in. I've been eying the cheesecake with fresh strawberries."

AJ clapped his hands. "I love to see a woman actually eat. In my business, women are dieting or purging. There's this crazy guilt associated with food."

"In mama's family we eat. We feel guilty about everything else."

AJ settled the tab and stood to leave. He leveled his eyes at me appreciatively. "I'll have the company driver take you to your hotel."

"I'll catch a cab when I'm ready. It's a beautiful afternoon. I'd like to walk along the water."

He smiled. "When I'm gone, you can schmooze the stars all you want. Maybe you'll snag an interview."

AJ kissed my cheek. He stopped at Lepore's table on his way out. She looked over and waved. He'd snagged an interview for Maddie Goldstein.

I quickly finished my cheesecake and polished off AJ's two hundred dollar bottle. Maybe the wine was smoother than my twenty dollar Merlot. Maybe it was the fine crystal wine glass that made the cool sparkling liquid slide down my throat like honey. But my Dr. Pepper Lip Smacker makes the same mark on the lip of a twenty dollar bottle.

I walked past the designer's table, tweaking a thumb and pinky by my ear. "Ms. Lepore," I gushed. "Call me." And I hot-smoked it out the door to rouse the Silver Bullet.

Chapter Seventeen

I parked across the street from Johnnie's restaurant and, keeping my head low, darted into Ozzie's a full ten minutes early. I took a table in a quiet corner, away from the window, with a view of the door. I ordered black coffee and a double shot of Crown Royal and a glass of ice.

I stared at the door and listened to the iconic sounds of the city. Cars honked and sirens blared. A parade of customers marched through the door but no grumpy guy wearing a plaid shirt and baseball cap. Four cups of coffee later, the ice had melted in the glass. I tossed the whiskey down my throat and dropped a ten on the table. Then I walked out the door into a whirl of flashing blue and red lights.

The people of Bridgeport love cop drama. I pushed through the crowd to a stream of yellow police tape securing the scene. There were three cops on crowd patrol, and Leo and Tommy were taking statements from witnesses. A medical examiner knelt over a body in the road. The rear doors of his van were open.

And there, in the thick of it all, was Captain Bob. I ducked but it was too late. He waved me over.

I scooched under the police tape and tried not to think about how much he wanted to arrest me.

"Captain Bob," I said in my professional voice. "What do we have here?"

"What we have here, Caterina, is an interruption of a very nice meal with my wife at your Johnnie's restaurant." Captain

Bob jerked his head toward the ground. He waited for me to look down. I didn't want to. I smelled blood. A lot of it.

Taking a steadying breath, I dragged my eyes to the ground. I took in the bald head, the red plaid shirt, the blood. The baseball cap, lost in flight, was twenty feet away on the street. An expression of terror was forever imprinted in his eyes. It's not how I remembered him.

The last time I saw the old man he was laughing. I was making my escape across Walter's alley, the tackle box hot in my hands. Detective Ettie Opsahl dangled from the upstairs window, itching to shoot.

"Hit-and-run," the captain said. "Your card was in his pocket. Why am I not surprised?"

I ignored the jab. "He and Walter Jones were neighbors. He was going to tell me who killed Walter."

"Right."

"His upstairs window is a straight shot to Walter's office."

Eyebrows shot up. "Why didn't he come forward before?"

"I dunno. It's a little late to ask him."

"Smartass. You're like the pied piper of death, Cat. Every time a body pops up, I look for you in the crowd."

"Really? If you'd *investigated* Walter's death instead of *assuming* Cleo did it, this man might still be laughing."

Captain Bob's eye twitched. "Cleo is a crazy, gun-happy psycho who shot her husband once before."

"I'm not gonna argue with the cold hard facts of the case, Bob. The thing is, everyone wanted to shoot Walter. This time someone beat her to it."

His face spasmed. "Is there any reason to think this hit-and-run was anything but a tragic accident?"

"Gee, Bob. The guy lived seventy-odd years. Last week he witnesses a murder. Today he decides to talk—and an hour later he's dead. You do the math."

"Did he tell you anything at all about the murder?"

"Yeah. He said Cleo didn't do it."

Bob snorted. "Nice try."

The coroner signaled his team. The old man's body was bagged, zipped and loaded into the van.

A deep sadness came over me. I promised the old man I would keep him safe. It was the last thing I'd said to him.

I felt like a putz.

I trudged down the street and plucked the Chicago White Sox cap from the concrete. I brushed it off and brought the fabric close to my face. It smelled like Old Spice. Carlos Torres had signed his name on the rim. A trace of mustard was smudged on the side. The old man had seen his last ballgame and eaten his last hotdog. I hoped there had been lots them.

I checked my watch. I should go home and get dressed for the rehearsal dinner. But I wasn't ready to be alone yet. I made my way to the Silver Honda and drove to Tino's deli.

A gold Hummer was parked by the window and I pulled in beside it. Max and Tino were inside, hunched over a chess board. Tino had been teaching Max the game.

Tino met me at the door. He opened his arms and held me tight against his ample girth. The deli meister gives the best hugs. My world felt safe and sane again.

"Not your fault, Caterina," he said softly. "You can't blame yourself for the old man's death."

I didn't ask Tino how he knew. He just does.

"We'll get this guy," Max said grimly. "I promise you that."

I told them about my phone conversation with the old man. Tino poured wine and I plopped down at their table. I didn't have to know a lot about chess to count the pieces on the board. Or to know that Max was losing.

I had to give it to Max. He was a new player and he played with heart. But he hadn't beat Tino yet.

"Tino's kicking your butt," I said unnecessarily.

Max's eyes gleamed. He grabbed his bishop. "Not for long."

"Checkmate," Tino smiled.

Max winced and looked over at me. "We have a bet. When I beat Tino at chess, he's closing the deli for a week and we're going to Istanbul."

"Ah…" I said. "Istanbul sounds more like a spy game than a tourist trap."

Tino chuckled. "Why don't you pack your cloak and dagger and come with us?"

"I might do that. Cleo can stay here and run your deli."

"If she's not terrifying the male population of Cuba," Max said.

"That goes without saying," I said.

Tino smiled. "Have dinner with us. I made chicken saltimbocca."

I patted my stomach. "Raincheck? We have Stella and Jake's rehearsal dinner tonight. And I'm still stuffed from my lunch with AJ."

Max scowled at me. "I warned you to stay away from him."

I tried counting to ten and started yelling at four. "You're not one of my interfering brothers, you know. If it was up to the male members of my family, I'd be a nun."

Max gave a lazy smile. "Kitty, let me make this crystal clear. The last thing on my mind is protecting your virtue."

Tino's eyes narrowed. "What do we know about this RJ?"

"It's AJ," I said.

"Initials!" Tino scoffed. "Don't these people have names?"

"He's RB's assistant. Max doesn't like him because he's flashy, sexy, and a hopeless flirt."

"He's an arrogant asshole," Max said. He met Tino's gaze and nodded.

"I'll check him out," Tino said quietly.

I threw my hands in the air. Tino laughed.

"Any luck with the people in the photograph?" I asked.

Max produced a small black notebook from his front pocket. "A total of six college students took that river trip that weekend. Four besides Barbara and Courtney," he said around a mouthful of cannoli. "I ran down three of the four."

"Superstar. What about the photograph? Was the camera set on a timer?"

"No, it was a male who took the photo. Someone the six picked up on the way."

I felt a thrill of excitement. "Tell me it was Hal Bjornsen."

Max grinned. "It was your missing man from Wisconsin."

"Sweet."

"It was a Woodstock kind of weekend. Booze, dope, kids discovering their inner Jim Morrison." Max referred to his notes. "After graduation they lost track of each other. Michelle Kane manages a pet cemetery in Shorewood."

"They have a degree for that?" Tino said.

Max ignored him. "James Matson is in Silicon Valley, and Corey Evans is one of those Wall Street pigs everyone loves to hate. The guys are corporate jocks with big mortgages and pin-striped suits."

"How about the guy that got a Mercedes Benz scar that weekend?"

"Aron Sikes spelled with one A. I haven't located him yet. James Matson thought he accepted a position with an overseas construction firm after college. But that hasn't been confirmed."

"Maybe he left the country and didn't come back."

"He did have limited ties here. On his university application he wrote: 'No next of kin'. But at eighteen, he could have been mad at his parents."

"I love that orphan dream," I said.

"However, if Sikes is out there, I'll find him. I've got mad skills, babe. And wait till I show you my hands-on techniques. They will blow your mind."

I turned the color of the red in the checkered tablecloths. Tino barked a laugh and Max looked pleased.

I returned to the subject at hand. "What did they say about the guy who took their picture? It's possible those six smiling faces were the last to see Hal alive."

"Two people didn't recall him at all. With a lot of prodding, a vague memory of a dorky guy emerged through a drug-induced fog. Michelle Kane had the best recollection. She remembered the guy. She said he tweeked on the raft when they hit white water. She saw something in the paper a few years later when they discovered Bjornsen's body. She said it looked like him but she couldn't be sure."

I nodded. It had been awhile.

"She said the guy they picked up camped out with them the first night. When she woke the next morning he was gone. Apparently Aron woke earlier and was searching for him when he fell down a ravine. That's when he cut his arm like a Mercedes Benz hood ornament."

"He has a Mercedes scar from a fall?" Tino scoffed. "You'd have to be pretty damned drugged out to accomplish that feat."

"One more thing," Max said. "Walter did time in juvie before he was eighteen."

"The records are sealed," I said.

"Tino got a look at them."

I narrowed my eyes. "Who are you, Tino?"

"A humble sausage maker."

"With a bulletproof car."

Tino shrugged. "Some would kill for such a recipe."

Max looked amused. "Walter got in trouble with a friend. Stole a couple cars. Joyriding, mostly. Here's the clincher. The friend's name was Sam Kane."

I blinked. "As in Michelle Kane?"

"The pet cemetery degree," Tino said.

"Sam is Michelle's brother. He managed to rack up a record as an adult. Did a few stretches for burglary and fraud. Last time he was released was two years ago."

"In time to reconnect with Walter and set up the blackmail," Tino said.

"Possibly. My guess is that Michelle showed Sam the article about finding Hal's body. She had to tell him about their weekend. Apparently her recollection of Hal Bjornsen wasn't as vague as she let on."

"It would explain how Walter was able to blackmail Roxanne," I said. "Do you suppose Sam was in on the blackmail?"

"I'd almost bet on it. With Walter gone, what will keep him from approaching Roxanne himself?"

"That would be me, chico," I said

"I hope you're tougher than you look."

"Do you have an address?"

"I do. We'll take the Hummer. I'd like to be there if there's trouble."

"Good. We can run him over with your tank."

The bell jingled and Officer Ettie Opsahl charged through the door, her short dark hair a wild friz of curls. Her mouth contorted with rage. I peered closely for foam. She appeared pretty much like the last time I saw her, screaming out Walter's bedroom window.

"Caterina DeLuca," she said in a voice oozing disdain. "If it was up to me, you'd have been locked up long ago."

Max stiffened. Tino lifted a brow.

"Not feeling the love here. How about you boys?"

"I don't know what kind of hold you DeLucas have on Captain Maxfield. But I know the truth about you. You helped your nut-job partner kill her husband. You'll pay dearly for the death of Walter Jones."

"You're out of your mind," Tino said.

"Yeah," Max said. "Cleo is her nut-job *assistant*."

Ettie's jaw worked overtime.

"You think this is funny?"

"I think your powers of deduction suck."

The detective took a bullying step toward me. "Caterina DeLuca, you have twenty-four hours to turn yourself in. After that, Captain Bob will issue a warrant for your arrest or I'll find one of his superiors who will."

Max's eyes went frigid. He edged toward the detective, dwarfing her with his tall, broad frame. His breath fanned her hair.

"You'd better leave now," Tino said.

"I'll leave when I'm damned good and ready," Ettie snapped back. Then she turned and slammed the door behind her.

Chapter Eighteen

Stella and Jake's rehearsal dinner was held in the church courtyard on a gloriously warm summer evening. The groom's mother had engaged a Chicago caterer who once served brunch for Michelle Obama's girlfriends. All the DeLucas weren't there, of course. Some were serving and protecting the good citizens and donut shops of Chicago. Dinner guests were given a choice of pan seared filet mignon, pineapple glazed chicken, or sage crusted trout.

The caterers provided their own china and silver. Nevertheless, a few church ladies stood guard on the sidelines, defending against a possible breech of the church's unremarkable flatware, a Betty Crocker coupon victory of the seventies.

As Maid of Honor, I sat at the bride and groom's table. I was flanked on each side by the Best Men: twins Michael and Vinny. They ordered the filet mignon. The plate was beautifully presented with Cabernet wine sauce, fresh sliced mushrooms, herbed rice and grilled asparagus.

My twin brothers stared at their portion of meat.

"Where's the beef," they demanded.

Where was the duct tape?

I kicked both of them under the table. "It's at Wendy's… later," I whispered. "Behave yourselves."

Their eyes glommed onto my chicken.

I wielded my fork. "Back off."

The server poured wine all around. The groom's mother, Margaret, stared at her glass. "I don't drink."

"You will," I said.

She sat primly beside her son. Margaret was a kind, uptight Baptist. Jake was her only child. Her husband was gone. She had one sister in California. She faced the DeLuca family all alone.

God help her.

Stella's mom is my crazy Aunt Francesca. She's married to Papa's brother, Rudy. Aunt Fran has been snippy since I started dating an FBI agent. When her son, Frankie, was turned down by the FBI for general insanity, she launched a personal campaign to put the FBI out of business. After a visit from three men in black suits and sunglasses, she began driving to Wisconsin to mail her threatening letters.

"Everything is lovely, Margaret," Mama said.

Margaret smiled wistfully. "I wanted this night to be perfect for the kids to remember."

Jake and Stella cooed to each other and played footsie under the table.

"Take a lot of pictures," I said.

"They're so happy," Margaret said.

"They'll get over it," Uncle Rudy said.

My cousin Frankie tapped his glass with a spoon. "I have an announcement to make as well. My sister Stella isn't the only one making a big change. I'm turning in my badge. I'm leaving the Chicago Police Force."

Uncle Rudy frowned. "What? Are you nuts?"

"Is that a trick question?" I said.

Frankie smiled broadly. "I've decided to take my job back with the FBI."

"You can't stop my letters," Aunt Fran said.

"You'll have to wear a suit." Papa scratched his scar. "G-men wear suits."

"I got a suit," Frankie said.

"Does the FBI have dental, dear?" Mama asked.

I glanced around the table. No one else seemed to think there was a flaw in Frankie's plan.

I turned to Frankie and laid out the facts. "You never had a job there, 'cuz. You applied with the FBI. You got turned down. Heck, I've been turned down for lots of jobs myself."

The family exchanged knowing looks.

"*What?* Oh, here we go with this again?"

"And now she takes dirty pictures," Mama wailed.

The lone Baptist paled.

Grandma DeLuca waggled a bony finger. "Did the government apologize for the marzipan shortage of 1945?"

Mama discreetly moved Grandma's wine out of reach. Mama is the acting matriarch of the DeLuca family. She took over the position the day Grandma DeLuca went to Mass wearing a bra over her dress.

The groom's mother stared bleakly at her plate. "Jake is a good boy. But he has his own family now. It's hard to let him go."

Mama, the poster mother of dysfunction, beamed. "I never let my sons go. They call me every day."

Mama swiped Michael's mouth with her napkin.

"You're not losing a son," I said. "You're gaining a loud, obnoxious Italian family."

Margaret seized her glass and slung the wine down her throat.

"Welcome to the family," Papa said.

I slipped away before dessert was served. I dropped by the kitchen and grabbed two slices of cheesecake to take with me. One was for Cleo if it survived the ride home.

The church ladies were whispering among themselves. I nudged closer and perked up my ears.

"Can you keep a secret?" the one with purple hair said.

"Oh yes!"

One woman turned up a hearing aid. The other crossed two fingers behind her back.

"Saturday I overheard Ken Millani talking to Father Timothy."

"Oh?"

"Ken just donated $490,000 to the church!"

The old women squealed. It couldn't be safe the way they jumped up and down.

I escaped to my car with two desserts and a big ol' helping of guilt. I climbed inside and banged my head on the steering wheel.

Becky Millani and I played Nancy Drew when we were kids. Sometimes, if Ken was home, he'd play the bad guy or Dr. Drew. Once he was Nancy's housekeeper, Mrs. Gruen. Becky had the coolest dad in school.

"My pop was studying to be a priest before he met my mother," Becky said to me once.

"What happened?"

"I told you," she laughed. "He met my mother."

Ken was a good guy. He was on the school board and he volunteered for the boys and girls club. I'd wasted too much time this week wondering if he was a murderer. What was wrong with me?

I ate Cleo's cheesecake first. And then I ate mine.

What the hell. I was headed there fast.

◇◇◇

I zoomed home and ran upstairs to get out of my dress and into my running gear. Inga was antsy after riding shotgun all day and I seriously needed to burn off some bad mojo.

We jogged easily for a while and then hit the running track at the high school. Inga and I lengthened our strides and I let my mind go to that place where there is nothing but breeze and rhythm and pounding feet. Father Timothy wouldn't like to hear it but this is the closest I'll probably ever get to meditation. I could have run forever.

Reluctantly, we started heading home. It was almost ten and I had a long day tomorrow. We'd just rounded onto Loomis Street when pins and needles started pricking the back of my neck. I reviewed the turn we'd just made in my mind and realized my peripheral vision had caught sight of a dark blue Volvo. I'd seen it before. It had passed us in the high school's parking lot.

We were still four blocks from my house so I started zig-zagging a few side streets to see if I was just being paranoid.

I snuck a peek at each turn. Nope. I was being followed. The dark outline of the vehicle was revealed by streetlights only. The car's lights were off. It was moving slowly, keeping almost a full block behind; just close enough to see my form in the distance.

My heart started racing and I could feel the sweat on the palm that was holding Inga's leash. As I got closer to my neighborhood, I took a quick left into Mrs. Pickens' back alley. Gladys Pickens is the neighborhood busybody and my plan was to cut across her yard.

But before I gave her the chance to light up the phone lines, I ducked behind a dumpster by the alley's entrance. I waited and soon heard the hum of a car's engine and the crunch of slowly rolling tires. I felt the driver's eyes peering down the alley as he let the car silently roll slowly by.

I eased around the dumpster and tiptoed to the alley's entrance. Poking my head around a wooden fence, I saw the Volvo ease toward the next intersection. It was the turn to my street.

When he came to the stop sign, he stepped on the brakes and paused. It was too far to read the license number in the red glare of his brake lights. But if he turned left, it was a good bet he knew where I lived.

He turned left.

I trotted down the street just far enough to see his brake lights again. He parked on my side of the street, in the middle of the block. My house was on a corner lot but he had a good enough sight line.

Damn it! I gave Inga a tug and we took off running north. We ran a long loop around him and entered my back alley, sight unseen.

I shut the back door, locked the dead bolt and set the alarm. I stood there gasping. We were in the kitchen and Inga was still on the leash. She was a bundle of nerves.

Who was this guy? Why was he tailing me? I hadn't pissed off anybody lately. At least not more than usual. Not that I knew of.

This incident had me freaked. It felt bad. Maybe it was the night. Maybe it was the dark. But my bones told me this was serious. It was so…stealthy. It was so…committed.

Get it together, DeLuca, I thought to myself. I reached down to let Inga off her leash when I heard the scratch of a key on a lock. The front door opened.

Both of us froze.

I did a quick inventory. My Glock nine MM was still keeping Victoria's Secrets safe in my dresser drawer at the end of the hall.

But before the door closed behind my intruder, I heard a low grunt and someone burp through his nose. Rocco! The king of boy noises. I knew that particular resonance.

I let Inga off her leash and practically stumbled into the front room with relief.

"Rocco!"

Rocco had kicked the door shut behind him. He was looking down at the two large paper bags in his arms filled with Chinese food.

"Hey, Sis, I…" Rocco began and then looked up. He stopped abruptly when he saw the look on my face. I saw his body suddenly lock up and his jaw set.

"What? What's happened, Cat?"

I was relieved enough to feel a little Catholic guilt. "Rocco, I'm just glad to see you, bro. Let me just reset the alarm. Chinese? You just ate at the rehearsal dinner."

"Did you see my beef? Cause I didn't."

"You're as bad as the twins. They're at Wendy's."

Rocco dumped the Chinese on the coffee table and headed to the fridge for a couple of beers. Chinese food is Rocco's and my thing. He handed me a Goose Island beer and started pulling out cartons of Mongolian beef and sweet and sour shrimp. I snagged the lemon chicken and a pair of chop sticks and wiggled into an end of the sofa.

"What are you doing here?"

"I'm here because I wanted to check up on you, that's all. It's been a hard day, what with the hit-and-run. Besides," he shrugged, "where else can I eat all the Chinese I want with no screaming kids? Okay, now it's your turn. You were using the alarm? I'm always nagging you to use that damn thing. What the hell happened?"

Rocco lobbed a shrimp toast into his mouth but I could see he was eyeing me. I dug into my lemon chicken but I had so much of the left-over adrenaline going that my chopsticks were swinging like a pole dancer.

"It's nothing. I'm probaboy making a mountain out of a molehill."

Rocco set down his carton. "Give it up, Sis. And I mean it. What happened?"

I shoved the chopsticks back into the carton and sighed. "OK. Someone followed Inga and me tonight on our run. It was a dark blue Volvo. I didn't notice it at first but he was there at the running track at the high school. He followed me on the way back. He already knew where I lived. I didn't get a read on his plates."

Rocco shot up and looked around. "Where'd you last see him?"

It so didn't help that Inga chose that minute to jump onto the sofa and crawl under a cushion with a whimper. My partner is such a drama queen.

"He was parked at the east end of the street, this side, in the middle of the block."

Rocco walked out the front door without another word. I heard his car start up in front and the squeal of tires on pavement. I locked the door and reset the alarm behind him.

Rocco returned forty-five minutes later. He'd searched the side streets and main streets. He'd done a foot search down my street and back alley.

"Nothing." Rocco flopped next to me on the couch. "Whoever that guy was, he's long gone by now."

Rocco snagged a carton of congealed egg foo young. He looked down at the fat globs floating on surface. Then he shrugged and dug in.

"So I made a few phone calls while I was out," Rocco chewed. "I called Tino to let him know about the Volvo guy. He said he'd keep his ear to the ground."

"Ah, Rocco. I wish you hadn't done that."

Rocco ignored me and slurped more egg foo young. "I also called some of the boys at the precinct to let them know your street needs more attention. At the very least, I want this guy to see some blue if he ever shows up again."

"No! Oh Rocco, you didn't! Who'd you talk to? Were any of them related to us?" I shuddered as the consequences hit me full force. My voice lowered to a snarl. "Did you speak to any *DeLucas?*"

Rocco's eyes widened innocently while he stuffed another huge bite into his mouth. His chin was glistening. "Honey, you do know where you live, right?"

"Ah crap! Ten minutes after you called, our family phone tree lit up like Christmas."

Rocco chuckled, digging deep into his carton. "Not even ten, I'd bet."

"Listen to me, Mr. Greasy-Lips-Egg-Foo-Young-Guy. You didn't need to do this. I was handling it. You know what this means, Rocco. It means that MAMA knows! She had Father Timothy on speed dial before…."

Rocco set the carton down and grabbed a napkin to wipe his chin. He turned full on to face me. "Reality check, Sis. This is nothing to play around with and you know it. I saw your face when I got here. And you don't overreact. If anything you blow everything off, which makes me freakin' nuts, by the way."

"*Pffft.*" I hate it when Rocco was right.

"Think about it, Cat. Think about where the real danger is here."

"You say that like there's even a contest. Who would *you* rather meet in a dark alley?" I challenged.

Rocco chuckled and put his arm around me. I rested my head on his shoulder and sighed.

"OK, let's walk through this so we can figure out who this guy is. Tell me about your cases, all of them. And anything else that comes to mind, no matter how inconsequential. You have such a knack for bringing out the killer instinct in people. For all we know this guy could be someone you cut off in line at the grocery store."

I rolled my eyes but started talking. I knew there had to be some clue out there, something that would lead me to who this Volvo stalker could be. I was so tired I could hardly keep my eyes open. My body had crashed after my panicked adrenaline rush and my mind felt numb. But I kept talking, telling Rocco everything about the Jones case and Steve Greger and other cases I was working. Rocco was silent for the most part, just asking a clarifying question once in a while. At some point I don't remember, I drifted into silence too.

When I awoke in the deep of night, I was laying on the couch with a pillow under my head and a blanket over me. Cleo had come home. Her bag was on the table. Rocco snored softly in the recliner. He must have called Maria after I'd fallen asleep to let her know he was playing watchdog tonight. I quietly got up and tucked the blanket around him. For a best friend and big brother, you couldn't do better than Rocco. I softly kissed his forehead and sent up a "thank you" to whoever was listening. Then I stumbled to my bed and slept the sleep of the dead.

Chapter Nineteen

I had to hand it to Mama. She held off from calling me until six in the morning. It was a record for her. Either she'd learned to hold her tongue or she was scheming and plotting a real zinger this time. I snorted to myself as I picked up the phone. *Yeah. Like that was even a question.*

"Is that you, Caterina? Are you dead yet?"

"You know it's me, Mama. You know I'm not dead yet."

"And how should I know that?"

"Because you don't talk to ghosts. You hate it when grandma does."

Mama expelled a long-suffering sigh. "Caterina DeLuca, what you've put me through. No mother. No mother in all the history of the world has gone through what *this* mother has with a daughter like you."

I wondered about the mother of Eva Braun. Or the Wicked Witch of the West. Those women should've had a priest on speed dial.

"I'm fine. Really, thank you for your concern."

"So is this what you want, Caterina? Police out patrolling your neighborhood. Father Timothy saying extra prayers for you. Do you *like* all this attention? Is that it?"

I sputtered. "I do *not* want Father Timothy saying extra prayers for me!"

"Well, you *should* want this. You should want Father Timothy praying for you every second of the day. Like I do, Caterina. On my knees I pray for you."

"Is this conversation going anywhere other than Oz?"

"Your brother Rocco had a good job for you. A job with insurance."

I'm not a dispatcher, Mama. I'm a private investigator."

"You take dirty pictures."

"That's my job."

Something in her voice made me wary. Uh-oh. Mama was just playing with her food before. Now she was circling in for the kill.

"Mrs. Gianni's daughter is hiring at the hospital. She will interview you today. I told her you have two years of experience."

"What kind of experience?"

"She does what you do," Mama zinged triumphantly. "She takes pictures. There's good money in the medical field today."

"What kind of pictures?"

"X-rays and MRsomethings."

"I'm not a radiologic technologist. You have to go to a school for that."

"What's to learn? You take pictures of naked people. She takes pictures of naked people." I could see Mama flapping the air dismissively.

"Mama, I love you. And I'm sorry you were worried about me. But I don't want to be anything other than what I am."

"A snoop with no insurance," Mama sniffed.

"Yeah."

"You're killing me, Caterina. My chest hurts. I can't breathe."

The doctor says Mama has the robust heart of an elephant.

"Maybe it's gas. Try Tums."

"It's not gas. It's a daughter who takes dirty pictures and consorts with murderers."

I knew where this was going. If I didn't end this conversation soon, Mama would remind me of the thirty-four grueling hours of hard labor she did when I was born. I'm grateful to her. Don't get me wrong. It's just that when Mama brings up the big *thirty-four*, I secretly feel guilty. As if maybe, on my way out, I looked at my impending life through that hole and put on the brakes.

"We're getting close to finding Walter's murderer," I said. "I need a little more time. I will prove to you that Cleo didn't kill anyone."

It wasn't exactly a lie, I told myself. Max said you know you're getting close to the murderer when someone tries to kill you. With the old man's tragic death and the stalking blue Volvo, we had to be closing in fast.

Mama made that clicking sound with her mouth again.

"Say hi to Papa. I'll see you both Saturday for Stella's wedding." She snorted. "If *that woman* doesn't kill you first."

"Don't make me haunt you, Mama."

I dragged myself out of bed feeling like I woke up inside an episode of *The Twilight Zone*. Mama's early morning phone calls can have that effect on me. I showered and dressed and scrunched my hair back in a clip. Then I followed the aroma of coffee and ham and pancakes to the kitchen.

Rocco sat at the table. Cleo scooted around him, flipping pancakes, pulling dishes from the cupboard, and OJ from the fridge. Rocco turned his body with hers as if he was dancing with her from his chair. He kept her in his sights. He was careful to not have his back to her.

Cleo whipped out an unnecessarily large butcher knife to cut the ham. Rocco quietly dropped his hand into his pocket. I guessed he was hiding an unnecessarily large cannon down there.

I couldn't blame Rocco. Cleo's infamous video had sent chills down the spine of every man in America. Sometimes I wondered if she would ever have a normal life again. I wondered if Lorena Bobbit ever gets laid.

I poured coffee in a mug and sat beside my brother.

"Thanks for staying over." I made a face. "I guess I was spooked last night. First somebody ran the old man down. And then the blue Volvo—"

"Old man? Blue Volvo? What's going on," Cleo demanded.

"Cleo spent the day at All Things Blue," I said.

"Marvin says I have what it takes to be a star."

"You should go to Vegas," Rocco said.

"Do you really think so?"

"Please go," Rocco said.

My brother faced me squarely. "I don't want you to be alone until we can figure this blue Volvo business out."

"Volvo? *Hello!*" Cleo said.

"I'll sleep over again tonight and keep watch."

"Watch what?" Cleo said. "I thought Maria threw you out."

"Thanks, bro, but I won't need you tonight," I said. "I have my premium platinum alarm system and my vicious guard dog."

"You do realize she's a beagle, don't you?"

"And I'll be home tonight," Cleo said.

Rocco looked at my assistant uncertainly. "I don't know."

"Do you want me to shoot somebody?" Cleo said eagerly.

"She'll do," Rocco said. "Call Uncle Joey if you need to dispose of a body."

Max drove and I rode shotgun to Sherwood. Michelle Kane, the third woman in the rafting picture, managed the pet cemetery there. We hoped she would connect us with her brother, Sam. Sam and Walter stole cars together in high school. Max and I suspected they teamed up again to blackmail Roxanne.

The Happy Trails Pet Cemetery is a big rambling theme park without the rides. It is twenty acres of eternal four-legged bliss. The Hummer pushed through an iron gate that read, *Until We Meet Again*. We followed a winding road past fanciful gardens, a mausoleum, and lots of lawn-art. St. Francis was everywhere.

Max grinned. "Would you bury Inga in a place like this?"

I poked him. "Do you think she can't hear you in the back seat?"

Inga wagged her tail and put her head on my shoulder. I reached in my pocket and gave her a sausage.

We pulled up to the park office. I patted Inga's head.

"You should wait in the car. The other dogs are taking a nap."

Max opened his mouth to say something. I glared at him and he closed it again.

The woman at the front desk was on the phone when we entered. She signaled with her index finger. She'd be with us in a moment. She had blond hair and porcelain skin. She wore a tag that said *Grief Counselor*. Her liquid eyes were the color of rain. I bet she was a good crier.

Over the other breast she wore a diamond/sapphire broach. It knocked my eyes out of their sockets.

Max mumbled from the side of his mouth. "Nine dogs, seven cats, and a mega plot for a kid's pony."

"What?"

"You were wondering what that piece of jewelry cost."

"Lucky guess," I mumbled back. "You're not psychic."

"You try." He smiled wickedly. "What am I thinking?"

I jabbed him hard with an elbow.

He laughed softly. "I'll take that as a *maybe*."

The woman finished her call and joined us by a St. Francis water fountain. She wore a soft plum silk suit and matching heels.

"Are you here to say goodbye to a special friend?"

"We're looking for a live one," Max said. "Michelle Kane."

Max's hard body and good looks weren't lost on the blonde. The liquid eyes dropped to his left hand. No ring. She flashed a sexy smile.

"Shelly's in the Slumber room with Frodo. She's making final preparations for this afternoon's service."

"Thank you," I said.

She didn't respond. I was invisible to her. Her eyes didn't waver from Max.

"What am I?" I said. "Chopped liver?"

She placed a card in his hand. The long, manicured fingers played on his palm. "My number. Call me sometime."

She turned on her heel and walked away with more wiggle than she came with.

"Puh-leeze," I said.

Max grinned. "You wanna know what *she* was thinking?"

"You're still not psychic. She's a neon sign."

"Sometimes it's refreshing not to get mixed signals," he said pointedly.

My cheeks felt hot.

"To the Slumber Room, Kitten." He held out an arm and I took it.

"I told you they were sleeping," I said.

We followed the signs and found Michelle Kane alone with the slumbering Frodo. The toy Pomeranian was laid out in a cherry coffin with blue satin lining. He had checked off the planet and was taking his favorite chew toys and a box of Scooby Snacks with him.

Michelle looked much as she did in her college photograph. She was older now and she'd lightened her hair. Today her eyes didn't match the smile.

"I'm surprised to see you here," she said coolly. "I told you everything that was relevant on the phone."

Max warmed her with a smile and shrugged. "You may have omitted something and not realized it. When we spoke earlier, you were vague about the discovery of Hal Bjornsen's body. You said you read the article but were uncertain whether he was the guy you camped with."

"So?"

I cut to the chase. "So you lied. You knew it was Hal's body they found by the river where you camped. Why dodge the truth?"

She looked at me coldly. "Who are you again?"

"Cat DeLuca." I whipped out my card. She took it.

"You catch cheaters."

"And liars," I jabbed. "I found Walter's body. I also found the whopping bag of cash Roxanne Barbara paid when the picture you saw in the paper was used to blackmail her."

"Blackmail?" She was genuinely astonished. "I don't know where you're going with this but it has nothing to do with me."

"It does have something to do with your brother."

Max stepped in. "We believe you told your brother about the rafting trip. You showed him the newspaper article. You were upset when you learned Hal died alone out there. You felt guilty. Your brother shared the information with Walter and they used it to blackmail Roxanne. She had the money and the most to lose if the story went public."

Max made quotes in the air with his fingers. "Famous designer's drug-crazed weekend results in suspicious death. Twenty year cover-up exposed."

"None of that is true."

"When did that stop the tabloids?"

Michelle threw up her arms. "What you're saying is preposterous. Maybe Walter Jones blackmailed Roxie. But I can assure you my brother was not involved."

Max's tone softened. "We'd like to hear that from him. We aren't here to make trouble. We can straighten this out without involving the cops."

She set her jaw. "My brother is finally getting his life together. I'm not going to let you screw it up."

"He doesn't need our help for that," I said. "Let us talk to him."

Michelle chewed her lip. "Walter was a piece of trash. He destroyed my brother's life. I'm glad he's dead."

My brows shot up and down. "Uh, where were you, Friday afternoon, when Walter died?"

Her withering look sent shivers down my spine. "Get out! If you come back, I'll call the cops myself."

She stomped out of the room and Max went after her.

I looked down at Frodo. His head was resting on a hand embroidered pillow. The hair around his mouth had turned white. He had been an old man when he died. I liked to think he had many adventures.

I reached into my pocket and pulled out one of Tino's sausages. I tucked it in the small cherry coffin beside the box of Scooby Snacks.

"Say good night, Frodo," I said.

I found Max in the parking lot punching a number on his cell. He held a small white card in his hand.

"Hi Stephanie. This is Max. We met a few minutes ago and you gave me your card…Yes, I am. I'm a huge Chicago Fire fan… You have tickets? Su-weet. Let me check my calendar and get back to you…I called because we missed Michelle in the Slumber Room. Maybe you can help me. I lost touch with her brother Sam a few years ago. Do you… *Really?* Thanks, Stephanie. I'll let you know about next weekend."

"What did she say?"

"She has tickets for the Chicago Fire against the Seattle Sounders game this weekend."

I gave him a look.

Max grinned. "Sam's sister gave him a job here at Happy Trails. He lives in a small caretaker apartment behind the office."

I gasped. "Is he here now?"

"We just missed him. He's out picking up. He's bringing in a dobie and a cocker spaniel. She said we can catch him in a few hours."

"Score. What was that about a game?"

"She has tickets for next week's game."

"I love soccer. Can I come?"

"You really had no idea what she was thinking earlier, did you."

I shrugged. "You said she wasn't your type."

"I know. She's tall. Blonde. Gorgeous. But now I know she likes soccer. I may have rushed to judgment."

"You're a dog, Max."

He laughed.

We had a couple hours to kill. We parked the Hummer at the Happy Trails gate and jogged into town with Inga. Max stocked up on sodas, chips and a pizza. I threw in two coffees and a fat bag of applesauce donuts. I don't do stakeouts unprepared.

Sam had been in no hurry to return to work. When the small, company hearse finally pulled up to the gate, we cut it off at the pass.

Sam rolled down his window. His eyes were bleary. He smelled like scotch.

"A long lunch at the bar?" Max asked.

He leaned his head out. "Is there a problem?"

"Just you."

The ex-spy jerked the door open, pulled him out, and shoved him against the car. Sam sputtered angrily. His eyes shifted fearfully between Max and me. Inga howled in the back seat, cheering Max on.

"Do you want to take this, Kitten?"

"You bet." I looked hard at Sam. "We know you and Walter blackmailed Roxanne. That felony can get you ten years in the slammer. This is your one *Stay Out Of Jail* pass. Leave Roxanne alone. If you contact her again—even to sell Girl Scout cookies—you will be busted. Do you understand?"

"I like that," Max said. "I thought you summed it up nicely."

Sam cast a defiant, sullen look. "Where's my money?"

I thought I hadn't heard him right. "*What?*"

Sam's lips sneered. He was pretty cocky for guy who had a Special Forces Operations leader in his face.

"I did some checking. The cops didn't find my money in Walter's house. They don't know anything about it. That tells me you two have my money. There's no way you're going to the cops. You're bluffing."

"Can't we just shoot him?" Max said.

"Maybe. Do you have an alibi for Friday?"

His eyes flashed anger. "You saying I offed my best friend?"

"Not saying. Just asking."

"I'll tell you this. If I'd been with Wally, he wouldn't be pushing up daisies today. His screwy wife would."

"Answer the question," Max said. "Where were you Friday?"

Sam scowled resentfully. "DePaul University. I'm in a computer program."

"Will the teacher remember you?"

"Yeah. We had an exam Friday. Ask her."

"We will."

"That money belongs to Wally and me. I won't let you keep it."

"You're a damn fool, Sam," I said. "You don't get a dime of Roxanne's money. And you're blowing your *Stay Out Of Jail* pass."

He glared defiantly. "Oh, I'm getting something out of this."

"OK. Have a donut."

I traipsed after Max to the Hummer. As I opened my door, I stole a look back at Sam Kane. The raw hatred on his face snatched my breath away.

Max cranked up the Hummer and whipped onto the road. "He put on a good act, but I think we got through to him."

Personally, I wasn't buying it.

Chapter Twenty

I felt restless later after Max dropped me off at home. I needed a break from murder. I needed less blood, more drama, and a paycheck. In short, I needed to stalk someone.

I put a fistful of cases on hold the day Cleo stole Walter's Corvette. I stuck my hand in a hat and pulled out a name.

Patty.

She contacted me last week saying her husband, Jim, had been acting strangely. She cited unexplained calls and large cash withdrawals from their savings. Most telling were the additional hours he spent "at work" that didn't add up on his paycheck.

Patty said she noticed changes in her husband as he approached his fiftieth birthday. She suspected a midlife crisis. The Pants On Fire Detective Agency handles many MLC's. Someone hears a time bomb and he/she is suddenly hell-bent to self-destruct. I wouldn't say MLC's are the Agency's bread and butter. But they're definitely the jam.

I didn't know a lot about Jim. I knew he worked in Bridgeport at a tool factory. And I knew his shift ended at five. I glanced at the kitchen clock. Four-twenty-four. I would have to hurry. I stuffed water bottles and a few slices of cold pizza in my surveillance cooler. I grabbed the rest of the applesauce donuts and my camera. I dropped Inga and Beau off at their Grandma's. I might be looking at a long night. Or I could be home for supper.

It was four-fifty-four when I blazed into the employee's parking lot. I knew Jim drove a white Ford F150 and I had the plate number. I found his truck parked in the far corner of the last row. Looked liked he had been last to arrive this morning. And he was first to burst through the door at five.

No overtime today.

I ducked behind a copy of this month's *Elle* as Jim hustled to the back of the lot. He cranked up the truck and I followed him onto the street. Jim pointed his nose south. I hummed to myself. His wife and home were due north.

I was careful to keep my distance. I lagged back, keeping a buffer of cars between us. Jim was on the lookout. He took a few silly detours, scanning the rearview mirror for a tail. I had to applaud the guy's effort. But he was an amateur. And no match for the stalking queen.

I followed Jim to the outer edges of Chicago's south suburbs. His destination was a windowless building with lots of neon and sleeze. He pulled into the lot and parked beneath a sign that flashed LIVE GIRLS. *Puh-leeze.*

Tick tock. Jim hears the time bomb ticking.

I sucked up my gut and resisted the urge to pull on rubber gloves. I grabbed my camera and followed him inside the cheesy strip club.

A few dozen customers were scattered through the smoke-infused bar. A beefy bartender doubled as a bouncer. Jim took a seat in front of the stage. I slid into a discreet booth near the back with a clear camera shot of his table.

Apart from the dancers and the server, I was the only woman in the bar. It was a hot summer day and I was dressed in a tangerine tank and white shorts. My legs felt bare in a really creepy way. If I'd known my destination, I'd have worn a NASA space suit.

Guys tried to buy me a drink and gave up after a while. Only one obnoxious drunk gave me trouble. I was going for my gun when the bartender dragged him away.

A server brought Jim a drink. He didn't order one but she knew what he wanted. Once when the bartender wasn't looking she gave him a quick kiss.

Snap. Kodak moment.

Jim was rather sweet with her. I've followed a lot of cheaters. I've learned to distinguish the "players" from those with an emotional bond. Jim may have been playing when he first went looking for "live girls". But for my money, he fell in love with the server.

My mark stepped outside when the server took her break. They went to his truck. I got the steamy window pictures. And her head disappearing from view. I got shots of them entering and leaving his truck. In the exit photo, Jim's fly is unzipped.

Snap!

I rushed home to blow up the 8x10 glossies. Then I dropped by Patty's. She said Jim was working late and she invited me inside. She made tea.

When she was ready, I laid the photos on the table for her. I watched her process the evidence.

Her eyes were dry. Her lips held tight. She didn't speak at first. When she did, her voice was calm.

"He's a dead man," she said.

As if on cue the dead man walked through the door. Jim felt the tension in the room first. He looked at me and swallowed hard. He'd seen me at the club.

"I can explain, sweetheart," he blubbered.

"Don't 'sweetheart' me," Patty said.

Jim's eyes fell to the pictures on the table. His lips paled. Patty walked calmly to the buffet and opened a drawer. I caught a glint of steel in her hand.

"No," I screamed.

Her husband didn't have time to cry out. She emptied the clip in his chest. She put the gun back in the drawer.

"Hurry," she said. "Help me drag him outside to the porch."

I was shaking. "You're out of your mind.'

She gave a satisfied nod. "I think I'd get off with temporary insanity. Unfortunately, he'll come around in a few minutes."

I looked down. There wasn't a drop of blood.

"Blanks," I said numbly. "He passed out cold."

Jim was only dreaming he was dead.

"I bought the gun to scare off an intruder. I've never wanted to kill anybody."

We dragged Jim's limp body out onto the porch. She threw his clothes, car keys, and collection of eight track tapes out with him. She smashed his golf clubs one by one against the cement porch. She dumped them on top of him.

Jim was beginning to stir. I thanked Patty for the tea. I stepped over Jim and all that was his and tromped to my car. I gave a satisfied grunt.

More drama, less blood, and a paycheck to come.

Oh yeah. This is what I was made for.

I ate a peach before bed. It was tucked inside one of Cleo's hot, buttery croissants. I was going to miss Cleo's cooking when she went home. Or to the slammer. Or to Cuba. I wondered if communists eat croissants. I was reasonably sure prisoners didn't.

I sat cross-legged on my bed, trying to piece together the puzzle of Walter's murder. I brought to mind everything I'd learned since Inga dropped that bloody sock at my feet. I squeezed my eyes shut and mentally tossed the pieces in the air. I didn't force them. I let them free fall and link together where they fit. Then I looked at all the scattered pictures. I got nothing.

A curious memory came to me. I was about thirteen. My favorite teacher, Sister Clara, found me crying after school. A girl stole my diary. She showed everyone. I was devastated. I swore I'd never go to school again.

Everyone knew my most intimate secrets. I was afraid of the dark. One of my boobs was bigger than the other. And worst of all, I really *really* wanted Joe Ridgeway to be my boyfriend.

I thought Sister Clara would share my outrage. She didn't. Instead, she gave me more homework to do. I was to memorize Jesus' teaching on forgiveness.

"Find it," Sister Clara said. "It's in Matthew."

I never forgot Sister Clara. And I never forgot my assignment. I forgot the name of the girl who stole my diary. I forgot Joe Ridgeway. My boobs eventually grew to the same size. I haven't learned forgiveness like Sister Clara yet. But I'm still working on it.

I pulled out the list Cleo made of people Walter conned. It was incomplete, but it was what we had to work with. Cleo had penciled in an estimate of how much each victim lost. Most numbers were relatively small. A few were staggering. Savino came up with the addresses.

After a while I heard Cleo talking to a voice I didn't recognize in the kitchen. I decided to check it out.

I trotted down the hall to the kitchen. Cleo was standing over a scrawny guy cowering in the corner. She had my frying pan in one hand. And his gun in her other. He smelled like cheap booze. His face had the crazed bug-eyed thing going. It could be drugs. Or the dazed look you'd expect if Cleo just hit your head with a cast iron pan.

I walked over to the refrigerator and pulled out a couple beers. I held one out to Cleo.

"Open it," she said. "My hands are a little busy here."

I cracked her beer and slid it on the counter. I plunked mine on the table and plopped on a chair.

"Gee, Sam," I said. "I can't believe you broke in my house. With a *gun?*"

"You know this piece of crap?" Cleo demanded.

Sam flinched. He wasn't nearly as cocky as he was a few hours ago in the Happy Trails Pet Cemetery hearse.

"Don't let her hit me with the frying pan again," he pleaded.

I took a swig of beer. "Max and I met Sam this afternoon. He and Walter go way back."

Cleo squinted her eyes. "If you know Walter, why weren't you at our wedding."

"I was in jail."

"Figures," she said affronted. "You could've sent a card."

"Like *I'm* rude? *I'm* not the one who killed him."

Cleo went perfectly still. Her voice, when she spoke, was chipped ice.

"What are you saying, Sam?"

"Forget it, Cleo," I said. "Sam's onto you. He knows too much. We can't trust him to keep his mouth shut."

"I don't know nothin'," Sam said nervously.

I held out my hand. "Gimme the gun. I'll take care of him right here."

"Whoa! Are you freakin' mental?"

Cleo gripped the gun tighter. "You can't shoot him here. I just mopped the floor. Have Rocco arrest him."

"Too much paperwork."

"There's not that much paper involved," Sam said eagerly. "I've been arrested before."

"Good tip," Cleo said. "But you're still not worth it. I say we call Uncle Joey. He'll dispose of the body."

"No bodies," Sam moaned.

"You think Joey will do it?"

"Are you kidding me. He has an industrial size meat grinder."

Sam was crying now. "No one was supposed to get hurt. I swear. I just wanted what was mine."

"Look around, Sam. The only thing you own here is the dirt on the floor."

Cleo's gaze riveted to Sam's shoes. "My clean floor!"

I thought she was going to clobber him again.

"I have another idea," I said. "I'll make a call."

Four minutes and twenty seconds later two ex-spies stormed the kitchen. They quickly assessed the situation. The handcuffed hearse driver was tied to a chair. Cleo stood over him, frying-pan and pistol-ready. Double-locked and loaded.

I was working on a bowl of chips and a second beer.

"Did he hurt you?" Max said quietly.

"Not even a little bit."

Max clutched Sam's hair in his fist and jerked his head back. There was an angry red welt on his forehead. His two blackened eyes jumped in fear.

Max sort of grinned. "Nice work, Cleo. You can lose the frying pan now."

He lifted Sam by the collar. The chair jerked off the floor.

"Listen up, brain surgeon. Cat doesn't have the money. I do. If you have a score to settle, you come looking for me. You got that?"

Sam swallowed hard.

"One more thing. If you come within a mile of these women again, I will rip you apart, limb by limb, with my bare hands. Is that understood?"

"Okay! I got it already," Sam choked looking sullen.

Max slammed the chair back to the floor again. Tino exchanged his handcuffs for mine and the ex-spies stepped outside. No one said a word. Max returned a few minutes later.

"Tino is making a call," he said.

Sam gulped. "What are you going to do to me?"

Max rummaged in the fridge and came out with a beer. "How do you like your goat?" he said.

Tino returned as Max was finishing his second peach croissant.

"We're in luck. The plane was delayed," Tino said. "They'll take a stowaway if we hurry."

Max jerked out a big syringe. It looked big enough to kill a horse.

"No!" Sam screamed.

He fought fiercely but Tino held him down.

I gasped. "You're not going to—"

"Say goodnight, Sam," Max said.

Sam didn't say anything. He was out cold.

"Oh my god," Cleo hugged herself. "You killed him."

"He'll wake up tomorrow," Tino said. "In Afghanistan."

Max hoisted Sam over his shoulder. "The guys he'll be traveling with are mercenaries. They're tougher than any guys Sam could meet in prison. Who knows? Maybe he'll get a backbone before he finds his way home."

I followed them outside to Tino's black Buick. Our neighborhood spy, Mrs. Pickens, pulled back her curtain.

"Throw him in here," Tino said. He opened the trunk.

Mrs. Pickens stiffened.

"Uhm, perhaps Sam could ride in the back seat," I said.

I opened the back door. Max chucked him inside.

"He'd better not throw up in my car," Tino growled.

I hugged them both. "Thanks for giving Sam another chance," I said.

The sausage maker grunted and lowered himself onto the driver's seat.

"Don't thank me," Tino said. "I wanted to shoot him."

Chapter Twenty-one

In the wee hours of the morning, Steve Greger weaseled into my dreams. I couldn't make out his face. But there were a lot of teeth behind the smirky grin and they were laughing at me.

I seized my camera and tore after him. A dark, blue Volvo closed fast behind me. The ghost of an old man hovered above me. His laugh was hollow and he reached for me with a hand of bones ....

I sat straight up, eyes wide open. My heart thundered in my chest.

I pushed out of bed and padded to the kitchen with Inga at my heels. I made a cup of cocoa and poured two bowls of Rice Chex. We sat together on the window seat and ate our cereal. When we crawled into bed again, Inga slept beneath my covers. And if I dreamed, I didn't remember.

I woke in the morning feeling stiff and bloated. I pinched my bum and decided it didn't feel bigger. I was thirty now. If I wasn't careful, Cleo's cooking would go straight to my ass. I briefly considered giving up sweets for a few days. Like that's gonna happen. So I dug my Nikes from the closet. I dressed in sweats and pony-tailed my hair.

Five days ago, my regular exercise routine went to hell with Walter. I gave Inga a shake. She opened an eye.

"Go wake up Beau and Cleo. We're going for a run."

After my nerve-racking run the other night, I knew the best thing for me to do was to get out there again. I wasn't going to let myself be intimidated by the blue Volvo guy. That didn't mean I couldn't use the extra company.

Inga bounced away and came back with her leash and Beau. Prying Cleo from the bed took a lot more effort. I stole her covers and threatened her with ice water and a fat, dumpy future.

The front porch was clear but we slipped out the back lest an over-achieving paparazzo was lurking. Beau and Inga were all smiles and wagged their tails. Cleo wore a carrot-colored wig, sunglasses and a big, grumpy frown on her face.

Less than two blocks out, Cleo lagged behind, winded, gasping for breath.

"Go ahead," she sucked air. "Beau and I will meet you at the school."

Inga and I zoomed ahead. We circled the school twice without a glimpse of the blue Volvo. There was also no sign of the wheezing red head and her little black dog.

"Your Aunt Cleo is a big fat liar." I thought Inga should know.

Inga wanted to circle the school again but I called her back. "The Pants On Fire Detective Agency will not be duped," I said. I was on a scent. And it smelled like chocolate.

We found them at a sidewalk table outside Isabella's Cafe. Who knew they serve ice cream for breakfast? Beau was on his second helping and he shared the bowl with Inga. Cleo held on to her double hot fudge sundae with a death grip.

"I'm putting a hex on you," I said. "That's going straight to your ass."

"You're too late. I got some voodoo curse already. I think my sister, the Ho, put it on me."

I eyed her sundae. "Double whipping cream. Are you going to share your breakfast or not?"

"Not. I've already lost everything else. Get your own breakfast."

"Pity party at table six," I said to a couple walking by.

Cleo sniffed. "Two months ago I had a home, security, money in the bank, and plans for my future."

"Yeah? Well two months ago I was in my twenties. This morning I'm measuring my butt. *My butt!* Talk about a crisis."

"Be serious. I'm facing a one way ticket to Cuba. Or twenty years fighting PMS-crazed felons for the cookies on my lunch tray."

I waffled a hand back and forth. "I gotta go with Cuba. They say Latinos are great lovers."

"Then why don't they say, *once you go Latino, you never go back?*"

"They do. It only rhymes in Spanish."

Cleo blew a sigh. "Face it, Cat, I'm screwed. Walter screwed me. The cops are screwin' me. Only nobody kissed me first."

"There was that salesman from Toledo."

Cleo smiled. "Mmm, his mustache tickled."

"And so will Big Bertha's." I snatched a huge spoonful of hot fudge gooeyness. When the server came by, I ordered a fu fu coffee, two jelly donuts, and a fat Italian sausage for the dogs to share.

My back pocket started to vibrate as "Fever" blared out.

"Hey, Savino."

"Hey, babe. I'm a ghost." That was standard code for "off the record."

"Got it." *Damn, that man had a sexy voice.*

"I have a name to match 'O Baby Man'," he said, referring to the man's mantra on Walter's blackmail sex tape. "His name is Gregory Hart and he lives in Hyde Park." Savino gave me the address and continued on. "Interesting thing about the guy. About a year ago he moved from the Gold Coast where he'd been a resident for over eight years. I know Hyde Park isn't exactly slumming it, but still it's a step down."

"Hmmm," I said. "Perhaps Walter's blackmail was making a serious hit on the guy's net worth."

"My thoughts exactly. I want you to bring someone with you. This guy has got to be aggravated and enraged. That's a dangerous cocktail, babe."

"Hmmmm," I said, trying to sound agreeable.

"Words, Cat. Promise me you'll bring somebody."

"Promise," I sulked. *Men are SO bossy.*

I flipped the phone shut and turned to Cleo. "Inga and I have a few errands to run. We'll be back in a few hours."

Cleo waved us off. Her face was buried in the sundae dish, licking the end of the hot fudge.

Inga and I looked at each other.

"C'mon, partner," I said. "You're somebody."

Inga and I ran home, got the car, and headed for Hyde Park.

The address Chance gave me led to a stunning Victorian with a wraparound porch that was probably considered a mansion back in the day. Today it was just a gorgeous, expensive home set in a gorgeous, expensive neighborhood in Hyde Park. *Some slumming.*

Inga and I trotted to the door. I rang the bell and Gregory Hart answered it. I recognized him right away, even with his clothes on. There's a trick to looking a man in the eye that you've never seen before except in a sex video. I wish I knew what it was.

"Mr. Hart?" I began. "My name is Cat DeLuca and I'm a private investigator. My partner and I are here to tell you that Walter Jones is dead."

He looked down at the beagle and back at me.

"Cockroaches don't live forever, Ms. DeLuca. But I already knew about Walter. It's all anybody sees on the news these days."

I nodded and kept my eyes firmly planted on a spot somewhere between "O Baby Man's" eyebrows. I focused hard and tried to squelch the vision of him naked.

"Yes, Mr. Hart. But what the news doesn't know yet, or the local police, for that matter, is that Walter Jones was blackmailing you. There is a video kept safely under lock and key. The real reason I'm here is to ask you some questions

Silence. It was one of those *I knew that he knew that I'd seen the icky video* moments. *Eeesh.*

This time I looked directly into his eyes. There was no rage or fear or embarrassment. No calculation even. Just resignation.

"Would you like to come in, Ms. DeLuca?"

"I'm good."

Hart shook his head and shoulders as if he was dusting himself off.

"You're wrong about something."

I lifted my chin and my eyes narrowed suspiciously. "What's that?"

"Ms. DeLuca, you're right that Walter Jones *tried* to blackmail me. And you're right that he had all the evidence to do so. But you're wrong that he was *successfully* blackmailing me." Hart drew in a big breath and let it out again. "Actually, Walter Jones' *attempt* at blackmail is the best thing that ever happened to me."

Hart left his station holding the screen door open and walked out onto the porch. He moved to the edge of the stoop, looking off into the distance.

"I was an unhappy man in a miserable marriage. I might not have done anything about it if it wasn't for Walter Jones. You see, I'd told myself it was better to stay in a bad marriage, loving another woman, than to let my wife get half my money.

"Two years ago, Jones came to me with a copy of the video. At first I was horrified, of course." He winced. "I'm sorry you had to see that by the way."

Awkward.

"I didn't really watch very much of it," I lied.

He exhaled, relieved. "So you didn't see the—"

"God no," I said quickly.

I knew what part he was worried about. I shuddered. Sex is *so* not a spectator sport.

I focused between the brows.

"When Walter showed me what he had, I knew there was no end to what he could do. How much can you fight for a life that you hate? How much can you fight for a life that's not yours?"

"You took a big hit in the divorce. You lost your house on the Gold Coast."

Hart called over his shoulder, "Cathy, would you come out here?"

The woman from the video had been listening. She stepped out from behind the door and walked onto the porch. She was the same but different. She had clothes on for one thing. She was also six months pregnant.

"We're far from destitute, Ms. DeLuca," Cathy said. She had clear, blue eyes and she held her head high. "It's true Greg lost some things. But he's happy now. And he has a woman who loves him."

"In spite of my failures." Greg gave a self deprecating laugh. "I gained self-respect in the process and now, I have a family in the making. I hope to be a better man; a man they will be proud of."

The look in his eyes gave me no doubt that he was telling the truth. I had only one more question to ask him.

"Where were you last Friday afternoon when Walter was killed, Mr. Hart?"

"I was at work, I suppose. Ask my secretary."

Cathy wrinkled her nose thoughtfully. "Friday? No, we were at the doctor's office. We were looking at live images of our son through an ultrasound screen."

Greg got a goofy grin on his face. "He was sucking his thumb. I couldn't believe it."

"A boy?" I smiled. "Congratulations."

Wow. I didn't see this coming. I came to the video guy's house expecting sleaze, and I got a real-life love story. Greg and Cathy were crazy-happy together. I hoped they would make it.

Life is funny. On another day it would have me, not Walter, taking pictures of the cheating Mr. Hart. Hart's ex-wife would have been my client, wondering perhaps, why Gregory was working so late every night. She had a new life now. I hoped she found happiness too.

"I wish you both well," I said. "If your alibi checks out, I'll destroy the video and you won't hear from me again."

It wouldn't be hard to check the court records and the OBGYN's appointment calendar. I am nothing if not thorough.

I tugged my partner's leash and walked away, confident we could soon scratch Gregory Hart off the suspect list.

◇◇◇

Cleo and I sat at my desk, hunched over the spilled contents of RB's blackmail envelope. A few newspaper clippings and photographs had scared serious cash out of the designer. I had no idea why.

There was a knock at the side door that opened to my office. I wasn't expecting anyone. I looked through the peep hole at a tall angular woman with short straight hair. Her face was scrunched. She was reading my sign.

Cleo pushed me aside and pressed her face to the door.

"She needs our help," she said grimly. "Her man is chasing skirts."

"You know this how?"

"Red and swollen eyes."

"I don't see that."

I swung the door open and the woman jumped.

"Hi," I said.

"I must have the wrong address. I'm looking for Cat DeLuca."

"You got her."

She examined the sign again. "Pants On Fire Detective Agency? You're not serious."

"Serious as your man breakin' your heart," Cleo said.

I shot Cleo a look that was just short of stuffing a sock in her mouth and showed the woman in.

"How can I help you?" I said.

"I received a call this morning from—"

Cleo butted in. "Cut to the chase, lady. You've got a dirty rotten cheater."

The woman threw Cleo a look most people reserve for the insane. It was, I thought, a fair assessment.

"I'm here about a murder," she said.

Cleo's trigger finger quivered. "You want us to off the slime-ball? It'll cost extra."

I pushed her aside. "Forget everything she said. We don't shoot people."

Recognition flickered in the woman's eyes. "It's the crazy video lady."

"Yes it is," I said. "How can I help you?"

"I'm former Deputy Nicole Rallen. I investigated the Bjornsen case."

I was astonished. "Hal Bjornsen was your case?"

"It was my first case. It didn't end well."

"You said former deputy?"

"Four years ago I turned in my badge and went private. I started up a security business. The hours are better. The pay is better. And I sleep better at night."

I eyed her black suit, very Dana Buchman.

"The clothes are definitely better."

She laughed. "Definitely. An FBI agent called this morning. Chance Savino. He said he knows you."

"In the Biblical sense," Cleo chortled.

"He mentioned you're investigating the Hal Bjornsen case,"

"Yes, I'm looking into it."

She opened her bag and pulled out a thick file.

"I want you to have this."

I looked at the file. The name *Hal Bjornsen* was written in bold black marker.

"That's a lot of pulp for an accidental death. What are you hoping I'll find?"

"I want you to find the son of a bitch who killed Hal."

Cleo's eyes got glassy. She leaned in. "Ooh, this is getting good."

Nicole shifted uncomfortably. "Is there somewhere we can talk?"

"I know just the place," I said. "We'll have lunch."

"Lunch!" Cleo scrambled for the door.

I pulled her back. "We'll bring you a hamburger."

Cleo pouted. I gave her a look.

"All right," she relented. "Make it a cheeseburger."

"Gotcha."

"I'll be at the shooting range. Working out." Cleo put a finger to her lips and blew. "So many cheaters. So little time."

"Oh my god!" Nicole said and followed me to the car. "You gave that woman *a gun?*"

I sighed. I didn't know where Cleo's small arsenal came from. She changes weapons like they are a fashion accessory.

"I really need to pump up my insurance."

Chapter Twenty-two

I brought Nicole to Mickey's, hoping to see Rocco. I didn't. But my Uncle Rudy sat at the bar flanked by my cop pals from Walter's crime scene, Leo and Tommy. I introduced them to Nicole and the guys played musical stools making room for her. They caught her scent when she walked in. She was one of them. Cops bond like denture adhesive.

We had a beer with the boys before finding our own table. Leo and Uncle Rudy immediately glommed on to Nicole and talked cop-shop. I took the stool next to Tommy.

"Hey, Tommy, how are the guys in the precinct treating you?"

Tommy gave a wry grin. "They're calling me Dummy. As in *crash* dummy, the ones they use for crashing cars. Because I caught the exploding car. 'Fraid *that* name's gonna stick."

I grimaced. "Sorry about that."

"It's OK, I'll be happy when I'm not the rookie anymore, though. They'll point their sites on the next newbie, ya' know?"

I gave what I hoped was an encouraging grunt. But I knew better. Once cops peg you with a name, the reputation and the story follow you everywhere. From here on out, even if Tommy moved to the Yukon and became a Canadian Mountie with the hat and jodhpurs, chances are he'd be known as Dummy.

I got up and pried Nicole from Leo and Uncle Rudy. I gave the two of them my best evil eye for picking on Tommy.

"What's up with that look, you got something stuck in your eye?"

I glared harder.

"She's probably got the PMS going on, Rudy." Leo paused. "See that deranged look she's got there—yeah, that's the PMS for sure."

"Hah. Hah!" I turned on my heel, and stomped off to our table. I *really* needed to work on my mean look.

The waitress appeared and we ordered grilled chicken salads with a shameless pile of Bridgeport's best onion rings. Nicole plopped the fat Hal Bjornsen file on the table.

"Isn't it unusual for cops to keep their files after they leave the department?" I asked.

"This is the only file I copied. Not that anyone would notice if I took the original. Once the coroner ruled an accidental death, the case was closed."

"You had issues with the coroner's conclusions."

"Big time."

She thumbed through the file and pulled out a photograph of an eight carat aquamarine gemstone with a classic emerald cut and gold band.

"The ring is a family heirloom. His grandmother gave it to Hal at his communion. He never took it off his finger. When he suffered paranoid episodes, he'd hold his other hand over his ring finger and rock back and forth."

"I'm guessing when his body was found, the ring was missing."

"No ring, no wallet."

"How did the sheriff justify an accidental death verdict?"

"The sheriff said Hal was unstable. He was bipolar/schizophrenic and in the sheriff's words, 'a spoiled rich brat'. He could have lost or given away these things."

"It's a stretch. But I suppose it's possible."

Her face soured. "It was an election year. The department was under a lot of pressure to end the case well. There was bad press surrounding Hal's death. The family was angry the sheriff hadn't done more to find their son. If the death was ruled a homicide, there would certainly be an investigation into the department's mishandling of the case. The Bjornsens had money and power and regular suppers with the governor."

"Were the family's accusations justified?"

"I dunno, Cat. When the parents reported their son missing, the sheriff didn't round up the posse. But Hal had disappeared before. He would stop taking his meds and behave erratically. He'd take off and eventually make his way home. The department chased after him a few times. After that, they just waited for him to come back."

"Only this time he didn't."

Nicole nodded grimly. "Hal was last seen having breakfast at a café on Highway 113. The waitress remembered he ordered ham, eggs, and pancakes with"—she tapped her chin and brought up the memory—"with strawberry syrup, as I recall. When he had finished eating, he asked the waitress for a phone. He said he wanted to call someone for a ride home."

"I'm guessing he didn't make the call."

"The waitress directed him outside to the payphone. The next time she looked out the window, he was climbing into a VW bus with a group of kids. A few days later she saw his picture in the paper and called the sheriff."

"Did the waitress say anything about seeing a raft tied to the van?

Nicole went bug-eyed. "How did you know?"

"I'll get back to you on that."

"You do that." She stared at her coffee. "Three years passed before some hunters discovered Hal's body near Baraboo, Wisconsin. Three very long, hard winters. There wasn't much forensic evidence to go on. Hal's neck was broken. The coroner said the fall could've snapped it."

"Or someone snapped it for him."

"When I left the department, I promised myself I would go to Florida one day and tell the parents the truth about their son's death. They live in Orlando now."

"I love Orlando. Disney World is there."

"Do this and we'll go together. The Bjornsen's have offered a large reward to know what really happened to their son. Something the department wouldn't give them."

"The high cost of closure."

Nicole raised her frosted glass. "We can buy Goofy with that kind of money, or at least one of the dwarfs."

I touched my glass to hers. They went *cha-ching*.

"I've always had a thing for Dopey's big ears," I said.

Uncle Joey was at my kitchen table when I breezed in with Cleo's double deluxe burger, fries, and Oreo shake. Cleo was feeding him Asian style pork chops with rice and coleslaw.

"I know people," Uncle Joey told Cleo. "Say the word and I'll open a restaurant for you."

Uncle Joey has friends in low places. He drives a Ferrari and lives a whole lot richer than a cop's salary. Joey is good to his family and generous with his money. He helped me get my house. I never ask questions.

"I like being a hotshot detective," Cleo said. "I like to shoot people."

"She's kidding." *I hope.* "What did your friend from the 23rd learn about Walter's dad?"

"He called me last night. I've got dates and details in my notebook for you. I'll make this easy for now."

He stabbed another pork chop and slapped it on his plate before continuing. "Cleo remembered her husband receiving some disturbing calls from a prisoner in Joliet. Turns out the caller's name was Jess Einman. He and Walter were childhood friends. Their dads used to hang out together."

Cleo shook her dark, pink-tipped curls. "I doubt Walter remembered Jess. He never talked about him."

"Walter remembered Jess alright. The night Walter's dad killed Jess' father, the boys were there."

A shudder ran through Cleo. "Why didn't he tell me?"

"It happened at Walter's house. He was ten. Jess was a few years younger. The men had been drinking and argued. The charge was reduced to manslaughter, partly because of Walter's testimony. Walter said the killing was self-defense. Jess believes Walter lied to help his dad."

"So that's when Walter went into foster care," Cleo said. "What about his mother?"

"Walter's dad was hot tempered, always in a scrap. A year earlier, he claimed his wife left him. She was never heard from again. My guess is he killed her and buried her in the backyard."

"In his letters, Walter's dad promised to come for him. He didn't."

"He didn't make it out. He died in a prison yard fight."

"That explains a lot," I said.

"There's more. Jess Einman was paroled two weeks ago. He did a nickel in Joliet for a string of liquor store burglaries. I met his cell mate this afternoon. Typical prick at first. After I put some serious cash on his books, he sang like a bird."

"Money sings," Cleo nodded wisely.

"According to the cellmate, Jess claimed his father was killed in cold blood. He was obsessed about evening the score. Einman said he'd kill Walter as soon as he was released."

"And now Walter's dead," Cleo said bleakly. "He wasn't even killed for any of the horrible things he did. He paid for something his dad did when he was a snot-nosed kid"

"The sins of the father," Uncle Joey said.

"I dunno," I said. "I'm having trouble with the cash on the dresser."

Uncle Joey shrugged. "Maybe he took most of the cash with him and left a wad on the dresser. It's a smart move. No jury would believe a man just released from prison wouldn't take the money."

"Maybe."

"I have the P.O.'s name if you want to talk to him."

Joey dragged some pages from a notebook and slapped them on the table.

"Thanks. Can we talk about RB now?"

"You got nothin' on RB. You need more than a few pictures and a bag of her money to get her talking."

"*My* money," Cleo said.

"We have to figure out why RB was willing to pay for Walter's silence," I said.

"She paid to stay out of prison," Cleo quipped. Prison was on Cleo's mind.

"Maybe," I said. "Or she might pay to avoid embarrassment about something she did in college."

Uncle Joey grinned. "There are skeletons in every college closet."

I raised a brow.

"Hey. I dated smart women before I met Linda."

Cleo waved a hand. "I could care less about embarrassing."

"Hence the video," I said.

"But I'd give away my big beautiful bag of cold hard cash to stay out of the slammer," she said.

"It belongs to RB." I reminded her.

"Ha. I found it, so technically its mine."

Uncle Joey looked at me and shook his head. "Don't go doin' that, missy."

I smiled. "What?.

"I know what you're thinking. Knock it off."

Cleo's eyes widened. "What's she thinking?"

"Cat's going all goody-goody on us. She wants to return the money."

This from my Uncle Joey who wears thousand dollar suits.

"*NO FREAKING WAY!*" Cleo squawked.

Uncle Joey shook his head sorrowfully. "It's a flaw in Caterina's character. Proof she's not my daughter."

Chapter Twenty-three

Jess Einman and Walter Jones were kids when Jim Jones murdered Jess' dad. Years later, in a twisted quest for justice, Jess wanted Walter to die. As wishes come true, Walter was very dead.

I wondered if the reality of Walter's death was as sweet as Jess imagined it. He would have played Walter's death out in his mind, killing him a thousand times in that cell. The question was, did Jess Einman pull the trigger? Or did someone beat him to it.

I called his parole officer. I said Einman attended our prison outreach services. When I explained a church member had a job opening in his hardware store, the parole officer nearly fell over himself spilling Jess' address and room number.

Jess was holed up in a scummy part of Chicago where even the cockroaches carry bug spray. Cleo and I hunkered down in the Silver Bullet outside his cheesy hotel. Cleo wore big fake eyelashes and a long, straight, platinum wig. I had big eighties-hair: poofed up and out and lacquered hard as a helmet. We wore our shortest skirts and hiked them up three more inches. It wasn't pretty. But we looked convincingly slutty.

I popped a piece of bubble gum in my mouth and drove around to the alley behind the hotel. I parked alongside the fire escapes and checked my watch. In this neighborhood I figured we'd have ten minutes, fifteen tops before the Silver Bullet lost all its tires or completely disappeared.

The alley was creepy and smelled like urine. We wobbled around to the front entrance in our heels. The street didn't smell much better. A late model Chevy with two fat, middle-aged men pulled over beside us. The passenger hung out the window.

"What does it cost to have you two pro's for a date?"

Cleo slung her bag and nailed him across the head. "What kind of girls do you think we are?"

"Ooh, this one is feisty. I'll pay extra for that piece of tail."

"You twisted perv!" She smacked him again.

The driver laughed. The passenger held his head and rocked. "Damn girl....You got a brick in that purse?"

Cleo swore and opened her bag.

"Cleo! No!" I shouted.

"Gun!" The driver screamed.

They burned rubber and we watched the tail lights until we lost them in the traffic.

Cleo brought the barrel to her lips and blew.

"Can you believe those guys?" Cleo said.

I cast an eye at her skanky attire. If the sun saw any more cleavage, her nipples would burn.

"What?" she said.

I snatched my Dr. Pepper Lip Smacker out and coated my lips. "You might want to lose the gun before someone calls the cops."

I grabbed her arm and dragged her into the sleazy hotel-no-tell. A greasy guy, wearing a filthy wife beater and polyester pants, sat behind a desk caged by bullet-proof glass. He looked fifty-something, but he could've been ten years younger. Too much time in this dark, depressing lobby would suck the life juices out of you. I hadn't been there five minutes and I wanted to go home and shower.

He didn't tear his eyes from the small black and white TV screen on the counter.

"Hour or day rate?"

I popped a bubble. "We don't need a room. We're visiting a friend."

He pointed to a sign on the wall behind him. "No visitors allowed," he said in case we couldn't read.

I palmed a fifty and slid it across the counter.

He pocketed the money and smiled. He was missing some teeth.

"You're registered." he said. His eyes returned to the screen.

We made a move for the elevator and he called us back. "*You* registered. She didn't."

"*What?*" Cleo squawked.

My hand slapped over her bag before she could brandish her weapon. "Okay. But you never saw us, understand?" I gave up another Grant, grabbed my assistant, and dragged her into the elevator. The door closed on his silly, toothless grin.

We got out on the third floor and teetered down the hall to Room 311.

I nodded and Cleo pounded the door with her fist.

"Barney!" I called. "Open the door. I know you're in there."

Footsteps and a hazel eye filled the peep hole. "Go away. There's no Barney here."

"You broke my heart, Barney," I wailed. "Why do you do me like that?"

"Beat it, lady. You got the wrong room."

I yelled louder. "I'm takin' you back, Barney. I need money for diapers."

He opened the door a crack. Jess wasn't a big guy. Cleo buffaloed past him and I followed her inside.

The one room studio held a small table, chair, and narrow bed. In one corner, a small icebox, sink, and hotplate formed a makeshift kitchen. I kicked the door closed behind me.

"Can we come in?"

"No. I'm not Barney. Get out."

"What's your name?"

"Jess."

Cleo looked at me. "Is that Barney?"

I squinted my eyes. "It was dark. I can't be sure."

"I would remember you," he said. "And I don't. Leave. Now."

A stray slip of paper was on the table. I sidled over that way.

"Can I have a glass of water?" Cleo said.

"You want to drink out of these pipes?"

"I'll take bottled water if you have it."

"I don't."

An address was scribbled on the paper. An address I knew too well. It was Walter's.

"Hey, what are you doing over there?"

"I parked in back. I'm checking my car to—Hey punks!" I hung out the open window, and waved my fist. "Get away from my car!"

Four kids surrounded the Silver Bullet. One had a bat. He was going for the kill.

"Stop!—Don't break my—"

Crash, then the sound of tinkling glass.

In a hot second Cleo pushed me aside. A glint of metal caught my eye.

"Cleo, no!" I shouted.

She fired into the alley. The pack leader defiantly nailed my fender with the bat before chasing after his friends.

"My car," I said numbly. And then the gravity of the situation sank in. I'd have to call my mechanic.

Something cold and hard pushed into my back. I turned and stared into the barrel of a Jennings. It was a small caliber. Not the gun used on Walter.

"This just keeps getting better and better," I said.

Jess waved his gun at Cleo. "You with the humongous boobs. Drop the gun on the floor."

"Hey! I've got boobs, too." I said.

In his other hand he dangled a pair of handcuffs.

"Too kinky for my taste, bucko." Cleo said.

"I was wearing these babies once when I escaped from a cop. I figured handcuffs would come in handy someday."

Cleo sniffed. "If you wanted us to leave, why didn't you say so."

"You're not going anywhere until you tell me who you are and why you're here."

"This is ridiculous," I said. "I won't be held against my will."

I made a motion to sweep past him and he jerked his arm out to shove me back. I snagged his arm, twisted my body around, jerked my knee in his groin. When he came up for air he was wearing the handcuffs.

"Bravo," Cleo clapped.

"Every girl should have brothers."

Cleo picked up her gun, dropped it in her purse, and smacked Einman over the head. He crumbled to the floor, out for the count.

"Candy ass. That's for killing Walter."

She stomped on his hand with her high heel.

"And that's for running over the old man, you big bully."

"Let's get him in the car before you remember something else," I said. "You think we can carry him down the fire escape?"

"No problem," Cleo said. "If we can't carry him, we'll drop him over the side."

Tino peered through the smashed window of the Silver Bullet at the guy passed out in the back.

"He looks bad. What happened to him?"

"He killed Walter," Cleo said. "I hit him over the head with my bag."

"Is he breathing?"

"I think so. He stirred a few times on the way over. So I zapped him good with my taser."

"Walter's dad shot his father when they were kids," I said. "For some reason Jess blamed Walter and wanted to settle the score. I found Walter's address on a slip of paper in his room. It's in his pocket with his gun."

"Without the bullets," Cleo said, patting her pocket.

Jess groaned softly and Cleo zapped him again.

"She enjoys that just a little too much," Tino said. "Drive around back and we'll dump this guy behind the store. He was mugged."

"I could fry him a few more times," Cleo offered.

"He's good," I said.

"Call Rocco," Tino said. "Tell him and Jackson to come right away. They should say they stopped by for lunch, found this guy in the alley. I'll make sure he has something on him to justify holding him and searching his apartment."

I made a face. "He won't come. Captain Bob ordered Rocco to stay away from my investigation."

"Rocco's your brother. He'll come."

A horn tooted and Father Timothy pedaled by on his bicycle. He waved. Then he rubbernecked. There I was dressed like a hooker and skanky as hell. The bike zigzagged and Father Timothy nearly lost control. He looked up at the sky, made the sign of the cross, and kept pedaling.

I cringed.

Tino gave a low, husky laugh. "You may want to put some clothes on before your mama sees you. That skirt will stop her heart for sure."

Chapter Twenty-four

I began stripping layers of sluthood the moment I walked through my door. I couldn't ditch the fishnet stockings fast enough. I tucked the nine mm in my underwear drawer and tossed everything else in a pile on the bed.

"Burn these when I'm in the shower," I told Inga.

The beagle's ears perked and she howled. My heart skipped. The front door closed. In an instant the nine mm trembled in my hand. A Victoria Secrets bra swung from the barrel.

"Caterina," my Uncle Joey called. "Are you home?"

Inga wagged her tail. "Does everybody have a key to my house?" I muttered.

I buried the gun and Victoria was safe once again. I tugged on mint green Liz Claiborne sweats and trotted behind Inga to the living room.

Uncle Joey wasn't alone. Cleo was there. And a fat balding man with eagle eyes and a slippery palm. He pumped my arm.

I didn't need an introduction. He was such a lawyer.

"Tony Beano," I smiled. "It's a pleasure to meet you."

"Your Uncle Joey tells me my job just got a whole lot easier, and you're the one to thank. The man who killed Walter Jones is behind bars."

I checked my watch. Einman should be booked and regaining consciousness any time now.

"It was a team effort," I said.

Tony Beano may have been talking to me, but his eyes were on the team cheerleader. Or I should say, on her pom poms. Cleo was in no hurry to lose the short, tight, slutty look. The girls were locked, loaded, and ready to burst from their cannons. Tony Beano was posed for fireworks.

I retrieved my hand and dragged Dr. Pepper Lip Smacker from a pocket.

"It's too early to know if we're out of the woods quite yet," Uncle Joey said. "The paparazzi will be around a few more days. I suggest we use them to our advantage."

"They're probably camped at Mama's, eating my cannoli," I said pettily.

"We have damage control to consider," Beano said. "We want to change Cleo's image, generate public sympathy. We want to make Cleo the victim here and open the world's-most-notorious-woman slot for some other sucker."

I replayed the video in my head. "Good luck with that."

Cleo ignored me. "What do you have in mind?"

Tony Beano grinned at the girls. "The paparazzi are looking for you and shooting film. Let them follow you to a food kitchen. Film you serving up a meal to the homeless."

Uncle Joey waffled a hand. "People annoy Cleo. A kitchen is a little too close to knives and frying pans."

"Fine." Bobby was undaunted. "Hospital visitation. Children's ward. She passes out teddy bears."

Cleo made a face. "Do their noses run? Because I'm not that crazy about kids and bodily fluids."

"You are that crazy," I said.

"Not to worry." Tony Beano scribbled something in his notebook. "Tomorrow afternoon, two to five. Cleo does Mother Teresa."

"*Cleo?*" Uncle Joey said.

"What do you want me to do?" Cleo squawked.

Beano smiled and spoke to the pom poms. "Stay home and close the curtains. I'm getting a stunt double."

◇◇◇

I stood under a long, steamy shower until every last drop of hot water was squeezed from the tank. It took three shampoos to wash the lacquer from my hair and lotsa bubbles on a loofa to scour Hotel Cockroach off my skin. But all the bubbles in Bridgeport couldn't scrub away the feeling that this wretched business with Walter's murder wasn't over yet.

I gave myself a shake and considered my damp reflection in the bathroom mirror. This was no time to be down. Cleo and I should be celebrating. Walter's murderer was in the slammer. Her fifteen minutes of fame on late night television would be forgotten. The paparazzi would go away. Mama would once again lavish me with pasta and guilt.

And Cleo would go home.

Those last words sang in my head.

Cleo was going home. Yippeeeeee!

A big ol' goofy grin spread across my face.

Time to crack the champagne.

I'd been saving an amazing bottle for such an occasion.

I dried my hair and skipped to the kitchen in my flannel pajamas, my skin was soft and pink like the fuzzy bunny slippers on my feet. Cleo and I would pop a big bowl of buttery popcorn. We'd stick in a DVD and watch a sexy comedy. And if we wanted a couple guys, we'd bring out Ben & Jerry.

It would be just Cleo and me. And Inga. And Beau.

And Frankie?

I did a double-take. Sitting at my kitchen table was my screwy cousin Frankie.

And sitting on his lap, sure as *crazy attracts crazy*, was my screwy assistant, Cleo.

"If I'm dreaming, don't wake me," Frankie said.

I pinched myself. No such luck.

I walked over to the refrigerator and stuck my head in the door. No champagne. A cork popped behind me and Cleo giggled. I spun around. Frankie was filling two crystal glasses with my amazing champagne.

Cleo giggled. "Gee, Cat, we're double dating the FBI."

"Gee, Cleo. You're an idiot."

I pulled a bottle of Chianti from the cupboard, opened it, and splashed some in a glass.

Cleo sighed and hunkered down on Frankie's lap.

Frankie rubbed his face in her hair. "We're the real thing, babe. Like Bogie and Bacall."

"Like Brad and Angelina," she giggled.

"Like John and Lorena Bobbitt," I said.

Frankie hooted. "Cat's jealous. Everyone knows she can't keep a man."

"Arrrggh!"

There are those rare, unexpected moments in life when the veil that guards the futures is lifted and we see our fates with unabashed clarity. This, for me, was such a moment. I watched Frankie and Cleo at my kitchen table and knew I was witnessing a train wreck.

My cell phone exploded in "Fever."

"Who can't keep a boyfriend?" I grinned.

"Babe, I was held up at the office," Savino said. "I'll be there in twenty minutes."

I racked my brain.

"Order a few appetizers."

Indian dinner! Holy crap.

I ran to my bedroom, peeling clothes on my way. Frankie's howl chased me down the hallway. "Keep a man? Cat can't keep a date."

"Ettie recommended the chicken vindaloo," Chance said

I yanked on a coral silk cami with a Calvin Klein printed skirt and stepped into a pair of wedge sandals. "Ettie can kiss my —"

"What? You faded out there, DeLucky."

Click.

The restaurant is a good ten minutes away. I grabbed a bottle of wine for our dinner and did my make-up in the car. I made it there in twelve.

Chicago Liquor Licenses are expensive and can be difficult to obtain. Bridgeport's new restaurant was BYOB. The server seated me by the window. Wine glasses were on the table. And the bulge in his pocket was the corkscrew.

My bottle of wine was breathing nicely when Chance stepped through the door. Tall and lean and utterly delicious. Like eye candy.

The cobalt blues danced and he moved toward me. My heart did flip flops.

"Wow," he said and kissed me.

He wasn't thinking about ordering take-out and having a romantic dinner in his condo.

"Wow backatcha."

I was.

"As promised." Chance passed over two manila folders. One was marked "Hal Bjornsen" in bold black marker. The other, "Courtney Kelly."

"These are the files you requested. They've gathered some dust in the last twenty years."

"Thanks, Savino."

"I know Nicole gave you her file on Hal. But you might find something new in here."

I peeked inside and my stomach lurched. Forensic pictures. I closed the cover quickly and set the folders aside.

"The two deaths were investigated independently by different law enforcement agencies," Chance said. "We don't know the exact date of Hal's death. But it's almost certain he died a few short months before Courtney was killed, less than three hours away. They were approximately the same age and their necks were both broken."

"There's almost too much coincidence there. Walter used both obituaries to blackmail Roxanne. There's a connection."

Our waiter poured the wine and we ordered shrimp masala, vegetable korma, chicken vindaloo, lemon rice and naan bread.

Savino touched his glass to mine. "How's the Agency holding up with Walter's murder? Cheaters are doing the nasty as we speak."

"I wrapped up one case last night. My other clients will wait a few days. They've seen the video. Some think Cleo is a folk hero. One woman wants a "Wally" done on her husband."

Chance's eyebrows shot up. "A Wally?"

"Like Cleo snuffing Walter."

"Tough customer. How's the Love Boat captain?"

I groaned. "Steve Greger is making me crazy. It's like a sickness. I can't help myself. I've chased him all over town and every time I think I've got him, he dodges my shot."

"He's an asshole. Don't let him get to you."

I shook my head miserably. "It's his freakishly toothy grin."

"If he's not man enough to keep it at home, he should ask for a divorce." He slugged down the last of his wine. "Maybe it's about the kids."

"It's about the money. Hers. Brenda's great-grandfather invented Saltines. The pre-nup was fierce. Steve can divorce her but he won't sail away in the Love Boat."

"Figures."

I filled our glasses. "How are your parents?"

"Fine."

"That's it? Give me a crumb here. I didn't even know you had parents until they showed up here."

"Everyone has parents, Cat."

"So where are they?"

"When I dropped them off at the airport, they were headed to a conference in Copenhagen. Greenpeace. Dad's delivering a speech."

"Are you kidding me? Does he know Al Gore?"

"They've met. Actually my folks were at Georgetown with Bill Clinton. They were hippies back then."

"Bill Clinton was a hippie?"

Chance laughed. "Not Bill, my parents. They wanted to name me Rainbow. "

"Rainbow?" I didn't try to swallow my laugh. I would have choked. "Let me get this straight. When my folks were doing hotdogs at Comiskey Park…" I had to catch my breath. "Yours

were smoking pot and singing "Give Peace a Chance." Maybe that's how you got your name."

He made a face. "At least they didn't name me Rainbow. Or Lennon."

My eyes drifted to the street. A traffic light on the corner turned red. Cars lined up outside our window in a long line of glimmering red lights. A driver turned his head my way. Our eyes locked. I stiffened. A broad, toothy grin spread across his face. He said something to the blonde hootchie beside him. She waved.

"Argggh!"

Chance splashed more wine in our glasses. He didn't bother to look outside.

"It's the Love Boat guy, isn't it."

I snarled through gritted teeth.

"He's laughing at you, isn't he?"

"Ar-rar-raggh!"

I wanted to extract the smirk from his face tooth by tooth. My camera was in the car. But I could capture his picture on my cell phone.

I reached for my purse but Chance was faster. He covered it with his hand.

"Let go," I gasped. "Greger's getting away."

The light turned green. Toothy Boy jetted off howling. I watched until his tail lights merged with all the others.

I dragged accusing eyes to Savino. "You let them get away. You made me lose my picture."

"Really?"

Savino was right. There had been no picture to take. Two people in a car can be easily explained away. Once again Steve Greger had made me crazy. And I'd acted like a fool.

I slugged down my wine and stared into my empty glass. "I'm an idiot."

Savino laughed. "You really can't help yourself, can you, DeLucky."

"No. I can't."

It was then I remembered my best intentions to leave my work and family at the door. The fact was, I'd talked about nothing else. It's no wonder I'd been in a dating slump since my divorce from Johnnie Rizzo. I had no life beyond dysfunction and infidelity.

I took a deep, centering breath. I locked my thumb and index finger together, and zipped my lips.

"I'm sorry, Savino. I wasn't going to talk about my clients or parents."

"What about my parents?"

I waved a dismissive hand. "Yours are fair game. And definitely more interesting than mine."

"They're not." His finger circled the rim of his glass and his gaze held mine. "What would be interesting though is one long, amazing night together. Just you and me. No distractions. No family."

I felt my eyes get glassy. "No switched-at-birth sister. No Mama speed dialing Father Timothy."

"If you want, we can role play that we're orphans."

"Orphans?" I caught my breath. "That is sooo hot."

Savino checked his watch. "Sixty seconds. It starts."

"Deal. But as an orphan, I can't worry where my next pasta dinner is coming from. In my fantasy, you cook for me. Naked."

He smiled. "That can be arranged."

"And you drive a Porche Boxster and take out the garbage."

"Gotcha."

"Your turn, Savino. "

"I'm good, babe."

"Seriously, Savino. What's your fantasy?"

He gave a crooked smile. "I wouldn't change anything. Not even your family. We're just leaving them home tonight."

Gee, I thought. I hardly scratched my fantasy list.

I knew men. I had brothers. I had been married to a schmuck. I stalk cheaters. Chance Savino was too good to be true.

"Last call. Fifteen seconds we begin."

"Anything else?"

I softened my voice to a purr, "So, what exactly did your parents say about Bill Clinton?"

Savino hooked an arm around me and pulled me to him. "Oh yeah. He inhaled."

Chapter Twenty-five

I drove back to Bridgeport the next morning feeling all warm and fuzzy inside. Savino and I spent a passion filled night of sheet-grabbing, toe-curling sex, mixed with hours of talking while wrapped in each other's arms. He had an early meeting. But before leaving, he brought me coffee, OJ, and toast in bed. Life was good.

I turned up the stereo and weaved in and out of traffic. Today murder and infidelity would take a back seat. I was giving myself the day off. My cousin Stella was getting married. I was her Maid of Honor. She would have her storybook wedding and I would be first in line to wish them both a happily ever after.

I had a hair appointment at ten. I was getting highlights and a shoulder-shag I'd seen on Heidi Klum. I scheduled a manicure and a pedicure, and if Roberto was working, I would sneak in a quick massage.

My cell phone vibrated as I was driving into Bridgeport. I answered without thinking. I should have let it go to voicemail.

It was Brenda Greger, the Love Boat guy's wife. You know that can't be good.

"Brenda," I answered.

Sob.

"Brenda!"

Sob, sob, sob.

"OK. Get it together, girlfriend. Are you hurt?"

I could hear her taking a deep breath, and then another.

"It's okay, I'm fine," her voice was doing that funny, sobby, hiccup thing. "I...I...I..."

I instantly turned into my yoga instructor. "Breathe, Brenda. That's good. Deep, cleansing breaths..."

"I...I heard Steve talking on the phone."

"Okay, can you tell me what's happened?"

A few more hiccups and it all came out in a rush.

"Steve was doing some work in his home office and I was leaving the house to go grocery shopping. I told him good-bye and went out to my car but then I realized I'd forgotten my list. So I came back in from the garage and grabbed the list. I heard him talking on the phone. He was...he was...*ordering flowers!*" Her voice went to a pitch where dogs bark.

"Okay," I said, matter-of-factly. "Tell me exactly what you heard." I wanted her to stay calm. "Talk like you're talking about somebody else."

"OK. I...I heard him order red roses to be delivered to the boat tomorrow at one thirty."

My ears perked up. *Ah ha!*

"Is that it?"

"What do you mean, *is that it?*" She shot back at me. Inga started to whine. "He has NEVER ordered red roses for me. NEVER!"

Whoa. Maybe Brenda was getting a backbone.

"Oh, it's all right." She immediately deflated back to her spineless self. "It's just that I didn't want to believe, you know *(sigh)*, that he could really be cheating on me."

This was the part of my job that I hated. Women don't generally believe anyone who tells them that in the end, they will be better off without the two-timing bum. I mean, really, who wants to hear *that* when your whole identity, as the wife of the husband-wife team, is about to disintegrate. Sometimes it's not even so much that these women are still in love with their husbands. It's that they've become the person who is half of a married couple. Nowhere to go from there.

But I couldn't say any of this to Brenda. I'd learned early in my detective career that women need to figure this all out on their own. So, I steered Brenda back to the job at hand.

"So, Brenda, from what you heard, it sounds like he'll be meeting someone at the boat tomorrow? Is that it?" I wanted to make sure she understood what I was going to do with this information.

I took her sigh for a yes.

"Okay then, what I'm going to do is I am going to the boat tomorrow and I'll see exactly what's going on. And I'll bring you proof. Just like we agreed, when you hired me."

She sighed again and hung up.

I have you now, toothy boy, I gloated to myself. Tomorrow I'd be waiting at the marina. I'd snag my 8x10 glossy and end this cat and mouse chase.

Immediately my arms and legs started to itch. What the heck? Then I knew….I was having an allergic reaction to all of Brenda's sighing. I hated the sound of women sighing. My Mama had it down to an art form. Need I say more?

I punched Mama's number on my phone and drove home to find the Benadryl.

"Is that you, Caterina?"

"It's me, Mama. The caller ID doesn't lie."

Mama made a noncommittal grunt. She doesn't trust technology.

"I'm calling to ask if you'll take Inga and Beau tomorrow night. Cleo is singing at All Things Blue. We may be late."

I heard her smile. "Papa will barbeque. We'll have a sleepover."

"Thanks, Mama. But no s'mores this time, OK? Dogs shouldn't have chocolate."

Mama sighed. "My chest hurts when I think what that terrible woman has put my poor grand-dog through."

"You know that terrible woman's name, Mama."

"I spoke to Captain Bob yesterday. I said *that woman* should not be allowed to take Beau to prison with her. Papa and I will adopt him."

"Cleo isn't going to prison, Mama. She's innocent."

"Ooh, the chest pain is getting worse."

"Captain Bob has the real killer in custody. His name is Jess Einman."

Mama sniffed. "If that's true, why hasn't he mentioned it to Papa."

"Maybe because Bob hasn't figured it out yet. But he will."

"Spasm," she choked.

"Take a deep breath, Mama. By next week, Cleo and I will be back for your Wednesday night suppers. I'll come by Tuesday with a nice pot roast."

"Don't plan your schedule around it, Miss Caterina."

"And you don't have to worry about your knives around Cleo."

"Maybe she should be worried about *my* knives around her!" I laughed. "So I'll tell Cleo we're on for Wednesday then."

Mama made her clicking sound. "It's like I speak and she doesn't hear a word that comes out of my mouth."

I was dressed for the wedding. I loved my hair. My nails were manicured and my body felt gloriously rubber-like after my massage. I examined my reflection in the full length mirror and asked myself the age-old question.

Why are bridesmaid dresses so god-awful ugly?

The color was nice. Emerald brings out my green eyes. But the fabric was stiff and shiny, not unlike the reflective tape on jogging shoes. Next to the bride, beneath the church spotlights, I could seriously blind people.

What I hated most about the dress were the two giant, hideous bows plastered to my hips. They added a lovely four inches to my derrière. I steeled myself from ripping them off.

"I now have all the facts I need. Stella hates me," I told Inga.

Inga opened an eye and closed it again. She likes Stella. And she doesn't take sides.

I pointed my rear to the mirror and twisted my head around to look. Yikes. There was acreage.

I finished my make-up and slipped on the final touch. An emerald necklace my friend Roger gave me last month for my birthday. It was stunning. Roger was dating my cousin Ginny and I hoped to see him at the wedding. I twirled around in the mirror. The necklace took my breath away. But it didn't make my butt look smaller.

"Fever" blared. It was the hot guy in the cool new car telling me he was on his way.

"I'm ready, Chance. Where are you?"

"Sorry, babe. I can't make the wedding."

"You didn't just say that."

"I'm at O'Hare right now catching a flight to Seattle."

"I can't believe you're ditching me at this wedding. Why not take a later flight? Is there blood involved?"

"Only mine if I miss my plane. I'm transporting a prisoner who's due in Federal court Monday."

"I'm not seeing the blood. Tomorrow's Sunday."

"I didn't make the reservations."

"When did you find out about this?"

"Earlier this morning."

"And it didn't occur to you to tell me sooner?"

"No. What good would it do?"

"I dunno. At least I'd be over it. I wouldn't be irritated with you now."

He laughed softly. "I'll make it up to you. I promise. Tomorrow night at All Things Blue."

"Like I'm holding my breath."

"Save a dance for me, DeLucky."

Click. I hung up on him.

OK. Call me childish.

But if there's one thing I hate more than standing in a barrel of snakes, it's going to a family wedding without a date.

Why? *Pity.* It's the wretched look of pity on every DeLuca face. And you know how my family breeds.

The truth is I'm happy with my life. I'm thirty, divorced, and I'm not thinking about kids. At least not yet. When someone says *morning sickness*, I think *hangover.*

I punched a number on my phone.

"Hey, Kitty," Max said. "What's up?"

"If you're available, I know a place we can get free cake."

"I love cake." I heard him smile. "Savino stood you up for the wedding, didn't he?"

"How did you know? He went to Seattle."

"Not smart. If he's not careful, someone could steal you away."

We arranged to meet at the church. Max was heading home to get all spiffy for his cake.

I put Inga and Beau in the backyard to play until I got home. Then I packed up the car.

I carried out a giant box wrapped in silver paper and pink ribbons. My wedding present to Stella and Jake were Terra e Fueco dishes from the village our grandparents came from in Italy. Stella and Jake wouldn't have a lot of use for fancy dishes while Jake was still in school. But someday they'd own one of these old Bridgeport houses and they'd have the DeLucas over for supper.

I carried out the two bunches of flowers and the book for guests to sign. Then I returned to the house one more time to grab my purse and shut the door.

My heels clacked on the sidewalk. Across the street, Mrs. Pickens craned her neck my way. She pretended to weed the yard. Her gardening tools were organized in a convenient carrier. They included a hoe, spade, and binoculars. They were a prop. I saw her landscaping service there yesterday.

I waved and stepped inside. Took three steps past the threshold and stopped dead in my tracks. Something wasn't right. It took me a moment to put my finger on it. And then it came to me. My purse wasn't by the door where I dropped it. It was on the small table a few steps further inside the door.

I'd left the door open only a moment. My throat caught. A voice screamed in my head. *Go back.* I tried to turn around but my legs twisted to lead. I was a kid again, having that awful dream. The one where the boogie man is coming and you can't run.

A long arm snaked behind me. It closed on my chest and wrenched around my throat. My assailant pushed me away from the door and kicked it closed.

He was breathing hard. His energy was exhilarated and dark. The snake arm shifted and he wrenched my neck in a sleeper hold. Black clouds closed in on me. I kicked savagely. I rammed a spiked heel to his shin and he swore. The death grip loosened on my throat and I gulped air. My left elbow jabbed his rib and I rammed my right fist behind me, crushing his groin. He screamed. But he held me tight. I couldn't glimpse his face.

A voice whispered hoarsely in my ear. "Forget Walter Jones."

I gasped. "You're the hit-and-run driver."

His grip tightened. I kicked him again.

"Don't mess with a girl who has three brothers."

A metal object pounded the door. I think it was the hoe.

"Caterina!" Mrs. Pickens said. "Is everything all right?"

"No!" I screamed. "Call nine one—"

The snake arm tightened around my neck. Black clouds swarmed my vision and this time I couldn't stop them.

Chapter Twenty-six

A big gnarly hand with a lion tattoo was examining my necklace when I regained consciousness.

"It wasn't a robbery," Leo said.

His rookie partner, Tommy, nodded. "Her purse is here too. Money and cards still there."

"What happened?" I sat up and my head pounded.

"Lie down," Leo said. "The paramedics are on the way."

I touched my head where it hit the floor. "Call them off. I'm good."

"You don't look so good," Tommy said.

The memory of my attacker flooded me. I felt nauseous.

"Where did he go?"

"A neighbor said he ran out the back."

I snorted. It made my head hurt more. "My guard dog ripped him to shreds."

Leo and Tommy exchanged looks. Inga lay on her back, tail wagging.

"There wasn't any blood in the backyard," Tommy said. "Your dog didn't try to stop us when we came through the gate. She led us straight to the refrigerator."

"Inga let you in because you're cops. She respects the uniform."

"Right," Leo said.

I was vaguely surprised no DeLucas responded to the call. Then it hit me.

The DeLucas are at the wedding. And the maid of honor is on the floor.

I struggled to my feet and tested my balance. I felt shaky and a little dizzy. But I wasn't going to throw up. I smoothed my dress and fluffed the two bows.

"That's a new look for you," Tommy said.

If my balance was better, I would have slapped him.

"Stella's getting married. I need a ride."

"I have to make a report," Leo said.

"Later. Just get me to the church on time." I groaned. "I can't believe I just said that."

Leo scooped up my purse. "I'll need a statement after the wedding."

The guys moved the flowers and silver box to the squad car. I rode shotgun and checked my face in the mirror. I looked pale. My hair was a mess. There were ugly red marks on my neck. I pinched my cheeks and smeared Dr. Pepper Lip Smacker on my mouth.

"Please be discreet, Leo," I said. "No flashing blue lights."

We passed the ambulance a block from my house. I waved.

Leo pulled up to the church, sirens blaring. Guests were gathering. Father Timothy, Papa, and Mama were waiting outside.

I pushed the car door open and spilled onto the sidewalk. Tommy caught me.

"I'm fine," I said all wobbly.

"Is she under arrest?" Father Timothy said.

"It's the pictures," Mama wailed.

I forced a smile. "It's nothing. I was late. Leo and Tommy gave me a ride."

Leo pulled me aside. "I'll see you after the wedding. And get someone to stay with you tonight."

"Thanks Leo," I said.

"Your dad and I go way back. I'll tell him the truth later." Leo peeled away, lights flashing.

"Now he's showing off," I said.

Mama and Father Timothy carried the flowers and the silver-papered box into the church.

Papa smiled at me. His eyes were moist.

"My beautiful Caterina. Something tells me the next wedding will be yours."

I listened. "Really? Cuz I'm not hearing that."

Papa emitted a long-suffering sigh. "Is it too much to expect the comfort of grandchildren when I'm old."

"Nice try, Papa. You're not even close to old."

He expelled a breath. "I worry about you, Caterina. This detective business is too dangerous. You should marry and have babies like your sister Sophie."

I cradled my head. "Papa, I can't talk about this now."

"You're right. I should talk to Savino."

"*No.* And I'm here with Max."

Papa looked confused. "Now I should talk to Max?"

"No!" I kicked him.

"Fanabola!" He exclaimed.

Mama trounced over. "What happened?"

"Your daughter kicked me."

Mama looked at Papa, then me, and back at Papa again. "She had a reason. The last time Caterina kicked you was when you told her not to marry Johnnie Rizzo."

"For the record, I'd like to take that kick back," I said.

"I told her she *should* marry Savino. Even Max will do."

Mama shook her finger at Papa. "I don't interfere with our children's lives. And neither should you."

"I'd like to get that in writing," I said.

The wedding was beautiful. Uncle Rudy walked Stella down the aisle. Aunt Fran cried. I suspected it had something to do with Frankie "returning" to the FBI. The twins were hunky Best Men. Their tuxedos itched and they scratched a bit during the ceremony. They reminded me of Papa rubbing his scar. I was a little shaky at first but I made it through the ceremony standing. I felt better after my first glass of champagne.

The reception was held at the Italian Club in Bridgeport. Max and I love cake. We each took two pieces. We danced but we never finished a song. The girls from the bachelorette party kept cutting in.

"Yoo-hoo! Mr. Pizza Delivery Man!"

Once they dragged him away. Max came back with lipstick on his face.

Tiffany's *Passion Pink* on one cheek. Tegan's *Endless Ruby* on the other.

Oh yeah. I'm a professional.

Max's eyes glazed over. "Great party."

"I ate your cake," I said.

Papa gave Max a disapproving frown. "I'm taking back my blessing," he said stiffly. "You won't father my grandchildren."

Max's relief was palpable. He bubbled like champagne. Commitment makes him nauseous.

Papa grunted with disgust. He limped away clutching his scar.

A pudgy finger tapped my shoulder. "May I have this dance?"

I whirled around and threw my arms around Roger's ample torso. My cousin Ginny pranced beside him like a school girl.

She flashed the boulder on her hand.

I gasped and hugged Ginny. "You go, girl! When's the big day?"

"Sometime next summer. We're planning our engagement party now."

"With a Star Trek theme," Roger beamed.

Ginny and Roger are perfect for each other. They're both Trekkies and computer geeks.

Ginny giggled. "Can't you just see Roger as Captain Kirk? He'll be smokin' hot."

I considered my chubby friend with his wild Einstein hair and mustache. Roger's body is a temple for Twinkies and super-sized fries. I mentally shoved, squeezed and packed every love-handle into Captain Kirk's sleek, form-fitting uniform. I got the Pillsbury dough boy in spandex.

Yowzah!

Max grinned. "What do you see in this big dope anyway?"

Ginny waved him off. "We're going to Italy for our honeymoon. Roger wants to buy my parents a vacation villa there."

"You know he's just trying to get them out of the country," I said. "I'll keep my mouth shut if my parents can go with them."

Roger looked stumped. "Why would I want to get rid of Ginny's parents?"

I laughed. "Max was right. You're a big, loveable dope. But I was serious about sending my parents."

The last time I danced with Roger was at my thirtieth birthday party. The Pillsbury dough boy made hamburger of my feet. I fixed a smile on my face and steeled my feet for torture.

This time was different. Roger was a chubby Fred Astaire. He'd learned some fancy footwork since the candles lit up my cake.

"Whoa," I said. "Someone's been giving you dance lessons."

He threw in a little rhumba. "*Dancing With The Stars*. I bought the DVD for every season. I'm working on the tango now. Do you…"

"I'll pass," I laughed.

He grinned. "Ginny's going to ask you to be her Maid of Honor."

I winced. "You have to talk to her, Roger. No bows."

"Why not?"

He spun me like a top, dipped me low, and gazed down at the hideous bows protruding from my thighs. "A big bottom is beautiful on a lady."

He pulled me to my feet. I smiled happily and rested my head on his chest.

"Now that, my friend, is music to every woman's ears."

I left the reception early, went home and changed into something without bows. Then I drove to the cop-shop to give my statement to Leo and Tommy. I didn't have a lot to tell them. I had no description of my assailant. What I had was a bruised neck and a throbbing head and some seriously wounded pride.

Leo didn't keep me long. He already knew what happened. He showed me where to sign my name. He said he'd fill in the blanks.

I paused at the door. "I'm a professional, Leo. The guys here respect the work I do."

Leo choked on a laugh.

"When you write your report, please don't make me look stupid."

"You don't need my help for that, Cat."

"Thank you."

"First you told me a blue Volvo has been stalking you."

"That's true."

"So you put out a *welcome* sign and left your door wide open. How do you spell *stupid?*"

"It's a welcome mat, Leo. It came with the house."

"Yeah? Well I'm still filing the report under S."

Tommy couldn't hold back a snigger.

"Hilarious, Crash Dummy," I said.

I dropped by Captain Bob's office on my way out. He asked if I was OK. I told him the guy who ran over the old man was stalking me. The Captain said I'm not the kind of person who takes a knock in the head well.

Bob congratulated me on my new job. Apparently Mama told him about my exciting new career taking MRI's of naked people. Captain Bob said his wife's neck is bothering her. He asked me to make her an appointment.

I cradled my head and trudged out the door to the parking lot. It was early yet. The sun was shining. The wedding guests were dancing. The twins were still at the buffet table. Stella would be too busy with the guests to notice I'd slipped away.

I needed a long, hot bubble bath and enough wine to wash down a bottle of aspirin. I threaded Cleo's Camry toward home.

I was tooling down West Thirty-Fifth Street, when I spotted Steve Greger's car heading east. It passed me and I got a good look at the blonde riding shot gun. And I saw all my bath bubbles disappear.

I couldn't help myself. I hit the brakes and flipped a U-ey.

Steve Greger made me crazy. I'd been off my game since the day he stranded me at the marina. I'd chased him around Bridgeport. He dodged my camera shots. And he cost me four hundred bucks for a flippin' coil wire.

I held the wheel in a white-knuckle grip. A zany, screwball grin seized my mouth.

"We finish this now, toothy boy."

I'd intended to scope out the Love Boat tomorrow when Steve's roses were delivered. But I could cancel those plans now. I'd have my Kodak moment tonight, on my terms.

The thing about Steve Greger is that he thinks he's smarter than everybody else. And he certainly thought he was smarter than me. He'd danced around me all week. But he hadn't met Cat DeLuca, P.I. yet. No one gets to fondle my coil wire without my saying so. Now this was personal. Payback was gonna be a bitch for tooth-face boy.

I slid my way up through the traffic until I had Greger's rear end in my sites. I followed him to a residential street not far from Donovan Park. When I saw him stop outside a house with a For Sale sign, I kept going and turned left onto the side street, then whipped into the back alley. I counted the houses down until I found the house I was looking for.

I gave myself a moment and groaned inwardly. Greger wasn't nearly as smart as he thought he was after all. I'd seen this cheater ploy before. Unfortunately it was with my cheating skank of an ex-husband, Johnnie Rizzo. It's not uncommon for a cheater to set up a rendezvous at a house on the market. All you need is a buddy who *one*. is a realtor—lacking any sense of professional or personal scruples and *two*. has the key. Yeah. Like that's hard to find.

I shuddered at the memory of following Johnnie to a place like this. It was a two-story "shotgun house," narrow and long. A style that is common to Bridgeport's older residential architecture. When these houses go up for sale, it's not uncommon for the owner's furniture to be in them. And that's, of course, the cheater-appeal. If you are looking for a low-risk tryst, an

192 K. J. Larsen

anonymous empty house with a bed and shower is the way to go. Your buddy will only ask you clean and straighten up afterward.

Shaking off the bad memory mojo, I got out of the car. I hot-footed it through the back gate and when I got to the back stoop, I decided to scout around the side of the house. Sure enough, the first floor lights had come on, where experience told me the living room was. I couldn't see through the curtains but I bet that Mr. Quick-Nasty-and-Unsatisfying would be settling for a downstairs couch. That way he wouldn't have to bother with remaking a bed upstairs.

I danced my way to the back door and B&E'd my way in. Tools are a good thing. I have no problem with that.

I thanked Mary and a whole host of other saints who may or may not have anything to do with squeaking doors and floors. I made my way in and through the hallway to the light.

I could hear low intimate murmurs coming from just feet away. I had him now.

I armed my camera and leaped out into the middle of the open hallway and started clicking my brains out.

It took me a second to register what I was clicking. But there in the lens was Greger on the couch, leaning toward a coffee table. There were papers on it. On the other side of the table was the blonde who was not Legs in platform shoes. She was probably a good twenty years older. This bleached version was obviously a realtor. They were eyeing a contract. I could die.

"What is going on here? I am calling the police." The realtor reached into her purse and grabbed the phone.

"Aaugghh!"

Greger tipped his head up to the chandelier and let out the loudest "Bwahaahaa…"

Oh, he was loving this!

But I swear to God and all that is holy, I saw a rainbow—a veritable spectrum of color—shooting off of that man's teeth.

I wondered as I hightailed it back to the car. "How does he DO that?"

Chapter Twenty-seven

I awoke to a symphony of drums and symbols crashing in my head. Maybe it was the champagne. Or the bump on my skull from an unexpected visitor. But I suspected it had more to do with the bride throwing the bouquet smack into my arms. And Mama sobbing with uncontrollable joy.

My eyes were gunked shut with last night's mascara. I pried them open. It took a moment for the numbers on my clock to come in focus. It read eight-twenty. I rolled out of my bed and into my slippers. I could smell something divine baking in the oven. I sighed happily and followed my nose toward the aroma of coffee.

Cleo pulled cinnamon rolls from the oven and placed them on the kitchen table. I poured two mugs of coffee. We each grabbed a fork and dug in.

Halfway through my first cup, the doorbell rang. It was Captain Bob. I opened the door and held my wrists out for the cuffs.

"I suppose my twenty-four hours are up. Do I get to wear those pretty silver bracelets?"

"Not yet." Captain Bob said, following the heady scent of cinnamon and coffee. "But I wouldn't give up hope."

I poured him a mug that read: *Kiss a Cop. Save a Donut.* Cleo put his cinnamon roll on a plate. Oh yeah. We go all out for company.

"I came by to give you an update," Bob said. "We've arrested a second suspect in the Jones case. We're in the initial stages of the investigation at this point and it's too early to draw conclusions. But it's possible Mrs. Jones could be absolved of all charges."

Cleo squealed and I cut in front of Captain Bob before she tackled him in a bear hug.

I gave him a cocky smile. "This is where I fight back the urge to say I told you so."

Captain Bob grunted. He scooped up another roll and we followed him to the door.

"This is where I point out that you didn't ask any questions about the suspect. You're not the least bit curious?"

I shoved a big bite in my mouth. "Of course. What did he say?"

"Funny you should ask. He's making crazy claims about two women, disguised as prostitutes, who forced their way into his apartment and—"

"Forced?" Cleo said.

I kicked her.

"—and kidnapped him, planting false evidence on him," the Captain finished.

"You're right. It's a crazy story," I said. "So, uh, did he say anything else about the women?"

"He said one had big boobs." He looked at Cleo.

"Why, thank you," she said adjusting the girls.

"Those were his words, not mine."

"You know, Cat has boobs, too." Cleo rushed to my defense.

I kicked her again.

"He also mentioned the women's car was thrashed on by some punks. A silver car with a broken window and damaged fender. He said if we find the car, we'll find the women." He paused a minute, then looked over the rim of his glasses. "I couldn't help but notice your Silver Honda wasn't out front."

"Uhm, it's getting some routine maintenance work done."

He took a final swallow and placed the cup in my hand. "So that was that *your* car I saw at Jack's earlier."

"I don't know, Bob. He has a lot of cars at his shop."

"Yeah. I almost didn't recognize it, you know, with the busted out window and damaged fender."

My lips didn't work. "Uh…" I stammered, but he was gone.

◇◇◇

I splayed the *Chicago Sun Times* on the kitchen table and rifled through pages until I found the Obituaries. Patrick Robertson was the third stiff listed. And I say that with respect.

The picture they ran of the old man was almost as old as he was. He looked about sixteen in the photo. Brave, cocky, and dressed for war. He did a stint in Korea. Came home with a Silver Star. He worked at a Bridgeport meat packing plant until it closed in the early nineties. There was other stuff about him. But I skipped over it and went straight to the good stuff.

The wake. It was today, beginning at eleven a.m., at the home Patrick shared with his son's family. Everyone was invited.

"Everyone?" I asked Inga.

Inga wagged her tail.

"You should probably wait here with Beau. We'll go for a run when I get back."

I checked my watch. It was ten-thirty-three. I wanted to be at the marina in two hours. That gave me an hour at the wake and twenty-seven minutes to get there.

I scuttled to my room, and threw my Suzi Chin one shoulder smoky-gray dress over my head while slipping on a pair of sling-back pumps.

I twisted my hair in a clip, gave a few strokes with a toothbrush, a good swirl of mouthwash, a dousing with perfume, two swipes at the raccoon eyes, and six sweeps of mascara. I scooped up my best bottle of wine and tripping over myself, I raced outside, smearing Dr. Pepper Lip Gloss all the way. I stopped at the curb, did a one-eighty, and stomped back into the house.

The Silver Bullet was being held captive in the shop.

"I need a ride," I screamed from the door.

Cleo appeared from the bathroom, keys dangling in one hand and curling iron pressed tight to her head in the other.

"Take it," she hummed. She tossed me the keys.

"OK."

I paused. Curiosity got the better of me. "I thought you wanted to rehearse once more before your hot debut tonight."

"I have a ride."

"You're not stealing Walter's Corvette again, are you? Because…"

Cleo wet her lips. "Frankie's driving me."

I groaned. "You do realize my cousin Frankie's a couple sandwiches short of a picnic, don't you?"

"I know he takes Prozac to control his blood pressure."

"Aurrrrgh!" I slammed the door behind me.

The old man had a lot of friends. There was already a crowd when I arrived at eleven-o-two. His daughter-in-law met me at the door. I handed her the bottle of wine.

"Thank you for coming. I'm Renee Robertson. Patrick's daughter-in-law."

"Cat DeLuca. Patrick was a great guy. I'm sorry for your loss."

"It was a terrible shock. A witness said the car deliberately ran him down. Who could be cruel enough to do something like that to an old man?"

I shook my head at a loss for words. I left her to arriving guests and slipped into the crowd. There were flowers everywhere. Cards and old photographs lined the mantle. The bar was well stocked. Looking at the time, I chose Irish coffee. Friends and neighbors had provided a mountain of food for Patrick's last party. Who knew there was so much diversity in casserole?

I drifted around the room, listening to the murmurings of Patrick's friends.

Who killed Patrick Robertson? Everyone wanted to know.

It was a question that had been twisting around my brain the past three days. My number one suspect was the guy who killed Walter. But somehow it didn't feel right. Jess Einman was a goofy, dumb guy, out to avenge the death of his father. It was no big secret. He told his cell mate. He told Walter. He probably told a dozen other guys. In his mind, his mission was a righteous one. Why cover his tracks now after he blazed a trail to Walter's door.

There was the possibility that Patrick's death was a random act after all. That there was no connecting thread to Walter's murder or Patrick's snitching. And the man in the blue Volvo that followed me that same day was a pouty cheater who didn't like his butt plastered on my photos. And the guy who attacked me in my house was a passing freak show.

And if you believe in fairies.....

I snaked through the crowd, picking up bits of conversation. Paying extra attention to the whispered ones. The word was that Junior wasn't holding up well. He and his dad were extremely close. Junior was laid off six months ago. He was a heavy machinery operator and construction jobs are tough to find these days. It wasn't hard for me to pick Pat Junior out in the crowd. He looked like a deer in headlights.

I waited for my chance and slipped upstairs. The old man's room was in the back of the house. It was exactly how he left it. His bed was made, square corners, a lingering habit from his army days. He made it halfway through a Robert Ludlum novel. A picture of his wife and a yellowing copy of her obituary were beside his bed. The rocking chair by the window had a straight shot to Walter's study. The last time I saw the old man alive he was sitting in this chair, laughing at my escape through Walter's window.

I opened my bag and pulled out the White Sox cap Patrick lost in flight on Morgan Street. I brushed it off and placed it on the rocker. And I placed a pint of Crown Royal beside it.

"I'm sorry I couldn't protect you, Patrick. And I wish we had that drink together. We might have been friends."

I looked out the window at the gentle slope of the roof line. It was made to order for a hotshot detective who makes her living scaling balconies, and too easy to resist. I opened the window and stepped onto the roof, slipped off my sling backs and shimmied down the drain pipe. I scampered into the alley and around the corner to my car. I could almost hear the old man laughing.

I got my Uncle Joey on the phone. He's the go-to man when you need something.

"Joey, do you know anyone in the union with pull?"

"Is that a trick question? What do you need?"

"A job for a heavy machinery operator. His name is Patrick Robertson, Jr."

"The old man's boy. Tough break."

"Yeah. Would you see what you can do?"

"I'll call in a favor," Uncle Joey said.

I left Bridgeport in a cloud of dust and slipped into Monroe Harbor a little past twelve. I grabbed my big white floppy hat, my white Keds and oval framed sunglasses. I wasn't exactly sure when Steve Greger and Legs would show but I wanted to be there first. I needed time to set up surveillance.

Jim Beam was on his boat and it looked like he was alone. Maybe he got stood up. That would explain why he wasn't bothering with a glass and he was drinking straight from the bottle. The Beam-Meister was moving around, stopping to take a swig every few minutes. He was naked except for a red strip of elastic over his privates. Ewww! No sober woman should have to see that. I turned my head quickly before it damaged my eyes.

That gave me two options to stake out Greger. The boat on the other side of Greger's was empty. That was until a small family showed up, all energetic and perky. They spent a lot of time moving things around, ropes and stuff.

The Leave It To Beaver family was, at this moment, getting ready to sail away on my First Option. Option two was to board Jim Beam's boat under the pretense of spying on a terrorist. I was really, *really* hoping to avoid that one.

At about ten after one, I realized I was going to explode. I couldn't hold in all that coffee I'd drunk this morning. With or without the whiskey at the Robertson wake. The flowers weren't coming until one-thirty and I figured Greger would come shortly before that. If I was quick, I'd be good.

I made the quickest dash to the club house. But not quick enough. When I got back, I saw I'd missed Greger's arrival. He was loading stuff onto the boat from a cart that was still on the slip. I could see him handing supplies to someone down below. All I could see were a pair of beautifully manicured hands. It looked like they were actually going to take the boat out this time. That meant I didn't have a lot of time because they would probably leave right after the flowers arrived.

Greger folded the cart and took it below. With no one in sight, I ran down the slip and crouched down by Jim Beam's boat. That's when I noticed Jim Beam himself….and heard him. He was lying on a towel, top side, on his stomach, legs splayed apart. Ewwww! The noise coming from his body sounded like a humpback whale throwing up.

Jim Beam was out for the count. I could jump on his boat stark naked, use the mast for my pole dance and sing "I Touch Myself" from the top of my lungs and he wouldn't have moved a muscle.

It was almost one-thirty and Greger was still below. I climbed aboard Jim Beam's boat and squatted down next to the wheel. I figured he and Legs were finished doing chores and were now doing each other, so it was time to take the picture. I was hoping they'd make it easier for me this time, like shagging on deck under the bright blue Chicago sky. But no such luck. I'd have to try to take the picture through the window again.

There was no way I was going to do the toes-clinging-to-the-rail thing if I could help it. I scanned the angles to Greger's cute little round window and came up with an idea.

I tiptoed my way along the side until I found handles to scamper up to the cabin's roof. I laid flat and pointed my camera to the window. Perfecto! There was Greger on the bed, naked and kneeling over Legs. I couldn't see her face, so I held the camera steady and in focus, waiting for that golden moment when he would move just a little to the side. I'd have my shot: Greger and Legs in flagrante delecto.

"Hey!"

I froze. I was hoping that whoever it was hadn't seen me and was heying someone else. I was hoping that if I stopped breathing and held myself completely still, they wouldn't see me.

"Hey Lady!" Louder this time.

I held my body still but quickly turned my head. I had to shut this person up before he disturbed Greger and I lost my shot. And then I saw him. Actually, I didn't zero in on him, but on the two dozen roses he was carrying.

"Hey," he yelled, "I have a delivery for you."

Stupidly, I turned my head to left, then right, as if to make sure he was talking to me. Since he was looking straight at me, and there was no one else in view except for the comatose JB, this just made him a little impatient.

"Are you deaf?" he bellowed. "I have a delivery for you."

Oh my god, I had to shut him up. I slowly crawled down off the roof and made my way down to the deck and onto the slip where he stood. Thinking quickly, I grabbed the roses, laid them on the back of Greger's boat, and handed the guy a tip, and hoped that no one else had heard him.

Camera still in hand, and Loud Mouth headed to his car, I started to move back toward my previous position, hoping I was not too late.

I was too late.

I heard Greger and Leg's as they climbed the stairs, talking and laughing. Damn. I couldn't leave this time without some kind of evidence, even if it was just to show Brenda that he was on the boat with someone else. The someone he was showering with red roses, the scumbag.

I stood on the slip, in clear sight of where they would surface, my camera aimed and focused.

I took several shots before I realized what I was capturing. Greger stood on deck, his arm lovingly around a blonde. But not The Blonde. Legs was nowhere in sight. Cuddled in his hairy, muscular arms, looking as if there had never been the slightest doubt in her mousy mind, was.....

Brenda?

Now, I'm usually not one to hesitate or hold back, but at that moment, I wasn't quite sure what to do. That, in itself, kind of threw me. Surely I could come up with some sarcastic remark or biting insult to fit the occasion. I mean, I've been throwing one liners since I was five. But I wasn't sure what to say or who to say it to. So I stood there.

That is, until Greger smiled. He smiled right at me, and then threw back his head and laughed into the sky. Beams of light reflected off his tooth enamel, causing passing seagulls to swerve. I squinted my eyes and fought the urge to throw my camera at his head.

But before venom could spew from my mouth or my arm wind up for a fast ball, Brenda spoke up.

"Cat, oh Cat," she twittered like a canary. "I'm so sorry, I should have called you."

She stepped away from Greger and leaned over the railing to talk to me.

"I was so wrong," she whispered airily. "I never should have doubted Steve. The red roses were for me. Can you believe it? The red roses were *for me!*"

I stared at her, at a loss for words.

"I should have called you once I knew he was bringing *me* to the boat today." Her voice dropped even lower. "I didn't have a minute alone to call you and I didn't want Steve to know I knew about the flowers. I didn't want to ruin his surprise."

I relaxed a little, and tried to muster a neutral expression but I knew that I couldn't hide the pity I was feeling. Because I knew what had happened. Greger, that low-life, suspected Brenda had heard him on the phone. Maybe he noticed some change in her manner or a comment she made. But he changed his plans and brought her to the boat instead of Legs. I knew Brenda had been right when she told me yesterday that he never buys red roses for her. He still hadn't. Not really.

I took a breath and let it out slowly. Still ignoring Greger, I kept my eyes on her.

"Okay, Brenda, I'm going to take off but we'll talk soon."

"Well, Cat," she hesitated and I knew what was coming. "I really don't think that I'll need your help anymore. I really appreciate it, but, really, I don't doubt Steve anymore."

It was then that I looked at Greger, his Donny Osmond smile still beaming up into the heavens. He winked at me.

I looked back at Brenda.

"Keep my card handy. You'll need it." And I walked away.

I drove home, sighing the whole way.

Chapter Twenty-eight

I stepped out of the shower, into my cushy terrycloth robe, and blow-dried my hair. Something was knocking around the back of my skull and it wasn't the ever present remnants of last month's concussion. Something wasn't right and I couldn't quite bring it to the surface.

In three short hours Cleo would be taking the stage at All Things Blue and I had one stop to make first. I straightened my hair, did my full throttle make-up routine. I put on a vibrant red Elie Tahari sleeveless blouse and black pants with full, flared legs. I popped in the pink diamond earrings Uncle Joey gave me for my thirtieth birthday and slipped on my Pelle Moda sandals to finish the look. One really must put in the effort when seeing a world-class fashion designer. And the outfit would do for tonight.

I pulled Roxanne's designer bag from the secret compartment behind the pantry. Then I called Inga and Beau to the car and we headed for RB's boutique on Chicago's Gold Coast.

The first spot in the parking garage was waiting for me. It was a lucky omen. I made a mental note to buy a lottery ticket. I grabbed the bag and told the dogs to guard the car.

Rounding the corner to the boutique, my feet staggered just a little as I glimpsed Roxanne's timeless little black dress once again. It was a study in leg and cleavage and it screamed to me from the mannequin in the window. It was like a siren call. It really was just the thing for tonight's gig. Here I was, all made up with someplace to go. Nevertheless, I folded. There's a shocker.

I charged recklessly through the door and flung the dress off the rack. I added black patent leather stilettos with peek-a-boo toes and a lusty-red clutch purse and paid the staggering bill. I refused to calculate how many 8x10 glossies would pay off my American Express. I dressed in the dressing room, stashed my clothes in the RB sale bag, and scooted upstairs to RB's office, with Walter's blackmail bag in hand. I felt almost giddy.

The receptionist greeted me with a wide smile. "You look perfectly *divine*," she gushed.

I spun around and the short skirt swirled around my legs. "Is Roxanne in?"

"She's at the new construction site in Bridgeport. She's leaving tonight for New York to prepare for the grand opening of the Fifth Avenue Boutique. She'll be back next week though. May I make an appointment for you?"

I checked my watch. "I have her bag. I'll try to catch her before she flies out."

OK, I suppose I could have waited a few days, but I really wanted to put this behind me. Mostly it was the whole Maddie Goldstein deception. The journalist's Twitter page had her flying to New York earlier today. I didn't know if she planned to do an article on RB's new boutique, but I definitely didn't want to take that chance. It was only right that I be the one to tell RB the truth.

In fact RB had some truth of her own to tell. I still had questions about the blackmail pictures that inspired the designer to pay that staggering chunk of change. One. How did the pictures connect? Two. Did RB's secret have something to do with Hal's death? Or Courtney's?

I clickity-clacked hurriedly in my black patent stilettos to the Camry and tossed Walter's blackmail booty on the passenger seat. As I cranked the ignition, I was glad I'd made an appointment for a tune-up. The poor car was sounding rough and I seriously doubted Cleo's manicured fingernail had ever dialed a mechanic's number in her life. The engine started with a roar and Beau and Inga each opened an eye in the back.

"Nice back-up you two are. We're hot on a case here. You're supposed to watch the car."

Beau stretched and the beagle rolled on her back, sighing blissfully.

"You're both fired."

I took Lake Shore Drive and hopped on the Stevenson to Bridgeport, dodging in and out of traffic, sailing past McGuane Park and Bridgeport Catholic Academy to RB's new construction. I whipped into the parking lot behind a stunning red Mercedes Benz CLS. The door opened and AJ emerged wearing a pewter colored Boss suit. Why was I not surprised?

I parked beside him and stepped outside. His eyes did the full lazy sweep, from my green eyes to my peek-a-booing red toenails.

He whistled. "You are one hot woman."

I whistled back. "Hot car. Hot suit."

"You forgot hot man," AJ grinned.

He was about to up the ante on our flirt-fest when he saw the bag in my hand. He stiffened. It didn't take a hot shot detective to know the last time he saw that bag, it was stuffed with green paper.

"Nice bag. It doesn't exactly go with the little black dress."

"It isn't mine. I'm returning it to RB. Is she in?"

"She's racing to catch a flight. I can deliver it if you'd like."

I made a *pretty please* face. "I need to tell her something. Just one quick minute?"

Blink, Blink.

He played along and chuckled easily. "Come on, Maddie. I'll see what I can do."

He held out his arm. I took it.

OK, I thought to myself. *I might as well just come clean.*

"I'm not Maddie," I blurted out. "I've never written an article in my life. And I don't live in New York City."

The *nice guy* look dashed from his face and he dropped my arm. My eyes widened at the one-eighty. He was suddenly annoyed and nasty. His eyes looked dead.

I privately cursed my Catholic upbringing for the impulse to confess.

"This is awkward," I said.

"So everything you said was a lie." AJ's icy voice could have eased global warming.

"Not *everything*. I like cheesecake."

"Who the hell are you?"

"Caterina DeLuca, Pants On Fire Detective Agency."

I thrust out a hand. He didn't take it.

"I'm investigating the murder of Walter Jones."

"The batty wife obviously did it."

"It's true Cleo Jones was an early suspect in the case. The police now have a man in custody they believe killed Walter. He'll be officially charged on Monday."

His face momentarily flickered surprise, and then hardened again.

"I don't care who you are. I don't like being played."

"Call me Cat."

He didn't call me anything. "And to bring Roxanne into this ridiculous charade is inexcuseable!"

"I don't play charades. I investigate. And just so we're clear, Roxanne was never a suspect. I knew she didn't kill Walter. But we have reason to believe she was at his house shortly before he died. It was possible she saw something that could lead us to his murderer."

AJ's breath had slowed. He was still pouty but calmer now.

"Sorry about dinner," I said.

His smile didn't reach his eyes. "If I knew who you were, I probably would have bought dinner anyway. But nix on the two-hundred bottle of wine."

"Fair enough."

AJ dragged out his phone. He had a text. I went ahead and followed the drone of voices. I got the feeling he might be letting me off the hook. But then again, he could be texting Roxanne. Tattling to RB first would make a more satisfying kill.

I walked past the unfinished staircase and framed walls and around the elevator shaft to a large area with a stone fireplace. RB was in dialogue with Ken Millani over structural changes she wanted in the blue print. A moment later, AJ stood beside me.

Roxanne gestured with her hands. "And I'd like these walls knocked down to create a bigger space for the conference room."

Ken nodded. "I'll meet with the architect tonight. I'll have the proposed changes ready when you return."

"Thanks, Ken. Call AJ with any questions."

"I will. Enjoy your trip."

Ken turned on his heel and walked past me. "Hello, Cat," he said stiffly.

RB scrunched her face. "Cat?"

"It's hard to explain," I said.

"Not really," AJ blabbed. "She lied. Her name is Cat DeLuca. She's a meddler snooping around Walter's murder."

"Oh my God," RB gasped. "You're disgusting!"

"I'm sorry, Roxanne. There was no other way."

"Get out!"

"If you'll let me explain …"

She stepped back and looked daggers at me. "You're that fraud designer-doctor! You've got some nerve intruding on Courtney's mother."

I was momentarily stunned by the repulsion in her eyes. I stammered like a school girl. "I've reopened Hal's case. There's new evidence. His death wasn't an accident. Someone murdered him."

OK. That wasn't exactly entirely a lie. There was new evidence. I just hadn't found it yet.

AJ's brows darted up and down. "Have the cops ordered a padded room for you?"

"Hah! They'll change their tune when I solve their case."

RB's face was a blank. "What the hell is she talking about?"

AJ twirled a finger around his ear.

"Whoa! I'm not whacko."

"We'll need a second opinion on that," AJ said.

"Yeah? Well don't ask my mother."

As quickly as it erupted, the anger drained from her face. Roxanne blew air. She looked deflated and small.

"I have a plane to catch."

I smiled brightly. "May I drive you to the airport?"

"Get out and don't come back. And take that bag with you."

"But it's your …"

"*Go*. It sickens me to look at you."

"That hurts," I said.

"And I hate seeing you in my dress."

Chapter Twenty-nine

Hot damn, that was ugly. I stomped to the Camry, threw the bag of money on the passenger seat, and slid behind the wheel. Inga and Beau nuzzled my neck. I opened the cooler. No Mama's cannoli. I dragged out two fat sausages and tossed them in the back. I dropped my head on the steering wheel and groaned.

RB hates me.

I shook myself but the *yuck* clung to my shoulders like a sticky cloud of doom.

"All right, then. If I can't shake it, I'll dance it off tonight at Cleo's debut. Or drown it, if necessary, in tequila."

Beau and Inga watched with soulful brown eyes.

"You're not fired anymore but you're on probation." I tossed them each another sausage.

A big black car appeared from behind the building and coasted onto the street. That would be Roxanne's driver taking her to the airport. I was more determined than ever to solve her friend's murder. We'd never be girlfriends now. She wouldn't share her crackers and cheese with me again. But maybe she wouldn't hate me wearing her clothes.

I decided to drop the dogs off at Mama's and head over to the club. If I hurried I would catch Cleo before the show.

I jammed the key in the ignition and cranked. Nothing. I crossed my fingers and tried again. Damn. Damn Cleo and her manicured fingernails.

So the case of Walter Jones' murder was to begin and end with a stalled car. At least this time I was in Bridgeport. I'd call Papa. He'd pick me up and drop me off at the club. If Mama wasn't watching, he'd bring cannoli.

First things first. I called my mechanic.

"Caterina," Jack answered, his voice slurred. He'd been drinking. "I'm still not loaning you Doris."

I cursed caller ID under my breath.

"I'm calling about Cleo's Camry. She has an appointment with you Monday. Her car's been running a little rough."

He grunted. "I told you I'll look at it but I can't promise how long it will take. If Devin were here…"

"Yeah, yeah. He's doin' the twelve steps with Jesus."

"Don't you start, miss. Devin's still sober."

"That's the beauty of rehab, Jack. They provide involuntary room and body cavity searches."

"You always gotta piss people off."

"The Camry's dead. It's at RB's new construction site. Can you pick it up before Monday?"

"Cleo can't have Doris either."

"Gee, Jack. Excessive amounts of alcohol should make a person happy."

"Doris never complained."

Click.

I bit my tongue and refrained from muttering something Father Timothy really didn't need to hear at confession.

AJ knocked on my window, eyes wide with concern. Maybe he thought I'd been spanked enough.

"Is everything all right?"

"The car won't start."

"You haven't called for a ride yet?"

"I'm calling Papa now. I arranged a tow."

"Where are you headed?"

"All Things Blue."

He smiled. "The best ribs in Chicago. I'll drop you off. It's right on my way."

"It's not necessary." I jerked my head at the backseat. "The pups are having a slumber party at Grandma's."

"I thought I smelled sausage. We'll drop them off on the way."

"What's this about, AJ? A minute ago you wanted to feed me to the fish."

"Well that was a minute ago. Now I know you're no threat to RB. She knows who you are and you've been kicked to the curb. Frankly, I tend to be a bit over-protective when it comes to Roxanne Barbara." AJ gave that easy grin I liked so much. "It's from years of habit. And from years of admiration and loyalty, I might add."

"Her boot's got some serious punch."

"Trust me," he laughed. "I know that boot from experience." AJ gave a self-effacing grimace and then that grin again. "So what do you say? You're stuck. It's not out of my way. Can I give you a ride?"

I slid the phone in a small pocket, where the fabric loosely hangs off the hips. "Thanks."

I grabbed the keys and stepped outside. AJ got another text.

He blew out slowly. "There goes my dream of ribs and blues. Roxanne wants me to bring the interior design samples home with me. There are two boxes on the top floor. I wish Otis would have delivered the elevator car by now."

"I'll help you."

"Do you mind?" AJ blinked, looking grateful. "It'll take two minutes."

I locked the car, and followed AJ into the lobby.

I walked ahead of him up the stairs, swung my head over my shoulder. "Knock it off. I can feel your eyes on my ass."

AJ gave a lecherous chuckle.

I laughed and raced him to the fourth floor in heels. He finished well behind me, huffing and puffing. I realized AJ was out of shape. He smoked, partied, and relied on designer clothes and tanning booths to look good. And a hundred-dollar haircut. My lips curled. I could arm wrestle him to the ground.

I walked around the upper level, beneath the sky light with a fabulous view of the clouds. I glanced up and saw the first raindrops on the glass.

I flexed my arms. "Point me to the boxes."

"Here's the thing." AJ flashed a perfect white smile. "There are no boxes."

"But you said Roxanne…"

He stood there, looking straight at me. The dead eyes were back again. "I lied."

Uh oh. "Is this about the Maddie thing? Because we can stop this right now before it gets too crazy."

AJ jerked something out of his pants. My mouth went dry.

"Wow, that's a big gun." I stared at the hard, cold steel in his hand.

A veil of ice filtered his eyes. He walked a circle. I turned on my heel. It was a dance, a wolf stalking his prey.

"You bastard! You screwed with my car," I said.

He shifted the gun to his other hand and pulled a black wire from his pocket.

I willed my voice to stay calm. "Jack's right," I squeaked. "I do piss people off."

I plunged my hand in my pocket in what I hoped was a nervous gesture. My cell phone felt hard and cool to my touch. I flipped it open and worked my fingers to the hard left, counting buttons, three down. I found *Send* and jabbed it twice.

Hello redial.

Here I was face to face with a psychopath. I had one lifeline. And I used it on a guy who would cheerfully kill me himself.

I was a dead woman.

"Put the gun away, AJ," I said loudly on the chance my drunk mechanic was listening. "The DeLuca men are Chicago cops. Any minute they'll see the Camry outside. They'll storm up here and kick your ass."

He blew me off. "You said you're investigating Hal Bjornsen. What new evidence were you talking about?"

"*Really? Are you freaking kidding me?* You need a *gun* to ask a lame ass question like that?"

"Humor me."

I turned my head to the window and sucked a breath. AJ swung around. I kicked my leg high, nailing his hand and punting the Glock through the air and four stories down to the ground.

I propelled my foot again, nailing his groin with my four inch stiletto. He crumbled to the ground in agony. I ditched my heels and ran. My heart raced and my vision blurred, bare feet pounding the cement floor. I set my sights on the stairwell ahead and didn't look back. I felt the dark energy closing in. He was coming for me. My breaths came in loud sobs and my heart thundered in my chest and above it all, footsteps roared behind me. Gucci's powered by rage, narrowing the gap. I took one last sailing leap for the stairs and a long arm snared my hair, jerking my head and whipping me back. We went down in a fighting heap.

I clawed at his neck as he slammed his fist into my cheek. I fought back with everything I had. I wouldn't allow myself to pass out. I focused on my breath, calling every saint I knew and making a few up as I went along. AJ was on top of me now. His hands bit into my shoulders. He pinned me against the cold cement floor. His face betrayed a measure of insanity I'd only seen when Uncle George had those Vietnam flashbacks. Twisting my hips to the side, I whipped my right leg over AJ's body. With a wild kick, I heard a snap, and then a howl. I'd disjointed AJ's knee.

My shoulders were instantly free. Pushing his weight off me, I scrambled to my feet. A hideous scar in the shape of a Mercedes Benz logo cut deep into his flesh where his forearm had been exposed.

I sucked air. "Aron?"

He roared.

He grabbed at his foot and I caught a flash of something in his ankle holster. He jerked it out and held it in his hand. A snub-nosed thirty-eight Detective Special.

I had underestimated him. He was definitely an overachiever in the weapons department.

AJ rose tentatively to his feet, testing weight on his dislocated knee.

I looked down at the tattered garment and moaned. "My dress. I'll be paying for it until Christmas."

His eyes were cold. "Yeah, I don't think you'll have worry about that."

The sound of a key twisting in a lock downstairs echoed throughout the unfinished cement walls. Then the thud of a door closing. Roxanne's voice sounded bitchy and tired.

"AJ?"

"Up here!"

"Thunderstorms in New York. My flight was delayed." Her heels clacked the cement floor. "What's *her* car doing here? Is *that woman* with you?"

You'd think she was talking about Cleo.

High heels tramped up the stairs.

AJ jabbed the barrel in my back and shoved me away from the edge of the staircase to stand beneath the giant glass ceiling.

"It's a beautiful night," AJ called to her, out of breath and panting. "We're under the skylight, watching the stars."

"It's not dark yet," she snapped. "And it's raining."

Her steps quickened and she ran the last two flights. She paused at the top and caught her breath. Her eyes took in my bruising cheek, bare feet, and AJ's gun. It was staring me down.

She walked toward us, her voice was surprisingly calm. "Have you lost your mind, AJ? She's irritating, I know. But it's no reason to point a gun at her. This is kidnapping, for God's sake."

"Thank you very much," I said and turned to AJ. "Do what she says, dammit. She's your boss."

He stared at the raindrops on the glass.

"Let her go. We'll pay her off. She has Walter's money. We'll give her more and hope she doesn't press charges."

"When it comes to keeping secrets, I'm the best. It's in my job description."

"I can't let her go," AJ said quietly.

"Why not?"

I answered for him. "Because he killed Hal Bjornsen."

She blinked. "Hal's death was an accident. He got mad and wandered off. We thought he'd follow the river out. I didn't know he died in those woods until Walter sent the article."

"So why pay off Walter?"

She sighed deeply. "I did it for Courtney. Walter was going to the gossip rags with lies about a drug orgy and Hal's death. It wasn't like that. We were kids. We drank beer and smoked a little pot. I didn't want to put her parents through those lies. It's been hard enough on them."

I made a clicking sound like Mama. Why someone didn't whack Walter years ago was beyond me.

AJ met the designer's gaze soberly. "I'm doing this for you. She's lying, don't you see? She was investigating *you*, Roxie. She *knows* you killed Walter."

RB couldn't appear more astonished if pigs were flying. "Are you out of your mind? I didn't kill Walter."

A gleam of bewilderment flickered across his face.

Scattered pieces of the puzzle fell into place. "It was you, AJ," I said. "You overheard my phone conversation at the restaurant. You ran down a harmless old man down just because you thought he saw Roxie kill Walter."

Roxanne massaged her temples. "What old man?"

"You stalked me in the blue Volvo," I said incredulously. "You attacked me in my home. You knew all along I wasn't Maddie. Your shock when I told you was a big act."

"Tell her none of this is true." RB was almost begging him.

"You thought Roxie killed Walter and you were willing to do *anything* to save your meal ticket."

"Are you finished?" AJ said.

"No." I kicked his bad knee with my foot. "I'm missing Cleo's singing debut."

AJ trembled with rage. "You really should leave now, Roxie."

"Oh, I'm leaving all right. And I'm taking Maddie, er, *whoever* she is with me."

"I can't let you do that." He moved the gun on her.

"I don't even know you," she said incredulously. "What is *wrong* with you?"

"You're a few decades late with that question," I said. "He killed Courtney."

"You're lying." Her voice was flat and the color drained from her face. "Tell me she's lying."

It came to me then. The nugget that hovered in the back of my skull these last few days surfaced. There was a picture in Roxanne's office taken in Paris, at Couture Fashion Week. AJ holding a glass of champagne, a huge rock on his finger.

"Courtney saw the ring, didn't she?" I said. "It was your fatal mistake. You couldn't resist taking it from Hal."

Roxanne stared at the gun in his hand. "What ring?"

"You blamed yourself all these years for not meeting Courtney in the library that night." She still didn't get it. "You didn't fall asleep, he drugged you. He needed you out of the way so he could kill Courtney."

"No!" she screamed. "You loved Courtney. We all did!"

"I'm not a monster." AJ's voice was low. "I had no choice. If she'd said anything, my life was over."

The wail of a wounded animal escaped RB's throat. She lunged at him, clawing at his eyes, raking her nails deep down his face and drawing blood. He screeched and pushed her off him with one hand, slamming her to the ground. The wounds on his face would scar like prison bars. I was considerably cheered.

"I never wanted to hurt Courtney," AJ panted as his hand cradled his face. "She wouldn't listen to me. Hal was an accident. That guy was a psycho."

She laughed harshly. "Psycho? Look in the mirror."

"I was twenty years old. I was scared."

"What about them? They were only *kids*."

"You couldn't man-up then, and you're still a coward today," I said. "For once in your life do the right thing."

He flashed a cold smile. "Oh I am doing the right thing, for me. They'll never have the evidence to convict me. And I sure as hell am not gonna turn my ass in."

"Walk away while you can," I said. "Take a boat to Cuba. I hear it's nice this time of year."

Roxie's eyes widened. "You killed Walter, didn't you?"

"No. That one's not on me."

I believed him.

"The first two gave me no choice. And now Cat will make three."

"Four," I said. "Don't forget the old man."

AJ let out a huff of air and raked his fingers through his hair. "Why did you have to come back, Roxie."

"What? You can't count to *five*?" she spat out.

I stared at the gun in AJ's hand. He had intended to kill me when he pulled the wire from the Camry. He didn't want me stirring the coals of Hal's "accidental" death. If I scooted through this night alive, I'd go to confession. I'd eat more ice cream. But mostly I'd learn to keep my big mouth shut.

Whatever plan he'd had for my demise needed to be adjusted now to accommodate a double whammy. His eyes scanned the large open space and clicked on the elevator shaft. A wicked smile turned the corners of his lips. His breath quickened, lips slightly parted. That's when I knew that AJ enjoyed the kill. And that he had hatched a plan.

I had to give it to him. It was a good plan. No risky gunfire. An easy cleanup with blood splatter confined to an easily bleached area. And with the heavy machinery around and Aron's construction background, our bodies might never be found.

He waved the gun. "Move."

Oblivious, Roxie trotted off. I dug my feet into the cement floor. It's not that I have a fear of elevators. But the big hole where this one was supposed to be scared the crap out of me.

He shoved the gun in my back and pushed. Gambling he wouldn't shoot, I kicked back, ramming his wounded knee. I whirled behind him. He stumbled and I braced myself, sweeping my foot against his legs. He crashed down hard. The momentum knocked me off balance and I went down on one knee. I scrambled to my feet. His hideously scarred arm struck like a snake. His hand cupped my calf and jerked sharply. The cement floor was brutal and my head was the punching bag. A whirl of colored lights surrounded me. I heard French horns. Nothing was making sense.

Clomp, clomp, clomp.

Roxanne was making her escape. Fashion queen Barbie should've ditched the heels.

AJ pushed my leg off him and clambered over me, the 38 glued to his palm. I closed my eyes and feigned death. It didn't require a lot of imagination.

Roxie didn't have a chance. Manolo Blahnik was no match for Mr. Gucci, even when he was limping. He pulled her back and dragged her kicking and screaming. It was a long chilling distance to the shaft. She put up a fierce fight and he laughed. She bit his arm, sinking her teeth deep into his flesh, drawing blood.

He yelped.

"*That's* how they nailed Ted Bundy," she screamed.

He swung an arm up, nailing her chin with his fist. Her head snapped back. She was out for the count.

He darted his head my way. I stopped breathing and played possum.

He bent down and tucked the gun into his ankle holster. Groaning, he lifted her up and hoisted her over his shoulder.

I rolled my eyes. *Wimp.*

AJ hobbled toward that big hole in the floor. Roxie's limp body blocked his left peripheral. I came at him from his blind side. If my feet touched the floor, I didn't know it. I flew at him. I was his Angel of Death. He could test his own wings on his flight down the shaft.

Maybe he caught a glimpse of my hands as I dove for his ankles; arms outstretched, grabbing for that gun. He twisted violently, too late. I wrestled the gun from his ankle holster, and rolled out as I jumped up. With my body's momentum, I swung my arm around and slammed the muzzle in his ear. Jason Bourne, eat your heart out.

Roxanne stirred in his arms. He put her down gingerly.

She opened her eyes and blinked at the gun in my hand. A crooked grin began to grow on her face.

"I get to shoot him first," she said.

I smiled at AJ. "You just missed your boat, *psycho man.*"

A sound erupted from the big hole in the floor and two hunky heads shot up. A couple Special Forces guys clung to the cables. It was a splashy entrance. My one lifeline call wasn't wasted after all.

Chance and Max hoisted themselves out of the shaft. AJ's eyes widened with fear. An involuntary whimper escaped his lips.

Max tramped over to AJ and smacked him in the jaw.

"You remember Max," I said. "He can kill you with his bare hands."

Chance glared. With one powerful blow he thumped AJ in the gut, punching the air out of him. AJ dropped on his bum knee. He wheezed. Chance hoisted him by the lapels of his suit jacket and carried him effortlessly away. He handcuffed him to a support beam.

Max knelt beside Roxie. "Are you all right?"

"Where did you come from?" Roxanne breathed smoothing her hair. "You saved us."

"Hello?" I said waving the gun.

Max helped her to her feet. "My legs are jello," she murmured and her mouth trembled.

I read her lips.

Hunka, Hunka, Hunka.

Max held her against him. "It'll pass in a few moments. It's the adrenaline crash."

Right.

Chance took my gun away before I shot somebody.

"How did you know?" I said.

"I dropped by Jack's to check on my El Dorado. He was drunk and crazy worried and mumbling something about a posse. I called Max. He beat me here."

I smiled and turned my gaze to the big hole in the floor. "You missed the stairs."

Max grinned. "Just the last flight. The shaft was a tactical maneuver. It's all about the element of surprise."

"*I* was surprised," Roxie murmured, sinking against him.

Chance held my face, his finger traced the outline of my bruised cheek. He exhaled deeply.

"You scared the crap out of me, DeLucky."

"I warned Cat to stay away from him," Max said. "She doesn't listen."

"Like that's a newsflash." Chance turned to Max.

"Get RB out of here and take her home. We'll try to keep her name out of the papers."

Max bristled. He didn't like taking orders.

"Please Max, stay with Roxanne," I said. "She's had a terrible shock."

His eyes darted uncertainly from me to Chance and back to me again. "If you're sure you're all right."

"I'm not at all. But I will be." I kissed his cheek. "Thank you."

Max gave Roxie a goofy grin. She smiled back. He lifted her in his arms and carried her effortlessly down the stairs.

"Max has a huge crush on Roxanne," I said. "He's gotta be happy."

Chance growled. "I can kill with my bare hands too."

"Jealous?"

"Of Max? *Pssssh.*"

"*Really?*"

The cobalt blues laughed softly.

Sirens wailed in the distance. Jack leading the cavalry. They were coming for me.

Chance caught my hand and pulled me under the skylight.

He was eye candy. I took a step toward him and he gathered me in his arms.

"I'll take that dance now, DeLucky. Under the stars."

A hard rain pelted the roof. Our feet moved to her rhythm. I tilted my head back and gazed at the sky.

"I don't see any stars."

His fingers touched my face. He closed my eyes and kissed me.

"Ahhh," I said.

Chapter Thirty

The screaming sirens stopped in the parking lot below and blue whirling lights flashed on the walls.

Ken Millani's voice boomed above the banter. "Wait!" Ken cried. "Don't break the—"

Crash! Smash!

And the musical *tinkle* of shattered glass.

Ken finished, irritated. "I was saying I have a key!"

"We're in," Rocco shouted.

"Stay here, Jack," Captain Bob's voice bellowed.

"Fugeddaboudit, chooch." Jack's voice slurred. "Cat owes me for repairs."

I thought that was sweet in a totally bizarre way.

"Gun on the floor," Uncle Joey's voice called. He'd spotted the Glock twenty-three I kicked from AJ's hand. "Hell of a nice piece too."

I know my Uncle Joey. I was sure he pocketed it.

"They're upstairs!" the twins shouted.

"Baby, we're coming!" Papa cried.

The Bridgeport Brigade stampeded the stairs. It was loud. There were a lot of them. I made out some voices. Tino, Uncle Joey, Frankie, Leo, Tommy, Uncle Rudy. Even Detective Ettie Opsahl who eats small children. It was the most beautiful sound I'd ever heard.

I smiled at AJ. "You should've swam to Cuba when you had the chance."

They exploded from the stairwell like a bad Spaghetti Western. Captain Bob and his posse, looking for someone to hang. And there he was, conveniently attached to a pole. I hoped someone brought a rope.

The DeLucas rushed to my side. The twins found me a chair. I gave it to Papa. He looked pale massaging his scar.

They ran off to find another chair and came back with my black stilettos with peek-a-boo toes. They were eating Skittles and the shoes were a little sticky when they handed them to me. AJ eyed the spiked heels and his face twitched.

I didn't even try to put them on. I was too sore and bruised. I'd done battle with a concrete floor and lost. I wanted to be home, soaking in a hot bubble bath with a glass of wine and a pint of Ben and Jerry's. And then I wanted to put on my flannel pajamas and crawl into bed.

Tino rushed over and hugged me. He held my face and kissed the red mark on my cheek. Then he marched over and thwacked the guy tied to the pole. AJ saw my stars.

"That's police brutality!" he wailed.

"He's not a cop." Uncle Joey yanked out a fistful of AJ's hair and jabbed him in the kidney.

AJ screamed.

"Now *that's* police brutality," Uncle Joey said.

Jack pressed a set of keys in my hand. "I brought you Doris. Don't blow her up, eh?"

I told Captain Bob my story. I answered his questions and he wrote a lot of words on the clip board.

"AJ told me he killed two people twenty years ago," I said. "A Hal Bjornsen and Courtney Kelly."

"Liar!" AJ shouted.. "Don't believe anything that woman says. She was impersonating a journalist."

Captain Bob peered over his glasses. "She looks like a journalist to me," he said.

He scribbled something on his report. And he scratched something else out. It looked like *Hootchie Stalker*.

"Is there any DNA or other physical evidence to connect AJ Nelson to these murders that you know of?" Captain Bob said.

I pondered the question. There was the matter of Hal's ring. But twenty years ago, the sheriff argued Hal probably gave the missing ring away. AJ would be quick to claim that defense.

"No," I said bleakly. "But you can get him for the hit and run. He killed the old man."

Bob whispered in my ear. "We'll try. We don't have a lot to go on. The car was stolen and wiped clean. Maybe he'll confess."

"Good luck with that."

AJ gave a cocky ear to ear grin. He'd do a little time for kidnapping but he was sure to skate on the murders. I wasn't surprised he passed on Cuba.

Captain Bob turned to AJ. "Were you acquainted with Walter Jones?"

"I was," AJ said uneasily.

"Do you have an alibi for the afternoon of the third? Can anyone verify your whereabouts?"

"No. No. And why?"

"What's going on?" I said.

"Your parolee didn't kill Walter. He fully intended to. In fact, he was all kinds of pissed that someone beat him to it. It took some digging but he has an alibi. Sorry, Cat. Your partner's head is back on the chopping block."

"Assistant," I sighed.

Ettie Opsahl smiled triumphantly.

Captain Bob watched me intently. "Cat, this is important. Did Mr. Nelson say anything to you about Walter Jones?"

I took a long moment to consider my response. AJ was a dangerous sociopath who might never go to trial for two twenty-year-old murders. It was a damn shame. Because I'd like Courtney's parents to know that the guy who ruined their lives isn't driving a Mercedes and drinking two hundred dollar wine. And I'd like to fly to Orlando and return Hal's ring to his mom and dad. And then I'd like go to Disney World.

I wasn't convinced we'd ever know who killed Walter. Far too many people were dancing on his grave. Too many would have cheerfully pulled the trigger.

Only one thing was certain. Cleo Jones was going down for the murder of her husband. And she was the only person I *absolutely knew* did not kill him.

"Caterina," Captain Bob said with less patience. "What did Mr. Nelson tell you?"

I met AJ's dark eyes levelly and I didn't stutter.

"He said he killed Walter Jones."

A few weeks later former Deputy Nicole Rallen and I flew to Florida. I returned Hal Bjornsen's ring to his parents. They didn't get the closure they deserved. There was a staggering lack of physical evidence surrounding their son's death. They understood Justice may never have her day. But their biggest questions had been answered. And they found a measure of peace.

The Bjornsen's gave us each an obscenely huge reward. Nicole purchased a condo near Cocoa Beach and she gave me a key. I didn't buy Dopey after all. But I held him down and tickled his ears.

The morning I returned from Disney World was the Fourth of July. Cleo wasn't at the airport to meet me. She'd left a text on my phone.

In the Bahamas with Frankie. Am as close to Cuba as I ever want to be. Hail a cab.

The cab driver stopped by Mama's before dropping me off at my door. Inga and Beau pretended they were glad to come home with me. They were both a little fat and spoiled. They wore new Chicago Bears doggie shirts and Mama painted their nails to match her own. They smelled like Tino's sausages.

I always knew what I would do with the RB/Bjornsen cache. I hefted the designer bag from the secret compartment behind the pantry wall and mixed it up with the reward from Hal's parents. It made one big ol' pile of blood money. And it never belonged to me.

I got out my GPS and the list of people Walter had screwed. I spent the afternoon dropping an anonymous envelope at each door. I mailed the ones that weren't local. Maybe the money wouldn't cover everyone's losses. And maybe it takes more than money to fix a sleazy betrayal. But it felt good spreading all that green around. I like to think it made somebody smile.

The Fourth of July celebration was at Bridgeport Park that night. Everyone was there. Papa and his Moose Lodge buddies dressed up as clowns. There was a carnival and pony rides. Vendors sold hotdogs and corn on the cob and cotton candy. The twins barbecued ribs. Mama made potato salad. And Rocco organized a softball game.

I joined Captain Bob and some of his guys. They were gathered around Uncle Joey's punch bowl. You know it had a kick.

Bob said his retirement was in good standing again. He got kudos from the department for his handling of the Walter Jones murder case. A second search of the crime scene produced strands of hair belonging to AJ Nelson.

I sucked a breath and looked at Uncle Joey. *"Really?"*

Captain Bob smiled widely. The twitch was gone. "AJ apparently lost them in the struggle. The prosecutor says a conviction is a slam dunk."

"That's *amazing*," I said.

"It's karma," Rocco said flatly.

Uncle Joey winked. "Well, it sure ain't police brutality."

I glimpsed Ken Millani across the park, sitting alone on the grass. I filled two big glasses with Uncle Joey's spiked punch and wandered over. I handed Ken one and sat down beside him.

The evening shadows were long. A lazy breeze rustled through Bridgeport. Ken watched his grandkids scoot down the long slide and up the ladder again.

When Ken's daughter and I were kids, he brought us to this park a few times. He chased us up the ladder and shot down the slide like a rocket. He was younger then. He made Becky and I laugh 'til our sides hurt. I wondered if he remembered.

I took one of Maria's giant chocolate chip cookies from my bag and broke it. I gave half to Ken.

"I know you killed Walter," I said.

Ken was silent a long time. But he didn't deny it.

"I figure you thought he wasn't home," I said.

Ken's voice was deep and sad. "Walter's Corvette was gone."

I nodded. "Cleo stole it."

"I wanted the tape from the confessional. I went there to talk to him. I brought papers promising I wouldn't press embezzlement charges."

"When you saw Walter wasn't home, you let yourself in."

"I thought maybe I could find the tape myself. I drove around back. I used my key to let myself in." He raked his hair with his fingers. "It was a dumb idea."

"Ya think?"

"And then Walter came in. He had a piece."

"And you didn't?"

Ken looked shocked. "I don't own a gun. I had *papers*."

"What happened?"

"I don't know. Walter went berserk. He was waving the gun— practically *foaming* at the mouth. He wouldn't listen. I tried to take it away from him and…"

Ken didn't finish. He didn't need to.

"It went off." I said it for him.

Ken's eyes were anguished. "I wouldn't have let Cleo go to the pen."

"That will be AJ's fate. He's a dangerous serial killer. He needs to be where he can't hurt anyone else."

Ken looked away. He was a decent man. He hadn't decided whether or not to turn himself in.

"How did you know?" he said.

"I did the math. The day after Walter died, you gave a huge donation to the church. $490,000. Four-hundred-ninety is not a random number. It's seventy times seven. It was Jesus' instruction on forgiveness."

I took the last gulp of punch and continued.

"Your business is in trouble. You couldn't afford to give a sum like that. The donation was remorse money. Penance. It was you screaming for forgiveness."

Ken almost smiled. "And you're so rarely in church. You surprise me, Caterina."

I made a face. "Sister Clara wanted me to learn about forgiveness. I memorized the entire eighteenth chapter of Matthew."

"She was a good teacher."

"She scared the crap out of me."

I hugged him hard. "What happened was a tragic accident. Buck up. Learn to live with it. Your family needs you. And you promised to put another story on my house."

I stood up and brushed myself off. Then I reached into my bag and pulled out the very last envelope. It felt fat and sweet in my hand. I dropped it on his lap.

"This is from Walter. He's sorry he was such a schmuck."

I didn't need twelve years in Catholic school to figure that out.

I walked away as the high school marching band struck up Yankee Doodle Dandy. Fireworks would begin soon.

My glass was empty. I made a beeline across the park for more punch and cookies. From a distance, I spotted a clown with his arms around Mama. They were talking to a ruggedly built guy in jeans and a tee shirt. He had an easy, powerful presence. He was hot. He oozed testosterone. And he was alone and unsupervised with my outrageous, interfering parents.

I wanted to die.

I shuddered, wondering what Papa was saying to Chance Savino. It almost certainly had something to do with virility and his willingness to produce multiple grandchildren. Mama would be drilling him about insurance. I stopped dead in my tracks, contemplating my escape.

The hunky FBI guy felt my eyes on his back—or more accurately, buns. His head shot around and the cobalt blues locked on mine. I felt a sudden weird exhilaration. My face grew warm.

I moved toward him. He met me half way. Chance caught my hands and a shudder ran through me.

His mouth twitched in a smile. "God, I missed you. How was Dopey?"

I stood on my toes and took his ears between my fingers. I brought his head down to mine.

"My god, DeLucky. Are you fondling my ears?"

"Mmhmm. Come here and kiss me."

To receive a free catalog of Poisoned Pen Press titles, please contact us in one of the following ways:

Phone: 1-800-421-3976
Facsimile: 1-480-949-1707
Email: info@poisonedpenpress.com
Website: www.poisonedpenpress.com

Poisoned Pen Press
6962 E. First Ave. Ste 103
Scottsdale, AZ 85251